Creatures of the Night

Vicious Vampire Tales

Kevin J. Kennedy
Gord Rollo
Simon Clark

DARK TIDE

BOOK 17 IN CRYSTAL LAKE'S DARK TIDE SERIES

Let the world know:
#IGotMyCLPBook!

Crystal Lake Publishing

Join the Crystal Lake community today
on our newsletter and Patreon!
https://linktr.ee/CrystalLakePublishing

Download our latest catalog here.
https://geni.us/CLPCatalog

ISBN: 978-1-964398-18-1

Cover art:
Ben Baldwin—http://www.benbaldwin.co.uk

Layout:
Lori Michelle—www.theauthorsalley.com

Edited and proofed by:
Jaime Powell, Sydney Ngxokela, Joseph VanBuren,
Paula Limbaugh, and Hasse Chacon

From The Bloodred World Of Vampyrrhic

Return Of The Blood-Feeders

Simon Clark

One

The tragedy, the whole heart-crushing terrible event, can be summed up as *I met her in March. Fell in love with her in April. Lost her in June.* But there is much more to those big life-changing incidents than can be expressed in three bittersweet sentences.

There are all the other things, too. Like first noticing Magenta in that big redbrick barn of a place called the Station Hotel. It's one of those market-town hotels that had seen the last of its big-money years a long, long time ago, and now clung on by its fingernails. Yet the redbrick building had embedded itself deep in the fabric of the town, hosting many a wedding reception, funeral tea, and the office Christmas 'do'. So, this venerable establishment had got by, paid its bills, occasionally replaced carpets and televisions in the faded grandeur of its lounge. And, barring meteor strikes, the Station Hotel would still be quietly doing business here in a hundred years' time. The hotel stands next to the new Aldi, pretty much in the centre of the Yorkshire town of Leppington. As for Leppington itself, it's a lonely backwater, eternally besieged by moorland, and barren hills, and cold-as-your-tomb winds that roar in hard from the North Sea that heaves and spumes just a few miles away. And when those winds blow from the East, they come racing across Europe, all the way from the vastness of the Russian Steppe. You can almost catch the whiff of bones of the old Soviet dead, growing ever more mouldy in their totalitarian graves.

I met her in March. Fell in love with her in April. Lost her in June. Now, I shall put some living flesh on those bare bones of three simple statements. Oh, and I'll talk about vampires, too. Not the vampires found prowling in horror films. Yes, granted, these vampires are violent, cruel, often red and wet from head-to-toe with the blood of people like you and me. But they are so much more than the make-believe vampires you might be familiar with—however, more about those vampiric monsters later.

First, I need to tell you about that June night, when a warm day had given way to cold winds and a hard rain, lashing against the windows of the Station Hotel. The storm made a sound not unlike sharp talons clattering at the panes—as if demons yearned to break into that one-hundred-and-fifty-year-old building and feast on our beating, bloody hearts.

Magenta worked at the hotel. In fact, she was running the place while its owner, Electra Charnwood, toured Europe. Magenta was tall, clear-eyed, with dark hair, and she possessed arms that were so strong you saw her biceps bunch, granite-hard, beneath her skin when she wrangled kegs full of beer. There are local legends that, many a time, she effortlessly chucked troublesome drunks out of the hotel into the street. Magenta always spoke softly, and had a way of looking at me, her dark eyes locking onto me, as if she read words written on my face. And, no doubt, she read the kind of hopes and fears we all carry so deeply engraved on our hearts.

Me? Mr Ordinary, I guess. When I left school, I got a job maintaining luggage carousel systems at airports, which took me around the world, seeing plenty of exotic locations, and some not-so exotic, especially at military airbases where service engineers were housed in barrack-style accommodation, and we weren't allowed off-base to visit the local bars. I enjoyed the job, though I acquired a steel pin in my right femur after riding a moped into a street-food shack in Hanoi (booze wasn't involved, heavy rain had fucked-up the moped's brakes). Six months later, a baboon stole my phone out of my pocket in Joburg. By some astonishing bit of fate, the monkey called my sister's number, and Tiffany enjoyed five minutes of crazy chit-chat, via a video call, with a dog-faced primate that was sitting in the top of a tree. Or maybe my big sister was just pulling my leg as she so often loves to do. For another example of her sense of humour, here's an absolute belter: when I was a kid, and I took a bath, and it was dark outside and I had the bathroom light on, Tiff would switch off the electric at the mains. With that act of domestic sabotage adroitly accomplished, she would make ghostly *whoo-whoo* sounds on the other side of the bathroom door, as I sat there in the dark, in the water, very nearly shitting myself in terror. Well . . . I say *very nearly* . . . but that's another story.

Return of the Blood-Feeders

Okay, back to a more recent segment of my life story. I was made redundant from the maintenance company after the growth in carry-on luggage saw the reduction in carousel facilities at some airports. Maybe the familiar hum of the motors that drive the belts around and around with their cargo of suitcases, baby buggies, and mysterious brown paper parcels tied up with hairy string, will one day become a thing of the past. Thereafter, a succession of casual jobs and equally casual relationships came my way. I had become completely rootless, drifting from town to town. My life reached a point where I became wary of allowing myself to love someone, because my relationships always ended in failure. In fact, as a relationship deepened, and I became more trusting, I'd start to feel a growing sense of panic, knowing the relationship would inevitably breakdown, and then I'd find myself alone, and lonely again. So, as a form of self-protection, I'd emotionally distance myself from what would be my current girlfriend. She'd pick up on that, then interpret my demeanour as a lack of interest in her on my part. Shortly thereafter, it would be the old story of me uttering that fatuous statement: "It's not you, it's me . . . "

Eventually, the tides of chance washed me up in Leppington where I met Magenta. She found me standing in the hotel bar, looking like an abandoned puppy, I guess. Even though we'd never met before, Magenta gently nipped my nose between her finger and thumb, smiled, then said, "Look, I've pinched your nose." She did that thing of showing me her thumb between two of her fingers, pretending it was my nose gripped there. That was the icebreaker. Then, as time went by, something magical happened. As I found myself falling in love with her, that panic of old never returned, where I'd convince myself that the relationship was doomed to failure. Soon we became a couple. We were very happy. What quality did Magenta possess that allowed me to fully commit to loving her, without this paralysing fear that we'd inevitably break up one day? I really don't know . . . Maybe it was something in her blood.

Two

That night—that emotionally explosive night—I remember her: naked, sitting astride me, her hair falling over her face as she pressed her lips together hard, feeling the movement inside of her that slowly . . . slowly . . . excited the nerves that a million years of evolution had tuned to exquisite sensitivity. Then that moment when her head whipped back, her eyes flashing, her hips moving backwards and forwards until . . .

Abruptly, she leapt from the bed. "Karl. Did you hear that? It came from downstairs, didn't it?"

Magenta panted, her lips were still full from the sexual rush of blood. Her breasts quivered as, from a chair, she snatched the black silk kimono with the gold dragon design on the back—the one I'd bought her after she asked me to stay for the summer. Magenta rushed towards the door. Meanwhile, cold winds from the faraway Russian Steppe threw a hard rain at the windowpanes. An entire legion of demons clawing at the glass, or so it seemed to me.

"Damn it, Karl, if this is another break-in . . . " She panted, still breathless from our lovemaking. "They'll be after the cash—second time this year!"

"Wait." I dragged on my tracksuit bottoms. "Don't go down there by yourself."

We were alone in the hotel, it being midweek. After all, hotels in places like Leppington rarely have paying guests at any other time but weekends.

"Magenta, wait." Anxiety for her safety prompted me to repeat my earlier statement: "Don't go down there by yourself."

But she did rush down the stairs by herself. And my fifteen-week paradise, living with her, laughing at each other's jokes, and the greatest sex of my life . . . well . . . it all ended in an absolute nightmare.

Return of the Blood-Feeders

Off I went after her, running barefoot and bare-chested, down a flight of stairs that are so thickly carpeted it's like running on memory foam. Magenta moved fast, so I only caught a brief glimpse of her before she vanished around the next turn in the broad staircase, down which ladies in long skirts would have sashayed a hundred and fifty years ago when the hotel was new.

Storm winds lashed the windows. Raindrops clattered, so adroitly imitating demon talons. The air had been warm, smelling pleasantly of the hotel's Tuesday-Night-Is-Curry-Night special. Now, however, the air turned cold. A breeze flowed up the staircase, like someone had left the outer doors open, admitting that savage easterly, gusting in from the hills. Not only did the bitingly cold air chase away fragrant aromas of Chicken Balti, the breeze carried with it the smell of wet soil—that heavy, thick odour you get when standing next to a ploughed field in the rain. At last, I'd closed the distance, and I caught sight of her again before the next twist in the stairs.

"Magenta," I called, "wait!"

She threw a glance back at me that blazed with such power. "When I get my hands on them, they'll wish they'd never been born."

Hair streaming out in the breeze, bare feet flashing across the carpet, her kimono rippling in a swish of ebony silk, she yet again vanished around the next turn in the stairs. My breath came in throaty gasps as I followed. Of course, she believed thieves had broken into the hotel. Probably feral youths in hooded jackets, reeking of skunk and vodka. They'd perhaps smashed a window and slithered in, expecting to find cash in a drawer or, if there was no cash, making off with bottles of whisky and gin to sell.

Moments later, I heard . . . well . . . what did I hear? Footsteps, I suppose. Running footsteps. But there was something wildly disordered about them, as if people stampeded through a sinking ship.

"Magenta!" I couldn't see her, even though I had now entered the hotel's reception area. "Magenta! Where are you?"

The lights had been burning brightly, yet now they began to dim as if someone operated a dimmer switch, starving the bulbs of voltage, turning the light yellow, then orange, then a dull red. I headed for the bar, expecting to find thieves there, but almost straight away, I spotted the cellar door yawning open. Strangely, the freezing blast of air came from that doorway. A vicious outpouring of cold that shrivelled my skin to bumpy goose flesh.

And now . . . I felt something *beyond* the five senses. Many people claim we humans have something called 'creature feeling', which is the ancient instinct that alerts us when danger is coming our way. Even if the danger is both unseen and unheard, our nerves still detect that aura of threat, hurtling towards us. Creature feeling then triggers warning flashes of alarm inside our skulls—that our lives are in immediate danger from who knows what.

A heartbeat later - the scream.

"Magenta!"

The light grew even more dim. Shadows flowed from the walls. They created tides of darkness, swirling across the floor towards me.

Another scream was followed by a terrifying yell of, "Karl! Don't come into the cellar!"

Of course, I went into the cellar, how could I not? That's when my comfortable opinion of what constituted reality was smashed to a million pieces.

Magenta struggled with a dozen figures. They were barefoot. They wore decaying clothes. Regardless of whether they were male or female, they did not have a single hair on their heads. I gazed down into that shadow-filled vault beneath the hotel, where beer kegs and crates of bottles are stored, and I saw men and women who moved with a furious energy. Horrifically, their heads resembled skulls. And those intruders focussed every shred of their concentration onto Magenta, who, time and again, would break free from their clutching hands only to be instantly caught once more. My impression was that they pawed at her in a frenzy of passion and carnal hunger.

I went down the steps, three at a time, my bare feet hitting the stone risers so hard my entire body jolted, causing my teeth to snap together, biting my tongue, releasing a powerful taste of blood into my mouth.

Magenta twisted around in the strangers' grasp. Her eyes locked onto mine. Incredibly, her face was radiating love for me, rather than the terror of her own fate. "Karl!" Her voice echoed around that tomb of a place. "Karl! Go back! Don't come any closer— don't you dare!"

By this time, I'd reached the bottom of the steps. Creature

feeling—alarm overload—portents of danger. Those visceral warnings blazed inside my head. Nevertheless, the need to save Magenta burned within me most brightly of all.

The light dimmed—the lightbulbs becoming just spots of red hanging from the ceiling. Yet, despite the gloom, I saw the figures clearly enough. I saw their savage, hungry faces, and the lust in their eyes. And what terrible eyes they were. Pure white eyeballs, no colour whatsoever, just a fierce black pupil in the centre of each sphere that was the colour of milk.

In desperation, I grabbed an empty champagne bottle from a table. Champagne bottles are heavy; they have thick glass, and their neck fits the palm of the hand as superbly as the hilt of a warrior's sword. There suddenly came shouting and yelling, the sound an outrush of fury and terror without words. I ran toward the dozen figures that were mauling the woman I loved. And using the champagne bottle as a weapon, I attacked those bald heads, slashing right and left.

Then . . . here's the odd thing . . . Well, the absolutely strange thing. The figures didn't even notice I was there. The bottle smacked against heads, inflicting cruel gashes in blue-white skin, but the people I struck did not react. Such was their fascination, *their obsession,* with Magenta, they did not notice I was there, even though I rained brutal blows down on them with that heavy bottle. There was no blood. At least, I don't remember any blood—when, by rights, crimson should have been gushing from headwounds. If anything, only a transparent liquid seeped out. And not much of that, either. Just enough to leave glistening smears on their skin.

By now, it was so gloomy, I could barely see. In fact, the brightest objects there were the eyes of the strangers. Those white eyes, centred with a single dot of hatred; that's how the small, hard pupils looked to me. Now, I glimpsed their black fingernails. Many of which were split and torn to the quick. Sometimes, their grey, bloodless lips would part to reveal teeth the colour of old bones you see in museums. Bones which belonged to the plague dead, from bleaker, disease-blighted eras of humanity. And in the centre of the vortex of writhing limbs, there was Magenta. Her beautiful face was striped with scratches from those black fingernails. Her hair was tousled into a black froth. And yet her eyes remained undeniably fierce as she battled her attackers.

I struck harder with the bottle. Sometimes the man or woman

I attacked would briefly glance at me, just for a second, almost a quizzical look, as if they asked themselves, 'Why is that man hitting me?' But then my victim's obsession with Magenta would force their gaze back to her. Magenta was the centre of their universe; she was the only object that existed for them. Even my muscular onslaught on their bald heads seemed little more violent to them than the gentle tickle of a cobweb would be against my own face.

Just then, more pandemonium. Five or six figures with the same bald heads came running down the cellar steps. Maybe these were the individuals who had been racing through the hotel corridors earlier? I hadn't seen them, but I had heard them. Now, they dashed towards the group that wrestled with Magenta. The new arrivals howled so loudly the sound hurt my ears; this was a howl of envy. They had seen Magenta. They wanted her, too.

As they ran across the cellar towards her, where she violently struggled with her captors, I moved to block their way. As I did so, I raised the champagne bottle above my head. They barely even noticed me, their focus was on Magenta, and Magenta alone.

Thud! The force of my blow, striking a bald man of around forty, succeeded in bursting one of his eyes. Clear gel began discharging from the socket down one cheek. The pain from the ruptured eye must have registered, because he swung out his arm, like a man opening a door in a bad temper. His forearm connected with my chest. The resulting impact knocked me backwards with such force that my feet left the floor, and I found myself flying through cold air that stank of wet soil.

I crashed into a line of beer kegs stacked on their side. A moment later, my skull smacked hard into one of the steel kegs. And there I lay, dazed on the floor, feeling hot blood rushing down my neck. The blow to my head had been immense. I couldn't stand. My legs were worryingly numb. I couldn't even open my mouth to scream out in rage and terror.

The strangers gathered Magenta up into their fierce grip. They each held onto a part of her body, as if she was the treasure they had always sought. One pale hand grasped her wrist, another hand grasped an ankle, another a thigh, and so on. Carrying her on her back, above their heads, they rushed to the far end of the cellar. There, a steel door abruptly swung open, revealing a black void beyond—a tunnel to God knows where. Thereafter, they carried Magenta through the doorway. That's when pale hands reached from the darkness to grab hold of the door, then they drew it shut once more.

I remember, that before she vanished into the tunnel, Magenta had turned her head as they carried her. Those dark eyes of hers fixed on me. In those eyes I'd seen love . . . and a last farewell.

I met her in March. Fell in love with her in April. Lost her in June. Yes, what happened could be summed up in sixteen words. But I could never express the totality of what I experienced on that night. Not in even a million words. And the worst was yet to come.

Three

Was I badly injured? Yes, absolutely. Following the attack in the Station Hotel, I spent ten days in hospital. Police officers interviewed me as I lay there in the hospital bed. My head was bandaged, and my brain was still surfing merrily along on a psychedelic wave of analgesia. As one doctor cheerfully admitted, as she regulated the flow of painkiller through the catheter into my arm: "What we do have here in hospital are plenty of big hammers."

I did laugh loudly at that. "Big Hammers. Ha-ha!" The drugs made me see her comment as outrageously hilarious.

Believe me, I am not laughing now.

Every couple of days, detectives visited me and began the interview with the same question. "Karl, the night Magenta disappeared, did you have an argument with her?"

You can see where they are going with that line of questioning, can't you?

And yes, as I lay there, awash with morphine, grinning, slurring my words, I muttered my story about intruders with bald heads and uncanny eyes. How they carried Magenta away into the tunnel that is accessed through the steel door in the hotel cellar. The police investigated. And the results of their findings are as follows:

"Karl. The tunnel only runs for twenty paces before it's blocked by a roof fall. Magenta can't possibly have been taken into the tunnel. Now . . . the night Magenta left the hotel, did you and her have a fight?"

On being discharged from hospital, I took my paper bag full of painkillers with me back to the Station Hotel. Without rationally working out why, I thought it important I reopen the place. Maybe I wanted to ensure there'd be money to pay the bills. Also, there was the cook, cleaner, and bar staff who depended on the hotel for their living. And maybe I needed to be right there in the building—the place where Magenta disappeared.

Within days, a new rhythm established itself in my life: waking early in a hotel, which was empty apart from me, and with its dead silence coldly haunting long corridors and deserted rooms. The staff arriving mid-morning. The hotel coming alive: drone of a vacuum cleaner, radio pumping out music as the cook prepped food for the day; the rattling of glassware as bar staff got busy. For a while, plenty of noise and activity as customers filled this quaint watering hole. When the bar closed, however, I was alone again in the hotel. Silence ruled: the all-powerful god of the building.

My head injury had been diagnosed as cerebral contusion; basically, a bruise to the brain, leading to that all-important grey stuff becoming swollen. The doctor explained that my head had struck the beer keg so hard that my brain would have rattled like a peanut being shaken inside a glass. My memory suffered, too. I instantly forgot customers' orders for drinks. Thankfully, writing the order down on a notepad as it was spoken, managed to circumvent that particular problem. Some customers tried it on. "Hey, I gave you a twenty-pound note for the beer. You've given me change for a tenner." *Parasites. Bloodsuckers.*

A pleasant woman, with short brown hair and a warm smile, sat at the bar one night, drinking her glass of white wine alone.

She asked, "Karl, are you okay?"

"Hmm, fine, why?"

"You've been staring into space for the last ten minutes."

"Oh."

"Is your head hurting?"

"No. The hospital gave me some big hammers."

"Big hammers?" Her puzzled frown melted in a heart-warming way as that smile of hers returned to her face. "Oh, 'big hammers'. I get it. Look, Karl, you must be lonely here, living by yourself, now that Magenta's . . . well . . . "

"Mysteriously vanished? Dead and buried?"

"Please, Karl. I'm just trying to be nice, okay?" Her warm smile notched up a few more degrees of erotic centigrade.

"Sorry."

"My name's Sarah."

“Pleased to meet you, Sarah. I’m sorry if I was, uh, grumpy, to say the least.”

“No worries, Karl. Look. I’m having a house party later. You’re more than welcome . . . I mean, you don’t have to spend every night here alone.” A smile to melt glaciers. Lights danced in her eyes as she fixed them on me.

“Oh,” I said, pleasantly. “Who will be at the party?”

“Just you and me, Karl. Just you and me.”

A guy with a silver beard and wet lips came up to the bar.

He gave me a hard stare. “Hey, you. I’ve just bought a beer and gave you a twenty. You gave me change for a tenner.”

Four

I did not go to Sarah's party for two. After the bar had closed, and I'd put the stools upside down on tables, ready for the cleaner's dance of the Hoover tomorrow, I noticed a man of around sixty. He was tucked away on a sofa in an alcove—one of those bar alcoves where lovers can meet at least semi-discretely. The man was a familiar customer; in fact, a daily one. His body was pencil-thin, and he had an abundance of curly white hair. He was distinguished-looking in a way that suggested he might have enjoyed a brief spell of fame a long time ago. Lead guitarist in a rock band, maybe? Sometimes, I imagined him, back when he was thirty years younger, his long hair blowing out, playing a huge, shrieking riff on a Gibson SG that was loud enough to shake bones in old tombs a mile away.

All that, if it ever did happen to the guy, took place a long time ago. Now, he came into the bar at noon, ordered a glass of red wine, which he would make last until two, as he read his newspaper. Then he would order his first beer of the day, which would be followed by many. Tonight, the man sat there, watching me with tired eyes that were edged with red skin. Booze was his metier now. Beer his chosen career. Drinking it, that is.

"Sir," I said, "I'm closing up now, so if you could finish your drink?"

"No problem. I'm on my way."

The man drained the glass, his Adam's Apple seemingly acting as a pump, visibly pushing the beer down his gullet. After that, he stood. He was swaying a little, not roaring drunk by any means, just tipsy.

The pain returned to my skull with a fierce enough jab to make me press the palm of my right hand against my forehead.

"My condolences." The man pulled on a brown jacket in

suede—and wore those slip-on shoes by John Galliano? "I know what happened to Magenta. You getting hurt. That's a rotten thing to happen."

The next words shot from my lips; I didn't plan to say them, but out they came anyway. "I will find her."

"Listen, young man, you mustn't do this on your own."

He didn't say anymore. He merely gave me a solemn nod, before heading out into the night.

Five

After the beer-drinker headed off, swaying into the darkness of Leppington's streets, I did replay his words inside my aching head. *"I know what happened to Magenta."* Did he mean that he believed she had intentionally left the hotel? This was the publicly circulating account; one that suggested Magenta had skedaddled, either with another lover, or to abandon me (of course, there were some who speculated I'd murdered her and buried her body up on the moor). Or did his *"I know what happened to Magenta"* indicate that he *actually* knew the circumstances of her disappearance? More importantly, did he know her location now?

I was alone again in the hotel . . . engulfed in silence and in gloom. As usual, I did my pre-bedtime rounds, checking lights were off, doors locked, bar takings carefully locked in the safe. As I padded along corridors, I thought about Magenta. Of course, I was always thinking about Magenta: what happened to her, where did she go? Who were those strange people who carried her off? Or, as the police suspected, had I simply dreamt it all, after falling against the beer keg and bashing my head? A decidedly brutal event, which had left me with fierce headaches, memory problems, episodes of blurred vision, along with bouts of irrational fury.

Up in my bedroom, the same one where I'd shared so many exciting times with Magenta, I swallowed prescription-strength painkillers. My head still ached. My brain felt swollen and sore inside its bone dome. In all honesty, I could not really feel my brain in that way, as if it were a sore finger, but that's the unsettling impression I had. After brushing my teeth, I went to lay on the bed.

Though the bed wasn't there anymore. I was in the cellar again. Standing in front of the steel door that sealed off the doorway into the tunnel. The very doorway those hairless, bare-foot creatures had carried Magenta through. This had happened to me before.

Just like all those occasions when I abruptly came to my senses in the stockroom, and not remembering what I'd gone to collect, I often found myself in the cellar without even realizing I'd decided to descend into that cold vault. Some instinct drove me down into the cellar to find Magenta, I'm sure.

As I stood there, I glanced around. What drew my eye first was the dried blood on the floor. My blood. The blood I'd spilled after my skull crunched into the beer keg.

Painkillers flowed through my veins, dulling my senses, making me feel woozy. *I shouldn't be down here . . . not at night . . . not alone . . .*

Now . . . had I locked the hotel's outer doors, and switched off the bar lights? I couldn't remember. Drowsily, as the analgesic dialled-down brain activity, I pulled a notepad from the back pocket of my jeans. (Had I gone to bed wearing jeans? Possibly so. After all, these days I was forgetting more than I was remembering.) Written there on the notepad, and in my handwriting was: *11.28 – yes – you switched off the lights and locked all doors*. At least, that saved me having to climb back up the cellar steps to check. Would my memory return properly? The doctor said, "Yes, probably. Just give it time." But I'd heard of people who had suffered a brain injury who were unable to dress themselves properly in the morning. Sometimes, they left the house wearing two coats, and with a shoe on one foot and a boot on the other. The thought of an injury-triggering dementia at the age of thirty-eight terrified me.

"Magenta, where are you?" This was another one of those occasions where I never even knew I was going to speak, and the words caught me by surprise. "Magenta, I do love you, you know that, don't you?" The air was so cold, I shivered constantly. Jabs of pain attacked my skull. I pictured my brain: swollen and veiny and purple inside my head, a sickening image to be sure.

I climbed the steps, telling myself I should be in bed. A moment later, I padded across thick carpet towards the main staircase. Two minutes later, I stood in the cellar. Yes, it had happened again. A breakdown of memory. I couldn't decide, at that moment, whether I had intended to return to the cellar, or whether instinct had taken over and, almost like sleepwalking, I had glided down the steps, into that gloomy mausoleum of a place, with its beer kegs, and with its conglomeration of old tables and chairs that had outlived their usefulness. Slowly, I approached the steel door. The police had replaced the old padlocks with new, shiny tungsten ones. They certainly didn't want anyone venturing into the ancient tunnels that ran under Leppington. Too dangerous, they claimed. Roof falls, bad air, liable to flooding: a death trap. I moved closer to the door, turned my head, then pressed my right ear to this steel slab that sealed off the labyrinth. The chill of the metal felt as cold as a corpse's kiss against my ear.

I listened.

Then I whispered, "Magenta."

At that moment, I pictured a figure on the other side of the door, there in the tunnel, flanked by walls of wet rock. A figure standing exactly as I was standing, ear pressed to the door, listening for sounds that might come ghosting through the metalwork.

"Magenta?"

I wanted to visualize the woman I loved standing there. But no. The mental image that swelled, so utterly malignant, and with repulsive clarity inside my own swollen brain, was of a monstrous thing. Some *thing* with a hairless head. Its scalp all wormy-looking due to thick, engorged veins running just beneath its grey skin. That uncanny creature would possess white eyes, centred with fierce black pupils. Those eyes would be staring into the darkness as the *thing* listened. In my mind's eye, I saw it tap its black fingernails against the steel.

At that moment, the door vibrated. A sound reached me that resembled far-off chimes. Fingernails striking metal, perhaps.

The drug that damped down the pain in my head damped down logic, too. After all, there could be no one at the other side of the metal barrier. The foul, slimy tunnel beyond the door couldn't support life. I knew that, yes.

But I had heard fingernails tapping the other side of the metalwork. I was sure of it.

I stepped back from the door. "Magenta," I whispered. "I will find you. I promise."

Six

The next day, the police searched the hotel again. They shot me quizzical glances as they moved from room to room, maybe trying to detect that momentary blanking of my eyes that guilty people employ to draw a sort of masking screen down over their faces. As if they fear their guilty thoughts will be exposed by those twin windows of the soul.

After refusing my offer of coffee, a pair of detectives—a man and a woman, looking more like accountants in their smart clothes—questioned me in a back room that served as the hotel office. Here, there were three monitors, linked to CCTV equipment. The police had already gone through CCTV footage of the night Magenta vanished. There were, however, no cameras inside the hotel. Magenta had once told me that many of her hotel guests preferred their faces remain off-camera when entertaining friends, or *very* close friends. Therefore, cameras only covered the front entrance of the hotel and the rear courtyard. There was no camera coverage, whatsoever, of the side door, which was used by clientele who wished to keep their hotel comings and goings a secret. Hardly surprising, therefore, that the cameras had revealed nothing to assist the detectives in their investigation.

The two detectives stared at me as I sat behind the desk. Because neither spoke for a while, the silence became so oppressive that I began to feel trapped. Meanwhile, CCTV monitors revealed the lunchtime crowd entering through the main doors. The cameras protecting the courtyard revealed a cat chasing a rat into a gap between stacks of plastic crates. Maybe the rat felt as trapped as I did? We were two creatures from different species that were united by the same sense of growing panic.

Eventually, the female detective said, "Karl, you do understand that Magenta could not have entered the old tunnel system? The roof has fallen in."

The male detective leaned forward, staring at me. "So . . . Karl . . . on the night of the incident, did you have an argument with Magenta? Was there a fight?"

My head began to ache again. Automatically, I reached for the packet of painkillers . . . and I wondered how I could prove to them that I had told the truth. That strangers had carried Magenta away.

Seven

The nightmare returned again that night. It delivered images that were fiercer, uglier, more terrifying than ever. Of course, it was the recurring nightmare of Magenta fighting those things in the cellar—those men and women with skull-like heads, grey teeth, eyes as white as milk, and their loathsome bodies stinking of wet mud. Magenta fought them, while her eyes fixed on mine. She wanted me to stay back from those violent creatures.

But I rushed at them, yelling, "Magenta!"

Then the nightmare was gone. I found myself out of bed and standing there, shivering. The bedroom was dark, absolutely dark. I couldn't see a thing. I extended my right hand, toward where I judged I'd find the light switch on the wall. My fingers moved through darkness, but they only pawed at cool air. I took a step in the direction of where I believed the switch should be.

No carpet beneath my bare feet. Only a cold, hard surface.

I thought my heart would burst with shock. That fist-sized chunk of muscle was pounding so hard with terror that it hurt so bloody much. Pain oscillated back and forth between head and heart. Where was I? Had I wandered away into the night, in a brainless zombie shuffle? Perhaps I was just ambling aimlessly through the backstreets of Leppington? I took another hesitant step forward . . . an oh-so cold floor against bare toes. Then I reached out – and I touched smooth metal.

Of course, like the spirits of the ancient Egyptian dead are supposed to return to their tombs at daybreak, after their nocturnal wanderings, a part of my bruised brain had compelled me to descend into the cellar again—it had to be the cellar, I was sure of it, even though I could not see anything in the darkness. My heart pumped blood to my brain so powerfully, that the pulse in my neck became as loud as thunder. At that moment, it seemed as if lightning had begun to flash. Yet this lightning was purple—dark purple, as dark a purple as the veins of your heart. The flashes of purple lightning did not reveal my surroundings in the cellar—I didn't even so much as glimpse the beer kegs, the old furniture—no, but, just for a second, that uncanny lightning rendered the steel door in front of me transparent. As if looking through a shop window, I saw grotesque figures. White, hairless heads—as absolutely white as skulls that had the skin peeled away. The creatures stared at me with white eyes, no colour whatsoever. Meanwhile, the fierce black pupils radiated total menace.

"We have her," their expressions seemed to say. *"We have your woman, and . . . oh, the things we have done to her . . . you wouldn't believe your eyes."*

Eight

I woke on the cellar floor. Daylight streamed in through the open doorway at the top of the steps. I was naked. Cold. My head ached. And I wondered about what had happened to me last night—where dreaming ended, where reality began. The swirl of blurred memories made me feel sick.

The reception desk clock told me it was five in the morning as I headed for the staircase. Within fifteen minutes, I'd showered in water so hot that I'd grunted with pain. After that, I lumbered unsteadily across the bedroom, took refuge under the duvet, and fell into a deep and, thankfully, nightmare-free sleep.

Nine

Stacks of empty plastic crates had been knocked over during the night. I saw them scattered in the courtyard when I gazed out of one of the staircase windows. The courtyard gates were shut and locked. So, had thieves come over the wall with the intention of breaking into the hotel, and accidentally upended the stacks? Maybe. Even so, a quick check satisfied me that none of the hotel doors or windows had been damaged. Everything was as it should be.

The bar had already opened to customers when I finally had the time to check the CCTV footage of the courtyard. That was one of those grim, blood-freezing times when, like driving past a car crash, you wished you'd looked the other way.

The camera was old and lacked a motion sensor, meaning I had to fast-forward through footage from when the hotel closed at eleven last night, the timer bar scrolling blurrily fast at the bottom of the screen. Briefly, speeded-up footage of a cat darting back and forth. A shower of rain, here and gone in the blink of an eye, as I moved through footage at x64. Then a figure appeared, climbing over the gates. The time: 24:00. Midnight—the witching hour.

I hit normal speed.

Ah . . . *her*. I watched the woman gracefully swing down from the high gates, which was an impressive feat of agility. When she dropped down onto the cobblestones, she lightly moved across the enclosed area, with its ten-foot-high brick walls, to the back door. There's no sound. These images are mute. The woman knocked on the back door, while glancing up at the windows of the higher floors as she did so. Of course, I recognised her. Sarah. The attractive woman with the heart-warming smile, who'd invited me to the party for just us two. Sarah had visited the bar earlier that evening, so why had she come back, climbing over the gate, returning like a thief in the night—or a clandestine lover? Yeah, without being overly boastful, the reason's obvious. Onscreen, Sarah stood there, part in shadow, part lit by the lamp in the street, her eyes catching the light, an expression of anticipation on her face.

Then, out of nowhere—five, six, seven figures—they were almost flowing across the ground, such was the smooth fluidity of their movements. Sarah noticed them. She reacted instantly, running back across the courtyard. Instead of heading for the high gates, she bounded up onto the stacks of plastic crates, using them like gigantic steps to take her up and above the outstretched hands of those creatures . . . those things with the hairless heads and brutish faces.

They followed, which caused stacks of crates to topple and fall under their frantic, explosive movements as they tried to catch the woman.

Then they had her. They dragged her away from where she tried scaling the wall to safety. Quickly, they hauled her down into the courtyard, where they forced her to the ground. The camera's sensitive lens made her face look as bright as a flashing lamp. Eyes, teeth, mouth—mouth opening so wide, revealing a void of blackness.

"She was screaming," I whispered to myself. "The poor woman was screaming."

The seven creatures pounced on her; they bit the bare skin of her face, neck, throat, arms, thighs. Seven sets of jaws working hard, gnawing. They opened wounds in her flesh. And, in the shadows, the blood formed streams of black rather than crimson. Those figures weren't eating. *But they were feeding.* They were frenziedly lapping with their tongues. Drinking her lifeblood.

Then the screen crashed to black. Maybe a hand had been clamped over the lens. Whatever the reason, I saw no more of that vile attack on Sarah. My heart pounded as I grabbed the phone.

"Calling the police won't do any good."

The voice startled me so much that I twisted around in the chair. There he was, the thin man, the one I referred to as the beer-drinker. He stood in the doorway, wearing the suede jacket, and the shoes styled by John Galliano—every inch the former rock star—and he possessed oh-so solemn eyes that were fixed on mine.

The man spoke again, with a voice as refined as his clothes: "We need to talk about Magenta. And vampires."

Ten

I finished my usual checks after the bar had closed. The last of the customers and the staff were heading off into the night. As always, my old friend, the perennial stab of pain in the head, had returned, so I went into the back office to grab a couple of those mind-swamping-sense-distorting painkillers the doctor had prescribed. I swallowed the medication dry. That done, I pressed the heel of my right hand against the back of my head, where my skull had crunched into the beer keg. After I down the pills, the muscles in my back would always writhe, like boa-constrictors beneath the skin, as if the muscles there protested my decision to dampen down body and mind with powerful chemicals.

Of course, by the time I'd swallowed those little pellets of pain relief, my busted memory circuits dumped any recollection of locking the hotel doors. However, in an attempt to get organized, I'd nurtured the habit of writing down virtually everything I did as a memory prompt, so I pulled the notepad from my back pocket, which listed orders for drinks that I'd scribbled down at the bar as I served customers:

2 gin and tonic (1 with lime slice).
2 pints Leppington Blonde.
1 Yorkist Porter and 1 medium red wine.

Yet instead of the usual reassuring message to myself that I'd switched off the bar lights and locked the doors, there was a mysterious note; one I had no recollection of writing:

Changed Clothes. Knives. Meet Joseph Krasten, 11.30. Be ready.

Astonished, I looked down at what I was wearing. At some point, I don't know when, I'd changed into an old pair of jeans; a thick fleece, which I usually wore outdoors, and rugged hiking boots.

I stared at the notepad. "Who the hell is Joseph Krasten?"

"That would be me."

I turned around to see the beer-drinker.

The man who claimed to be Joseph Krasten stood there in the office doorway. He had swapped John Galliano for rigger boots, and he'd paired a black leather jacket with black corduroys. In one hand, he carried a muddy shovel.

"Karl," he began, "I've opened the door in the basement, and cleared the roof fall that blocked the tunnel." He took a swig of whisky from a bottle he carried in his other hand. "Karl, you do remember our conversation this afternoon?"

I indicated that I did with a nod, but could I remember a single word of that conversation? No, I could not.

Joseph continued: "I ask whether you recall our discussion, because you told me that due to your head injury you suffer memory lapses."

My brain had fogged with that old painkiller magic; nevertheless, I sussed that Joseph Krasten and I had agreed to do something important. If I went along with all this, pretended I remembered every word of our earlier conversation, then I'd probably dredge up the relevant memory soon anyway. So, with a smile, I told him I was fine.

Joseph nodded. "Come on," he said in a decidedly sombre tone. "We're running late, it's after midnight. We need to go in fast and hard if this is going to work."

"Yes." I spoke in a way that was maybe too stiffly am-dram, because I could remember nothing at all of our conversation, and, okay, consider me vain, but I didn't want this stranger to perceive me as being dim-witted. "Yes. Time we got going."

Going where? The tunnel, apparently. But why? Of course, I remembered that's where those creatures had carried Magenta. Even so . . . the tunnel? What if I had accidentally knocked myself out in the cellar, then dreamt about the skull-head beasties?

Joseph took another pull on the whisky bottle. "I won't offer you any booze," he told me. "You've swallowed four of those pills, just while we've been talking now."

Had I? The dosage was two every four hours.

Return of the Blood-Feeders

Joseph led the way into the cellar. The stack of beer kegs raised comparisons in my mind to drum-shaped coffins—morbid canisters for assorted body parts from mutilated victims of war—arms and legs dripping red, stuffed into the barrel, then . . .

"Karl, you sure you're okay?"

A drug sweat made my face as slick as if I'd daubed myself with olive oil. The back of my skull hurt. A sharp-toothed rat was striving to gnaw through the bone to the squishy stuff inside. That's what it felt like to me.

"Yes, fine, Joseph." A whopping great lie, of course. But, my God, at least I successfully remembered his name.

We crossed the floor to the tunnel's doorway. Beyond which lay darkness, nothing but darkness.

Sarcastically, I thought, *"We're okay here, aren't we? We're on some kind of mission. And there's me, remembering bugger-all half the time . . . and there's him, Joseph, an alcoholic, necking booze straight from the bottle."*

He paused and stared right at me. "You know, you did say that out loud? You didn't just think it. Yes. I am an alcoholic. What happened to me in that tunnel fifteen years ago turned me into one. But now I've got a chance to do something of value again."

"Sorry."

"Don't be. Here . . . time to tool up." On a table earlier, he must have set out flashlights and small lights fixed to headbands. "Put on a headtorch." He then lugged a heavy-duty lump of equipment up from the floor. "Earlier, you told me that you know how to handle one of these?"

"A chainsaw . . . yes."

What's with the chainsaw? I must have stared at it with an expression of total confusion.

"Karl. You told me you spent all of January cutting up logs with one of these. Is that true?"

"Yes. It's true. I do know how to use a chainsaw."

"Good. Because garlic doesn't repel them. Crucifixes don't frighten them. They aren't like the ones in films. And you can forget stakes. Stakes don't even slow them down."

"Vampires . . . Joseph? Are you talking about vampires?"

"I am, Karl. And we are just about to go to war against a whole vampire army. They are ancient vampires, from the time of the Vikings. There'll be modern ones, too. New recruits, as it were.

Watch the new vampires. They're sly creatures. And as fast as rats in a pantry."

He handed me the chainsaw.

"Start your engine, Karl."

From his jacket pocket, he pulled out a large kitchen knife, the kind the hotel cook wields to hack through frozen meat. That done, he picked up a pistol-grip flashlight from the table.

Joseph gave a grim laugh that sounded so morbid in that echoing tomb of a place. "A man filled to gills with painkillers, plus a worn-out alcoholic. We make a formidable duo of vampire killers, don't we?"

Okay, the scorn was rich in his voice, yet my mind had started to clear—a hard, focussed certainty was beginning to form inside my head. "Whatever it takes, I'll find Magenta. Because that's why we're doing this. Am I right?"

"Absolutely, Karl. Though, be warned, even if we do bring Magenta back, she might not be as you remember her."

I switched on my headtorch before starting the chainsaw motor. Then, holding the thing with the blade up at a ninety-degree angle, like it had become a sword of vengeance, I entered the tunnel. No going back now. This felt like being swallowed into the forever-dark of Death itself.

Eleven

The tunnel had been carved from bedrock; it was a dark rock, oozing shining moisture. The lights from my headtorch, and the pistol-grip flashlight Joseph Krasten held, lit the way ahead with a searing brilliance that hurt my eyes. In my two-handed grip, the chainsaw puttered away, blowing out puffs of blue smoke. Why had Joseph given me the chainsaw? Would I be expected to cut through barriers down here beneath Leppington? I glanced up, picturing the underside of streets and houses and shops above me. Just then, we had to climb over a mound of stones that must have been the site of the roof fall that Joseph had cleared today.

Pausing, just a for a moment, Joseph said, "I had to shift the rubble in order for us to get through. The vampires, though . . . they're like snakes. They can squirm through the narrowest of gaps. They'd finally created an aperture that was big enough for them to access the part of the tunnel that terminates at the hotel. That allowed them to force open the steel door into the cellar." After he'd uttered those words, he continued walking. And I followed. Admittedly, the painkillers were making me wobble a bit as I moved, but I was managing to keep my balance.

The tunnel wasn't at all large. I could reach up and touch the roof. And, if I had wanted to, I could stand in the middle of the tunnel, then reach out at either side, and my fingertips would brush the walls.

Seeing Joseph take repeated swigs from the whisky bottle didn't reassure me at all. Had we both been consumed by some mutual fantasy, generated by his alcoholic mania and my head injury?

I needed reassurance. "We will find Magenta down here? You're sure?"

"Oh, she will be down here, Karl. I fought those monsters fifteen years ago. I succeeded in containing them in the tunnel. I became their prison warden. That's the real reason I return to the Station Hotel every day." He shot a strange grin at me. "Sentry duty. Though every good sentry deserves refreshment." He took another swallow of amber charm.

"And those monsters are vampires?"

"Indeed, so. They are ancient ones, from the age of the Vikings a thousand years ago, when Christianity forced the old Norse gods into exile. The likes of Odin and Thor, you know? Well, those gods just ignited—ignited with a lust for vengeance. That's why they wouldn't let dead Viking warriors remain dead . . . the pagan gods created a vampire army, which they concealed in caves beneath Leppington. And that is where they'd wait until the time was right to punish the cohort of humanity that embraced the teachings of Christ—something which resulted in the majority of English people turning their backs on Viking deities." The man's whisky-lubed words had slipped quickly from his mouth as we walked. The air smelt of wet soil, and of exhaust fumes from the chainsaw's motor. "The vampires want Magenta. Special blood, you see. They could smell it from down here, even though she lived high above them in the hotel. Her blood is the key . . . the liquid crimson key to their prison cell. Now they are breaking out, Karl. The gods will have their vengeance on humanity . . . and it's happening now." Joseph stumbled. Debris tripping him? Or drunkenness? He used the wall to steady himself, planting his hand against an oval patch of milk-white mould that uncannily resembled a human face. I could even make out the shape of closed eyes, a nose, delicate lips.

That's when our lights went out. Blackness thrust itself hard into my eyes. I gasped, because this darkness was terrifying, and it filled my mind with stark images of the end of the world. I pictured skull-headed vampires. Those macabre creatures were building profane altars out of living men, women and children before setting them on fire, and dancing around in the flickering light to the grim music of agony-driven screams.

Joseph whispered from the darkness: "They can do that, Karl. They have the power to rob batteries of their power."

"We need to go back . . . fetch a gas lantern."

"No, it's temporary. They can't choke off the electricity for long."

Return of the Blood-Feeders

"The night they took Magenta, the hotel lights went out."

"The vampires did that. Don't worry, Karl, the light will come back."

"Joseph, why not just tell the police about this? Let them sort it."

"Do you really think they'll believe us?"

I shook my head. "I told the detectives what happened, Magenta being abducted in the cellar, but they thought I'd dreamt the whole thing."

"Therefore, it's down to us. Okay, we must get going. Time's running out."

So, we moved forward by touch alone, the chainsaw pulsating in my hand, its motor idling on the minimum throttle setting, the fingers of my other hand stroking along the wall. It was cold, hard, wet. Then I found myself touching an inexplicably spongy growth in the darkness. What was that? Mould? Fungus? A face? My heart hurt so much, like it was being gripped by an iron fist . . . tighter, tighter, constricting the blood flow; that's how it felt to me.

"Magenta. Magenta." This was the charm I murmured to give me the courage to continue. "I will find you, Magenta. I will."

Cobwebs were the subtlest of presences touching my face. At least, I assumed they were cobwebs because I could see nothing.

Then came one of those sensations that seem as if it has been drawn, squirming, writhing, from the bleakest of nightmares. I even found myself holding my breath, trying to blot out the sensation. I couldn't, though. I felt everything.

You see, things, – *things* that were soft and cold and moist - had begun touching the bare skin of my forehead, my throat and then, worst of all, my lips. Sometimes those *things*, which were unseen in the darkness, felt like tongues. They were like tongues that were more slimy than wet, and which, with their own brand of unsettling eroticism, licked my mouth. When I attempted to claw those *things* away from me in the darkness, my fingers raked nothing but cold air.

"Joseph," I murmured, "can those vampires make us feel things that aren't there?"

Joseph did not answer.

"Joseph . . . Joseph? Where are you?"

Despair and panic filled me. I could see nothing, nothing at all. At that moment, I experienced the same emotions that my ancestors must have felt a hundred thousand years ago when they were lost in the dark and they heard the rustling sounds of predators closing in. I expected my own death very soon. A death that would be violent, painful, and terrible. And, in this darkness, I would not even know what had slaughtered me.

Twelve

Just as Joseph Krasten promised, the vampires couldn't kill our lights permanently, and abruptly the electricity returned to the devices we carried. Light blazed from the lamp attached to my headband. For a panic-stricken moment, I'd thought that Joseph had deserted me in the tunnel, that he'd left me alone down there. However, there he was. Maybe terror, or the effects of the Scotch, had silenced him momentarily. In any event, he was still by my side. He held the pistol-grip flashlight as if aiming a gun. In that dazzling cascade of light, the tunnel ahead was revealed.

And here is Sarah . . .

She stood there in the tunnel. Her eyes were shut. She smiled that heart-warming smile of hers.

"Karl," she murmured. "I knew you'd find me."

Sarah's dress was smeared with dirt and torn; one of the rips exposed the bare skin of her belly. Her flesh was blue with cold.

Joseph stared at me, his eyes bright with worry. "Karl. Can you continue?"

"Yes."

Joseph put his hand on my shoulder, a gesture of compassion. "You keep fading out on me. Do you remember cutting through the gate back there?"

I shook my head.

"Try to keep a grip on your mind."

"Says you with the whisky." I swayed there, feeling like I could fall asleep on my feet. "Sorry," I muttered at the sight of his hurt expression. "Too many painkillers . . . I lost count . . . swallow them like chocolate drops." Muscles writhed beneath the skin of my back, as angry as serpents that had been goaded with sharpened sticks. My body rebelled against the copious intake of drugs. Apparently, the flesh preferred the mind to feel the agony of that head injury. I bit my top lip, trying to use pain to blow the mind fog away. *Okay, Karl. Time to take control of events. Time to be the pilot of your destiny . . . not the passenger.*

"Sarah." I moved closer to the woman. "Sarah. I'll take you back to the hotel."

"No." Still with her eyes closed, she gently shook her head. "No, Karl, you lovely man." Then she opened her eyes. "No. I am here to show you something amazing."

Sarah's eyes were all white. All white, that is, apart from a fierce black pupil in the centre of each eye.

"I did warn you, Karl. Don't you remember?" Joseph's voice rose as fear gripped him. "She's a vampire. They made her into one. Don't let her touch you!"

Sarah held out her arms as if she wanted to embrace me.

Joseph spoke loudly, "Karl, the chainsaw. Remember what I told you, and how you should use it."

What has Joseph told me about the chainsaw? I can't remember . . .

Sarah's lips parted in a smile. Her teeth were grey . . . somehow dry-looking, too . . . her lips, though, were still red—a bright, striking red. She took a step toward me, whereupon Joseph immediately shone the powerful flashlight into her face as if he believed the flashlight had become a ray gun that could destroy her. The bizarre act of a drunk? No, maybe not . . . because the light was so powerful it seemed to hurt Sarah's white eyes that bulged from their sockets like boiled eggs. A strange comparison, I know, but that's what they reminded me of. Her eyes really did resemble boiled eggs, which had been peeled of their shell, leaving soft egg white. When Joseph moved closer to the woman, she backstepped, trying to avoid the powerful intensity of the light, even raising her hand to shield her face.

But then she made this statement with such force that the echoes of her voice raced away into the forbidding distances of this subterranean labyrinth: "Karl. They waited for you. They want to show you what they can do. They crave to demonstrate their power."

The harsh glare of the flashlight revealed bite marks on her neck, face, and the bare expanse of belly, which was exposed by the torn dress.

As she walked away, she said: "And if you want to see Magenta again, follow me."

Thirteen

The tunnel grew larger as it stretched ahead of me. Now it was perhaps four metres wide, and three high. Blue-white fungus bulged out from the rock walls in soft shapes that mimicked faces. Sometimes those pulpy shapes quivered. I'm sure of it, as if pulsating with some primeval form of life. The woman skipped ahead of us, while occasionally glancing back. The 'knowing' expression on her face made my skin crawl. She knew what would happen to Joseph and me, and that knowledge fed something vile that gestated inside of her.

My hands tightened around the grips of the chainsaw. Its motor beat out a slow rhythm so strongly it felt as if I carried a beating heart. Our lights were reflected back at us from the walls, hurting my eyes, triggering one of those cruel headaches that I'd experienced time and again of late—headaches that often had the power to force me down to my knees, with my head in my hands, and panting with the sheer agony of it all.

Not this time. Keep moving forward. Find Magenta. She's down here. I know she is.

Sarah walked backwards now, as if playfully teasing me. Erotically teasing me, at that. Her smile poured a cupful of warmth into my chest. Those lips . . . what would it be like to kiss those red lips?

A hand gripped my forearm powerfully enough to hurt. This was Joseph, forcing me to pause.

"She's a vampire." Joseph pointed at the smiling woman. "I know you are forgetful, Karl, just don't forget what she has become. She is leading us to other vampires. If they can, they will rip holes in our veins so that they can drink our blood."

"Don't worry. My memory is better than you think."

"I'm glad to hear that, Karl."

His expression told me that he didn't believe a word. He knew memory leaked from my skull like water through a cullender.

Sarah continued walking backwards, making 'follow me, darling' gestures with her hands—a gesture that must please her lovers when she beckoned them to her bed.

And so, we travelled ever deeper into the tunnel, which ran beneath Leppington town. As I walked, I exercised memory muscle. *My name is Karl Upton. I am thirty-eight. My first pet was a goldfish called Jaws. My grandad named the fish. Planets in order of distance from the sun: Mercury, Venus, Earth, Mars, Jupiter . . .*

We turned a corner in the tunnel to find it full of figures. They stood side-by-side, blocking the passageway, bald heads glinting in the glare of Joseph's flashlight. Their clothes hung in frayed strips, revealing patches of blue-white skin.

"Vampires." I raised the chainsaw, as if that machine, built for ripping through trees, was my sword of annihilation, my Excalibur.

"Vampires," agreed Joseph. "Now . . . you do remember what I told you about the chainsaw?"

What instructions had he given me? I fiercely searched for that elusive memory. *Come on, Karl, think. Think, because . . .*

Because things suddenly started to happen at a furious speed. Certainly, too fast for me to say, *"Sorry, Joseph, remind me about the chainsaw. How am I supposed to use it?"* because the vampires surged forward, bare feet pounding against the floor of the tunnel.

Joseph yelled, "Now, Karl! Fight them!"

The vampires ran towards us. Sarah jumped to one side. She forced her spine against wet rock as if she avoided a truck barrelling through. A huge grin blazed from her face. She—or the monstrous thing she had become—was exhilarated by the violent, headlong charge of the vampires. There were dozens of the things, possibly hundreds. Joseph's flashlight revealed a river of bobbing heads, way back along the tunnel.

Then the truth of what I saw hit me. "Joseph! They're joined together! They've fused!"

Joseph shouted, "In Viking mythology, when the dead of the battlefield were piled up in mounds, the corpses sometimes had the power to merge into a single creature, which would then run amok. The Vikings had a name for the corpse monster—Helsvir!"

Helsvir. That first syllable seemed grotesquely apt.

Return of the Blood-Feeders

These had been mortal human beings once. However, they had become conjoined. Merging with one another, as if parts of their bodies had melted into the flesh of the man or woman next to them. Perhaps these vampires had lain together in a mound for years until there had been a confluence of nerves and blood vessels and skin and intestine and bowel.

"The chainsaw!" Joseph roared. "Use the chainsaw!"

The abomination that was named Helsvir, forced itself through the stone throat of the tunnel. It moved like a millipede on hundreds of once human legs—twelve metres away, ten, nine . . .

I yelled, *"Joseph! Remind me! How should I use the chainsaw?"*

Then this huge clot of human flesh changed direction—not left, not right, but up!

Helsvir moved with such power and speed that even the roof presented no obstacle. The creature, which was the size of a truck, smashed through the rock above our heads, driving up toward the surface, and the cool night air.

"Karl! You must stop it!"

No. My mission wasn't stopping Helsvir from doing whatever it planned, my mission was to find Magenta and bring her home.

"Grab hold," I yelled to Joseph. "Grab hold and hang on!"

I hurled myself at the creature, as that pale leviathan flowed upwards. I flung an arm around a neck, which connected one of those bald heads to blue-while shoulders. Then I was riding the beast—up, up, up.

Relentlessly, Helsvir was breaking out of its prison, ripping a way through with a hundred hands. We emerged into the graveyard of a church, just a hundred metres from the Station Hotel. I hung on, watching in amazement and horror, as Helsvir erupted from the cemetery in a fountain of grave soil, along with a shower of white bones from old tombs. Seconds later, Helsvir moved with the smooth undulating motion of a millipede, through the cemetery, its sheer weight splintering headstones into a million fragments of stone.

I clung to Helsvir's loathsome back, which was formed from dozens of vampires. Arms by the hundred swayed—stumpy blue-white tentacles, of sorts, that terminated in hands with grasping fingers and blackened fingernails. Heads by the dozen, too, budded from the back of the creature where I succeeded in clinging on.

And, by some miracle of desperate strength, I still gripped the chainsaw. Its motor had died, but I refused to abandon what was my only weapon.

Joseph, I saw, had also managed to leap onto the broad back of the monster, which now glided smoothly through the cemetery toward the road. There, streetlamps blazed bright, illuminating rows of shops, pubs, the new Aldi supermarket, the train station, and the Station Hotel itself. Although I couldn't see Helsvir in its entirety (thereby allowing me to describe it fully), I had the impression that the thing was roughly barrel-shaped, flattened at both ends, with no discernible front or rear, and no actual head, other than the dozens of once-human heads that extended from its body. Its back formed something like a boat deck or a platform that was perhaps ten metres in length and five metres wide. It was on this expanse of back, composed of fused-together vampires, that I rode the creature.

Joseph called out: "Karl. Magenta's feeding the beast. They're keeping Magenta alive for her blood!"

Then, in the light of a streetlamp, I saw Magenta. At first, she appeared to be riding Helsvir, like someone rides a horse. However, then I realized she did not sit with her legs astride the back. No, the bottom half of her body was submerged as far as the waist in the vile thing. Legs, hips—they were embedded in pale, conjoined vampire flesh.

Joseph had abandoned his flashlight by now; he used both hands to grip one of the many arms that protruded from the monster. Constantly, he had to squirm from side to side, as he endeavoured to avoid heads that budded from Helsvir—all those heads with snapping mouths that tried to bite him.

He shouted, "Magenta's blood . . . there must be a special quality in its composition. It has become a catalyst for their metamorphosis."

"How do you know this?" I yelled those words at him as Helsvir crunched loudly over parked cars (fortunately empty of people). "How can you possibly know the . . . the biology of these things? You're never bloody sober! You're the town drunk!"

"I told you! I've fought these things before . . . you've got to keep a grip on your memories, Karl. If you don't, you're a dead man. Or, worse, you become one of these things."

Helsvir sped along a line of trees, the branches almost scraping me off that glistening back. I saw a lock of Magenta's dark hair fluttering from a branch as it whipped by me, low-hanging boughs having clawed at Magenta's head as she rode Helsvir's brute flesh.

Streetlamps revealed Magenta's face. Her eyes were dull, out of focus. She appeared to be in a trance. My God, I hoped she was insensible to all that had happened to her. If she knew about her grim situation, how could she remain sane?

A sudden pain in my ankle prompted me to drag my knee up to my chest as I lay there, hanging onto one of the cold necks. I realized that a head, bulging from the body, had bitten my ankle. Fortunately, my boots had protected me. Even so, the grip of those jaws had been so fierce it had bloody well hurt.

The chainsaw . . . at last, I remembered. But it had stopped working. Nevertheless, I risked kneeling up on the monster's heaving back to restart the motor. I gripped the T-handle and pulled. Nothing. The motor remained lifeless.

"Karl," yelled Joseph. "Use the chainsaw. If you don't, they'll tear us to pieces!"

I tugged the starter cord again. The thing spluttered; a single puff of blue smoke shot from the exhaust outlet. The recalcitrant motor, however, refused to fire into life, the chainsaw blade remained still . . . utterly useless. No more harmful than a plastic spoon.

By this time, Helsvir moved along Leppington's main street. There was no traffic, thankfully. However, a man emerged from an alleyway, pulling up the zip of his fly. Helsvir struck—those dozens of arms extending from the creature's five-metre-high flank—a mass of hands grabbed the man. They pulled him toward that glistening, blue-white skin, where dozens of heads clustered like sea anemones budding from a rock in the sea. Jaws opened wide before biting, then they were feeding as the man writhed and screamed. Hard teeth bit into his face, shoulders, arms. And those teeth crunched deep into the soft bulge of his belly. I knew the mouths were gulping blood from the wounds. Shudders of pleasure ran through Helsvir. I sensed its physical ecstasy, its gratification, that shivery bliss, and yet . . . and yet the hunger still burned. Just as Joseph could never fully quench his thirst with whisky, no amount of blood would ever satisfy the eternal hunger of Helsvir.

The dozens of hands, which had grasped the stranger and pulled him to those chomping mouths, now flung the body away.

The cadaver was drained of nourishment; just a piece of garbage to them now. The body rolled over for a dozen metres, due to the force of the throw, arms, legs, and head loosely flapping. The rolling corpse smacked into a lamppost and lay still. All around me, dozens of heads opened their mouths before releasing a long sigh of gratification. No doubt, the man's blood flowed through interconnected arteries, reaching all the parts of that composite body.

The arms that emerged from Helsvir then tried to grab me. They did the same to Joseph as he lay there, now clinging to one of the heads, so he did not slip off the monster's wet back. The smell of damp soil filled my nostrils; these creatures must have lain in the sopping mud of the tunnel floor for years.

Helsvir moved toward a line of houses near the hotel. These eighteenth-century homes did not have front gardens, their doors opened directly onto the street's pavement. With it being after midnight, the houses were in darkness. Mercifully, there was still no traffic on the streets.

Joseph let out a moan of anguish. "Please, Karl . . . you must stop Helsvir. If you don't, it will slaughter everyone in the town."

Once again, I gripped the chainsaw's T-handle, then pulled hard at the starter cord.

Success! The engine roared into life. An enormous din battered my ears. Blue smoke jetted from the exhaust outlet. The rich odour of exhaust fumes filled my nose.

"I did it," I called to Joseph. "The chainsaw's working!"

Then . . . nothing . . . just moments of blankness. Eventually, I realized I stood on the back of the beast. All around me, arms were sprouting from its hide like stubby tentacles. Blue-white fists pounded at my legs, while hands with black fingernails clawed at my shins and thighs.

"For God's sake!" roared Joseph. "Keep a grip on your mind. Keep remembering what happened to you. Magenta was taken by these creatures. There she is, embedded in its back. Do you remember what you must do with the chainsaw?"

I stood there on the creature that moved smoothly—dozens of legs rippling in undulating waves. Purple lightning began to flicker in the air around me—veins of red fire streaking through the purple. The smell of burnt hair (surely, that must be my hair that had been singed). A flash of purple stung my face. Could this be yet another display of the vampires' occult power? No doubt it was. They demonstrated their superiority over us. And they milked Magenta of her blood. They'd plugged her into the monster. Then they sucked at her like the parasites they were.

Rage blazed inside of me. Suddenly my skin felt so hot I thought it would ignite.

"Joseph! I remember! I know what to do!"

I opened the throttle wide. The chainsaw screamed, the enormous sound blasting away the mind fog that the painkillers had created. Now, the chainsaw's metal teeth spun so fast they became a halo of pulsating silver.

Out of the dark sky, out of the flashing daggers of purple lightning, the chainsaw blade swung downward. I dropped to one knee. And the chainsaw became a scythe that cut through necks, arms, and jaws. Sometimes, I hacked off the upper part of a vampire head above the nose, leaving exposed brain, and ruptured blood vessels that drenched me with a clear liquid, not mortal blood.

"That's it," shouted Joseph. "That's how to destroy these creatures. Off with their heads!"

Heads, which bulged from the back of Helsvir, opened their black-lipped mouths and screamed—white eyes, swelling obscene and glistening from sockets, stared at me.

Then the madness erupted.

Helsvir torpedoed toward the line of houses. My blade flashed left, right, left again, cutting away heads. Magenta, a mute totem figure. She remained embedded up to her waist in monster flesh. Streetlamps flashed by at the same height as me. Helsvir, taller than an elephant, many tons of vampire flesh moving at speed. My chainsaw ripped the face off a woman with a birthmark shaped like a strawberry on her forehead. I cut away arms.

Then something rotten happened; something cruel, unfair—the bastard trick of all bastard tricks. When my chainsaw's whirling teeth ripped away heads, they left raw neck wounds that revealed trachea stubs and white fragments of spine. But then Helsvir's back would quickly form mounds. Seconds later, horrifically, more heads would push out through newly formed slits in the monstrous body. Fresh vampire heads, birthed from openings in the creature's hide—an effect not unlike a child forcing its head through the tight neck-hole of a sweater. Briefly distorting the face, pulling down eyes, and then the mouth at the corners, before fully emerging.

The chainsaw—my sabre, my Excalibur—roared its bloody battle cry before steel teeth ripped away new heads. This was a gory harvest indeed.

Yet even though I made gruesome progress of sorts, a wave of despair roared through me. *Karl, you're wasting your time. If you hoped that shearing off heads would weaken the brute, then you're mistaken.*

Because Helsvir, despite the devastation I inflicted upon its budding skulls, targeted the row of houses. Hands, attached to hundreds of sprouting arms, ripped down walls, exposing people asleep in their beds. Instantly, the people sat up, and they screamed at the terrible sight of the creature. A moment later, its hands darted inwards, snatching men and women from their beds. Soon human beings, either in pyjamas, nightdresses or naked, were dragged from their ruined homes to be held to chomping jaws. Jaws that gnawed with frantic speed until the gush of blood filled their mouths, then they sucked—importing more nutrition into the monster.

My mind side-slipped again; my memory was still being smothered by painkillers. I found myself standing there, unable to recall my purpose on the creature's back. *Force yourself to remember. Heal ruptured memory. Recall what happened today. Drive thoughts through their proper channels, so you can function again with clinical efficiency. My name is Karl Upton. Earlier today, Joseph changed out of John Galliano shoes and put on rigger boots with orange laces. Joseph has a bottle of whisky in his pocket. Tonight, we entered the tunnel. We are fighting vampires. And . . . and he gave me this chainsaw to slaughter those creatures!*

Yes, I remembered again. I remembered everything. The chainsaw swung in a curve as I moved with the rhythm of a farmer from olden times, who reaps corn with a scythe. I cut away more heads that tried to bite me. I sheared off arms that would grab me and hold me down if they could. I moved forward to the part of the monster's back where I could begin cutting away the heads and arms that battled with Joseph.

He called out to me, "Karl, you don't have long. The fuel will run out soon! If you plan on doing something to save us, you need to do it now!"

Helsvir continued its own harvest of townsfolk. Breaking down house walls, extracting writhing, screaming victims. A woman with long red hair slipped out of Helsvir's grasp and fell five metres to the street below. Her head burst against hard blacktop to create a sunburst pattern of blood and brain.

Purple lightning crackled about the creature—a dark purple, veined with spitting streaks of crimson fire. A human brain produces electricity. Therefore, how much voltage would a thousand linked brains generate? Was this purple lightning that flashed through the air around the creature a by-product of its mental activity? Did Helsvir's interlocking minds disgorge this evil-looking lightning? Although I wasn't harmed, its heat continued to scorch my hair. And now the muddy odours of the vampires mingled with the stench of burnt hair. Yet, threaded through that, the scent of musk—a heavy, aromatic musk. Is that the smell of the clear syrup that I released from vampire veins when I carved their bodies?

Meanwhile, a small part of my own mind became the dispassionate narrator of events: *Horror thunders onward, like a runaway train. Helsvir moves to the next house. Crash! More walls collapse, exposing screaming human beings that beg for their lives. Helsvir needs more blood. Therefore, it scoops out those living morsels of humanity from within the crust of stonework.*

"Stop it! Don't touch them!" I screamed this at Helsvir. "Leave those people alone!"

Helsvir didn't respond. It didn't even seem to hear my shout, proving to me that trying to reason with the creature was as pointless as trying to persuade a maggot to stop feeding on rotting meat. The many arms of Helsvir reached into a bedroom, through a hole it had torn in a roof. An elderly man, with a remarkable splash of silver hair, reared up from the bed. The man was holding aloft a wooden crucifix, his shield of Faith. Helsvir lunged at him. One of the mouths snipped away the man's head, releasing spurting crimson from the gaping neck.

Above the din of a hundred furious hands, ripping stonework, searching for fresh blood, I heard the chainsaw's motor begin to falter.

"Fuel's running low," I shouted. "It could stop at any minute!"

"Then do what you have to do, Karl."

"What is that?"

"I'm sorry. I don't know."

"What the hell can I do, Joseph?"

"Let your instinct guide you."

I felt the vibration of the motor change, its rhythm wasn't as regular, the motor was being starved of fuel. *Probably running on fumes. Soon it will cut out.*

A hundred metres away, a bus appeared. It was a coach full of people, perhaps coming back from a party or a wedding. Faces peered out through the windows; mouths were dropping open in shock when they saw the monster tearing open buildings.

Helsvir, through its hundreds of eyes, saw the coach full of men and women. Immediately, the brute pushed itself back out of the ruined house. *Food,* it must have thought. *Food, and new recruits for the vampire army.* Seconds later, with that millipede-like undulating grace, Helsvir moved in for the kill. The bus driver tried to reverse. In his panic, he stalled the engine. Above the ecstatic sighs of freshly budded heads all around me, I heard the vehicle's starter motor cranking away. Yet the engine would not fire.

I have twenty seconds to save them. I told myself this as the chainsaw motor began to falter. I pictured the last trickle of fuel draining from the fuel tank toward the piston. Nevertheless, I continued my harvest, opening the throttle wide as I did so. Ten heads were shredded by the speeding chain that carried saw teeth. A tongue, ripped from a mouth, hit my thigh; it stuck there, a pellet of dark matter.

Joseph, meanwhile, pulled the knife from his jacket, then began hacking at the hands that tried to grab hold of him.

I called out, "I'm not even slowing this monster, let alone stopping it."

"Think of something, Karl. For the sake of everyone on that bus!"

My gaze found Magenta. She was a living implant embedded in the spine of the beast. Intravenously, she supplied blood that was infused with some exquisite quality—a rare chemical, an enzyme? I don't know what exactly, but I did know one shining, inescapable fact.

"Joseph," I shouted. "I'm going to get Magenta out."

"You can't. Her blood vessels have merged with those of Helsvir. You'll kill her."

"It'll work . . . I'll make it work." But doubt rose, like a sinister phantom, inside my own head. What I planned was tantamount to surgery. But what if I experienced one of those incidents of memory rupture? What if I had a mental blackout partway through the operation? Magenta would die. Helsvir would kill everyone on the bus. Then Joseph and I would be next.

Helsvir had, in fact, almost reached the vehicle. And still, the driver hadn't been able to start the motor. At that moment, everyone remained onboard, perhaps trusting that the steel bodywork would shield them. Not a chance. Not a hope in hell. They would die. But the worst thing is this: death might not be the end for them. Maybe their future lay in becoming part of Helsvir.

The vehicle's lights illuminated the scene more brightly than the streetlamps. Heads still pushed through slits in Helsvir's flesh to replace the ones I had cut away. The chainsaw dripped with that transparent vampire blood. Its engine stuttered as the fuel tank ran dry. Just then, a naked man raced from the ruins of a house. Helsvir's crop of arms on its right flank caught him, swept him up to its cluster of heads. There the man screamed as teeth crunched through skin to release the blood beneath.

Heart pounding, pain spearing my own skull, as my bruised brain became engorged with blood and adrenalin, I slithered along Helsvir's back until I reached Magenta.

I shouted, "Joseph. I need your help. Get ready to pull her clear!"

The engine's *putt-putt-putt* grew slower. If the engine should fail now, I might as well cut my own throat to escape this whirlpool of terror. Above me, the sky was a black dome, streetlamps swept by; an overhanging branch clawed at my head.

Joseph squirmed forward over heads with chomping mouths that snapped at him, trying to bite the man. Hands that belonged to protruding arms grabbed him. Once more, he used the knife, slashing at those limbs. Then a hand snatched the knife from his grasp and flung it away before trying to grip Joseph by the throat. Nevertheless, he managed to join me, right where Magenta's upper half protruded from the body of Helsvir. By now, Helsvir had reached the coach. Hands by the dozen tore at the metalwork, making small holes in the roof, then ripping at them with strong fingers to make those small holes larger.

Instead of using the chainsaw like a scythe now, I pointed it vertically downwards, then I shook it hard in the hope of coaxing the last drops of fuel from the tank, down into the carburettor. Thank Heaven. The motor roared with such power the sound hurt my ears. Immediately, I drove the chainsaw down, just centimetres from Magenta's belly. I had no way of knowing whether her legs, hidden by the creature's flesh, would be clear of the spinning chain with its dangerously sharp teeth.

As the blade went deep, the heads around me screamed in agony. The interconnected nervous systems were transmitting the pain signal to their fellow vampires.

I worked quickly. Cutting vertically downward into the brute's flesh, as deep as the chainsaw blade would go. Then I worked my way around Magenta's waist at a distance of just five or six centimetres. My plan was brutally simple: to cut out a plug of monster flesh with Magenta still enclosed in the plug. Purple lightning crackled all around us. A flash struck Joseph's ear—the lobe instantly turned black and charred. Yet he did not flinch. He gripped Magenta's left arm.

"Karl! Stop it! I won't let you!" This was a woman's voice.

I turned to see Sarah climbing onto Helsvir's back. Evidently, she had seen what I was doing and knew the danger my actions posed to her vile lord.

"Leave Helsvir!" she yelled, "I won't let you hurt him."

The chainsaw sang out its own savage battle cry. I swung the blade from left to right—a scything motion. Sarah's head, now no longer fixed to her neck, bounced onto the creature's back where eager hands grabbed it, the brains inside the heads believing this was food. The headless body of the woman slithered from the creature, falling to the street below.

That is when the motor died. With the chainsaw dead, I had no further use for it and flung the machine aside.

"Help me, Joseph." I grabbed Magenta's right arm, which hung limply. "Help me pull!"

Meanwhile, the limbs that swarmed out of Helsvir still worked furiously to break into the bus. Any moment now, there would be more slaughter.

Joseph grunted. "You didn't cut all the way around. There's still flesh connected."

"We don't have any other options now. Pull!"

We pulled so hard I heard my tendons crackle. My brain

seemed to beat like a heart against the bone of my skull. Waves of pain engulfed me.

But the pain gave me energy, too.

"Pull!"

We both pulled so hard that our knees buckled. Then, finally . . . at last . . . Magenta began to move upwards. Upwards and out. A woman encased in a plug of evil flesh . . . flesh that oozed clear-as-water vampire blood. Suddenly, Magenta emerged from the wet cavity. Veins that extended from her own legs into the body of Helsvir snapped. The blood running from the veins was red—very red. Human blood. Magenta's blood.

The monster stopped. As suddenly and as finally as that. Helsvir no longer tried to rip its way into the bus.

Every single mouth belonging to every single head that budded from the creature began to howl with such pain and immense despair. A powerful indication that the creature knew the end had come. Robbed of Magenta's blood, whatever forces that held all the vampires together into a single body evaporated into the darkness of the night.

Helsvir began to break apart. It became individual bodies—all cohesion gone. Whatever glued the vampires together, to form the entity had dissolved. Many of the vampires, even though they struggled to disengage themselves from the once-unified mass, appeared to be dying. And as they expired, they gradually melted into a substance that was more slush than solid flesh.

With the dissolution of Helsvir, the three of us on its back sank quite gently down through dissolving mush until we found our feet on solid ground. None of the vampires attacked us. A few opened steel manhole covers in the street then hurried back down underground, perhaps seeking a route into the tunnel. Maybe that is where they needed to be to survive. Other vampires—in fact, hundreds of them—did not make it to their underground lair. They staggered away, a mass of blue-white figures with bald heads. They tottered, then fell onto their hands and knees, heads hanging wearingly down. Their flesh turned to water, then the bones liquified, before trickling away along gutters and into drains.

Joseph spoke almost matter-of-factly, as he helped me hold the unconscious form of Magenta. "It's over, Karl. Come on, we'll take Magenta back to the hotel."

Fourteen

Life returned to something like normal. The public inquiry would take years to reach suitably non-committal and diplomatically ambiguous conclusions about what had happened in Leppington the night so many of its inhabitants died. An earthquake, poor building construction, fear and hysteria leading to collective hallucination. Commentators on social media fed the public morsels of truth about a creature rampaging through the town. But those scant morsels of truth were soon swept into oblivion by a tidal wave of increasingly wild theories, involving alien invaders, or mind-altering bacteria, or military brainwashing experiments. What's more, you can add thousands of comments that are either sceptical, witty, sarcastic, or downright insulting.

Joseph Krasten has retired as the vampires' jailor and resides in a hospice where he accommodates stage three cancer of the stomach—something which he had previously hidden from me, the only man he refers to as his friend.

I work in the hotel. Welcoming guests, changing over beer kegs, serving drinks in the bar. I don't need the notepad anymore to list customers' drink orders.

Magenta did not suffer any harm after the blood vessels that connected her to Helsvir were severed. Maybe her blood does possess some miraculous quality; perhaps the elixir of life, itself? Magenta is full of vigour, and both of us are happy to be living together. When she falls asleep at night, I pad down to the cellar, check the steel door—and its padlocks—making sure that formidable barrier is securely locked. Occasionally, I hear faint scraping sounds from the other side of the door—fingernails scratching metal, that's what it sounds like to me. Yes, I know there are survivors in the tunnel. The vampires are healing themselves. They are slowly regaining their strength.

Return of the Blood-Feeders

From time to time, I drop a hint to Magenta about one strange night, many years ago, when something odd happened in the cellar. She remembers nothing.

As for me? I remember everything.

Perspective

Kevin J. Kennedy

It's fair to say I should be the last person telling a story like this. I was never an academic. I was never one for writing down my thoughts. I was a low achiever. I suppose I spent most of my life wondering what I was supposed to be doing. I always thought I should have had a purpose, but other times I felt like my purpose was to sit on the couch and get fat. My resolve in living a life of achievement wavered quickly, and often, when I had any delusions of success.

I continually achieved nothing of worth in the eyes of the world around me. People wanted you to have wealth, contacts, assets, looks, or something else that they could use. If most people were honest, they wouldn't be your friend or associate if they weren't getting something from you.

You see, that's the thing about vampires. They suck your blood, and sometimes, your life force, but you know where you stand with them. There is no false sense of what the vampire wants.

It's easy to look at your life and decide that you understand other people are in similar types of pain, but when you doubt your own worth, it's easy to think that their problems are more genuine than your own. It's a conundrum, and I question if you are even allowed to feel depressed. It's a sad day when you must question your own right to feel down, but it is the world we live in in 2024.

As a human, my mood was somewhat of a roller coaster. It was out of my control. There were ups and downs that became part of my normal routine. I had tried various types of pills. Some brought me up, some brought me down, some did nothing, and some just took me away for a while. Those were the best ones. Those were the ones that made me feel complete inside.

Those were the ones that made me feel like I could stay in bed every day, in a darkened room, with no one around me, forever. The secret, though, was that I would enjoy it. That I needed it. The good ones stop you from caring. You can continue through the meaninglessness of life relatively unscathed. One day, though, you might just wake up enough that you want some feeling back. You might see some glimmers of hope and decide you must take the bad with the good.

You want to give life a chance. It's not easy getting to that stage.

The stage of being willing to take a risk and knowing no matter how good you make your life, it will come with pain. It always does.

Anyway, enough reflection. This is not a self-pity story. Far from it. It's a story of my re-awakening and vampires.

There are many different types of vampires, and I will enlighten you about some of them in these pages but that's not where the story begins, but don't worry. It doesn't start with me steeped in depression either. It begins with a woman, like so many stories before.

I had come off all the anti-depressants I had been dependent on for several years and the world was starting to make sense again. I had been eating better and I had gone back to the gym. While I still had dips in my mood, I found that if I was disciplined, I could manage my moods to an extent most of the time.

Motivation was still hard to come by, so being regimented in what I did was the only plan. It took a while, but as I shed the pounds, my energy levels began to rise. I found myself actually caring about how I dressed again, as my physique moved away from my slob-like state. I was never massive, but I did have a lot of meat on the bone. Jogging bottoms and a hoodie were comfy and my chosen clothes for almost any type of event you can imagine. As my body started to take a more human shape, I found that I started pulling on a pair of jeans, a T-shirt or a nice jumper.

I'm not going to tell you that I went out and bought a three-piece suit and got a haircut, because I didn't. Very much not my style. A haircut was also out of the question as my head was kept shaved close to the bone with a clipper.

It was at the gym I went to that I met the woman I mentioned. It had really become the only place I ever went apart from work. I had stopped eating fast food as I got fitter, so rarely ventured out apart from the once a week to the supermarket to stock up. Some days I would go to the gym twice just to kill the boredom of my newfound fit life.

Before work in the morning was my preference but when I got home in the evenings, my newfound energy battled with me when I tried to laze on the couch or to lie in bed and watch movies. Enter Samantha.

I never spoke to anyone when I was in the gym. I had become a bit of an introvert as the years passed by. In my younger days, I think most people would have described me as an extrovert but depression, anxiety, and my lifestyle had buried that version of myself.

Even as I was growing stronger and living a better life, no part of me wanted to return to the party days of my early twenties. Although I had ditched the hoodies and jogging bottoms, I still wore them to the gym. I'd often have my hood up and my head down as I moved from machine to machine, or from the free weights to the treadmill.

If I didn't have a hood, I was in a beanie hat and had my headphones in. I liked to keep to myself. I had my routine, and it was working. I bothered no one and no one bothered me. The odd guy who frequented the gym at the same times that I went would often give me a nod. I would nod in response but never more. When Samantha found me, there would be none of that.

Samantha was one of those girls who was a force to be reckoned with. She had an otherworldliness about her that in hindsight makes sense, but at the time I just found her mesmerising. She was a natural redhead. Small at 5' 2" and had the brightest green eyes I had ever seen. I had seen too many guys ogle women in the gym, so I always kept my eyes straight ahead or on my phone when I was training.

Samantha, however, always seemed to manage to get herself right in my line of vision and would always make sure she caught my eye. Each time, without fail, she would give me a massive smile before going back to doing whatever she was doing. That went on for a few weeks. I grew comfortable with the routine.

I also noticed how much attention she got from the other guys in the gym, but she seemed uninterested.

I surmised she was just being friendly towards me as I never bothered her. I was working on the notion that we may never talk, though, and a warm smile may be the extent of our relationship. How wrong I was.

The first time we spoke wasn't in the gym. It was outside and it was under circumstances I would never have imagined. I had mainly always seen Samantha in the gym in the mornings, but I was there late one Friday night after a particularly hellish week at work, burning off some steam.

I had worked every muscle in my body and after a good two

hours, I was ready to go home and was confident I would be able to chill on my couch without feeling guilty about relaxing. I wasn't going anywhere so I didn't need a shower. I travelled light. I had my car keys, phone, and headphones. As I had everything on me, I made my way to the exit and outside. It was a bitter February evening, and was made worse by the fact that my clothes were soaked to my body with sweat.

You could never get parked near the gym when you came on a Friday night because the bingo crowd was next door, and they maxed out the car park. I would always park at the outdoors store on the other side of the gym. The car park was empty if you left the gym late enough. The pensioner crew that played bingo were not night owls.

I was about to break into a jog across the parking lot to my car when I heard shouting. I turned quickly to see two guys standing beside a Subaru, pulling at Samantha. I'm not going to try and big myself up here and suggest I am some sort of hero, but I always did fucking hate a bully. I had no idea what they wanted with her or if they knew her, but I knew I had to intervene.

I woke up on my back. I didn't realise it at first, but it was the night sky I was staring at. Well, the night sky and an upside-down view of Samantha's head. She was standing over me, feet at my shoulders.

"Are you okay?"

Was I okay? Did she ask me that question or did I imagine it?

"Hey, hello. Can you hear me?"

She waved her hand right in front of my face.

I started to come 'round a little. There was a ringing in my ears.

"What happened?" I couldn't remember a thing. It wasn't until later that I remembered running towards the argument, but at that moment I couldn't remember leaving the gym.

"You kinda got in the middle of an argument with me and my ex. Him and his mate fucked you up a bit."

She reached out her arm and I took it. She pulled me to my feet with surprising ease. I was fifteen stone and in fairly good shape by that point. She seemed strong for her size, even for a gym girl. I wobbled a little and she grabbed my arm and steadied me.

"Did I at least get a few good digs in?" I asked, giving her the best cheeky grin I could muster at that point.

Her smile was warm as always and then she burst out laughing.

Perspective

"You got hit from behind and hit the deck like a sack of potatoes. No shame in it. You could never have seen it coming. If it makes you feel any better, I broke two of Stephen's fingers and then smashed his nose into his face. His mate would never touch me and Stephen knows if he touched me back, he would be dead before the night is out."

"Um, violent much?"

"He has a big mouth. I have a bit of a temper. Anyway, sorry you got caught up in it all. Thanks for the chivalry. Unusual these days. Come on, I'll drive you home."

She was pretty forward, a little mental and seemed just as bolshy as she was inside the gym. I told her I had my car and she told me not to be stupid. That I could come back for it tomorrow.

"You can't drive after being knocked out, stupid!"

She had wiped her finger across my scalp, brought it in front of her face. We both saw the blood on it, then she stuck it in her mouth and sucked it clean.

Was she trying to be sexy? Was she just cleaning me up and had no real sense of normal boundaries? Did I have a concussion and imagined it?

The next thing I remember I was in her car. She practically dragged me there. I could come back for my car in the morning, she told me. The night continued in a mostly strange manner. When we got to mine, she had me invite her in. It was weird. We had a sort of conversation where by the end of it, I felt like I was speaking the words she wanted me to speak and not the ones that would have naturally come into my head. I was inviting her into my place.

A place I never invited anyone. I could not for the life of me remember the last time I had a guest and yet I was inviting an almost stranger into my home who I had just gotten knocked out for. Admittedly, she didn't ask me to get knocked out for her and in an ideal world I would have done something worthy of a beautiful female's attention but nonetheless, we were going into my place.

Luckily, I was mostly tidy for a single guy and had been looking after the place since I started to get myself back together. I had found that doing things I didn't particularly want to do, kept me feeling like I was having constant little wins. It helped.

I'm not convinced Samantha would have noticed, though. She

made her way straight to the couch and flopped down on it as if we were long-term buddies and it was her spot. I can remember standing there, a little dumbfounded as she grabbed the remote from the coffee table and switched on the TV.

"What do you fancy watching?" she asked.

She seemed a little too comfortable, but she had driven me home to make sure I was okay, and I was thinking she was one of those girls who was just entirely comfortable in their own skin. I had only ever met a few in my time but they were always easy to be around. No bullshit with that sort of girl. I was still standing in the doorway thinking that I had not planned on her coming in, never mind getting herself comfy.

I decided it was just me. I had been reclusive for too long and someone trying to be friendly seemed strange as it was out of the norm for me. At least, that's what I was telling myself.

She slapped the cushion on the couch next to her and nodded towards it at the same time. I found myself taking the spot next to her as she searched through my viewing apps. She stopped on the original Hills Have Eyes movie and hit play.

"You do like horror movies, right?"

I did, not that it seemed to have mattered. The gorgeous half-stranger sitting next to me seemed to have made her decision. I wondered if she was really a stranger. I mean, I had been going to the same gym as her for a while and we had been nodding and smiling for a while but until I got myself knocked out by her ex-boyfriend's pal, we had never spoken.

Not a stranger I decided but not quite a full acquaintance either. I loved all four of the Hills Have Eyes movies but I struggled to concentrate as we sat quietly watching it. I kinda felt like we should be talking. I had no idea what we ought to be talking about but sitting not talking to her was awkward. I don't think the feeling was mutual though.

She had kicked her trainers off, put her feet up on the coffee table and looked like she belonged where she lay. Admittedly, there was something nice about having a beautiful girl in my place. It had been an age since I had dated or even had a one-night stand.

They were frequent in my younger days, but I got bored of the bullshit. I reached a stage where I literally met women simply to sleep with them and could no longer bear the repeated mundane chat that would lead up to the inevitable intercourse, and then the pain of waiting on them to leave afterwards.

It was unfulfilling at best and downright soul-destroying at worst. I'm not going to lie and say that I didn't miss the sex. The casualness of it and what surrounded obtaining the sex was what killed me. Most likely it was one of the main things keeping me drinking, too. Most women who want to sleep with you on night one, like to get together for a drink first. I'm not suggesting this is a hard rule, but the odds most definitely weigh towards alcohol being an encouraging factor for any promiscuity. Some people use it as an excuse and others just need it to relax their nerves a bit.

I needn't have worried too much about anything like that with Samantha, though. I can't remember actually trying to start any sort of conversation, although my mind was wandering about it. I recollect almost nothing of watching the movie because my focus was shot.

I can't even remember her leaning in against me and getting herself comfortable, but I can recall the softness of her body. It was bliss. I had enjoyed being alone for a while but having a beautiful girl's body pressed against me changed all of that in an instant. I could smell coconut shampoo coming from her hair and thought about walking down a beach with her in a warm country.

That's the last thing I really thought of before I came out of what must have been an intensely deep daze, and we were in bed. Samatha was on top of me, and she was riding me hard. Her hands were on my chest and her nails were digging in deep. The skin was broken and I could feel the blood running down into my armpits.

I felt like I had literally just woken from a deep sleep. I couldn't recall us leaving the couch, kissing, undressing, even coming to the bedroom. None of it. We were watching a movie, and I was thinking of us on a beach and the next thing I knew I was inside her. While my memory seemed to have abandoned me, clarity had come crashing back.

She was slipping up my cock slowly and then thrusting herself back down. I felt like her pussy was locked onto me and trying to suck me deeper inside her. She stared at me intently. There was no throwing her head around and screaming at the ceiling. She had her eyes locked on me and I felt somewhat like prey. Not that she was trying to hurt me. Far from it. She was taking me to levels of ecstasy I had never felt before. The pain of her nails digging into my chest coupled with the tightest pussy I had ever been inside was mind-blowing. The next thing I knew she had locked her hand around my throat and leant in close.

"Fuck me harder!" she moaned in my ear.

I lifted my hips from the bed and began to thrust into her as I grabbed her ass. She kept her hand on my throat and squeezed tighter. I rode her hard and she started panting into my ear as I pulled her against me while I thrust. She growled and that's when I felt her bite me.

Now, there are a few things you should know about vampires. When a vampire bites someone, they will always turn into a vampire unless the vampire kills them. It's not a sometimes thing. It's 100% guaranteed. It's as simple as the fang piercing the skin and touching your blood. You will be a vampire within twenty-four hours. Vampires do need to drink blood.

Likely not quite as often as you would imagine but it is necessary for their survival. When a vampire drinks, they must always dispatch their victim. No one wants a horde of vampires taking over and drinking the world dry in a few weeks. We cannot turn into fucking bats. Stories about ancient vampires who possessed the ability are most likely myth, but who really knows.

Some vampires are stronger than others, some are faster, and some are smarter than others. Becoming a vampire does amplify certain aspects of yourself. Some vampires are tolerant of other vampires and others are more apt to seek a rather solitary life. I didn't know all of this upon being bitten, or even for a while after, but we learn as we grow older, vampire or human, life is a journey.

There was no mind gift that explained it all to me and Samantha wasn't the most adept at informing me of the things that I wanted to know. She had seen something she had liked in me, and she had wanted me to be like her. She wanted me to be hers. Forever.

I can remember pestering her about why she chose me. She was aloof but overall, I don't think it was much deeper than the reasons that humans use to choose a partner. She thought I was hot, she liked the fact I had tried to come to her rescue like some knight in shining armor, even though I did fuck it up, and she liked that I was regularly in the gym trying to improve myself.

When I had asked her why a vampire bothered going to the gym, she laughed and told me that we could improve our speed, strength, or bodies just like everyone else. It made sense. I still wanted to look good, and nothing had come over my mind to give an overriding sense of clarity when I became a vampire. I still had ups and downs in my moods.

I still had questions. I mean, if you think about it, I was now one of the undead. It's likely a lot for anyone to swallow but I did fall in love with Samantha quickly. She was an impressive distraction, and she knew how to keep me happy. Not something I had been overly successful in doing myself, so I had decided that being a happy vampire beat being a miserable human.

Some of the stuff you have seen in movies or read in books is true. That's always the case, though. People get some stuff right then exaggerate other bits to bring in the crowds. Life isn't always as exciting as fiction, but it can certainly be as strange.

I no longer needed to eat food, but I still needed to drink water. No other liquid, apart from blood, was any use to me, but water was still a requirement. Again, I could likely last without water for much longer than the average human, but I would still die without it, or maybe lay in an almost dead state until I got some. I'm not sure if we can fully die in that way. Sunlight did not affect me in any way, or any other vamps I had heard of. I think the biggest change for me was my perspective. You go from knowing you will die one day, to knowing you will most likely live for as long as you want to.

Nothing is guaranteed, and vampires still die. Mostly by being killed one way or another, or suicide when they have lived too long or lost too much.

After Samantha turned me, things went on as normal for a little while. At first, I still went into work each day and we continued going to the gym. We spent evenings watching old horror movies and then we would hunt. Not every single night but there was a thrill in it for me at first. I felt no guilt at taking lives. I'm not even going to tell you that we only hunted bad guys, or that we fed on the destitute, or that I tried to drink the blood of animals instead of people.

We hunted who we wanted. I don't particularly care if you

judge me. It's no different from a meat eater, eating meat. Blood nourished us and there was something more in the kill. Vampires are more animalistic than humans. Less emotional. Hunting feels natural. If I am completely honest, most people waste their life. Work a third, sleep a third and waste a third.

Some of those we killed barely even put up a fight. They were beaten by life. They had so little will to live, the struggle was nonexistent. Those were the worst. No thrill of the hunt whatsoever but the blood was still exquisite.

As the weeks passed by, I was still asking Samantha questions and gaining the odd snippet of information here and there. While I was learning and embracing my new life, I watched Samantha get bored and restless. She had never stayed in any one place for very long, I found out.

I questioned if she had stayed here for so long with the intention of turning me all along but when I questioned her on it, she told me not to be stupid. I still wonder. She told me vampires always move on. While people went missing all over the world every single day, it wasn't wise to stay put for too long. We often travelled to kill and rarely hunted near our home, so I think she was using it as an excuse to get us to move on.

I had little in the way of belongings, so I sold some shit that pulled in a few quid, and decided not to give any notice on my place that I was renting. I figured the landlord was getting to keep my deposit so that should cover him while he got another tenant. I wasn't really bothered either way.

A few weeks after we decided we were going to move on, we had booked some tickets and were on a plane to Amsterdam. Samantha had been before, but I hadn't. I had never really gone anywhere but Samantha wanted us to travel to Europe before deciding where to settle.

It all seemed pretty exciting to me. It was an adventure I would never in a million years have considered if it hadn't been for her. All I knew about Amsterdam was it was famous for weed and prostitutes. When we got there, I realized it had a lot more than that. It was a quaint little place with cobbled streets. Trams ran everywhere and there were an insane amount of bicycles.

They had these huge multi-story carparks but they were exclusively for bikes. Thousands of them lined up next to each other. I refuse to believe they were all in use. People must just abandon them eventually and they stay there for all time.

I'm actually quite confident that there are enough bicycles in Amsterdam to give one to every single person on planet Earth. Anyway, enough about the bicycles. I found it to be a beautiful country if not a little cold. I'm not sure vampires are undead. I think we are something else, because we feel the cold just like you do. Again, it may take longer to kill us but I'm sure we could freeze.

We did partake in the weed and the prostitutes. In fact, we partied quite a bit when we were there. We had nights full of alcohol accompanied by coke, ecstasy or MDMA. Other nights on mushrooms and space cakes. There were nights where we would share one of the working girls and other nights where we would party with a few of them.

We never drank from those girls. It was entirely carnal. It was too small of an area the red-light district covered, and it would have brought too much attention if those girls had gone missing. Similar to when we were in Scotland, we travelled a good distance from where we were staying before we found our next victim.

It was in Amsterdam that I met my first other supernatural. I never really liked the word supernatural but it's likely best placed to describe vampires among other non-human species. Samantha and I had never spoken much about other vampires, and it had never really crossed my mind that there might be something other than vampires out there.

There was. In a small shitty bar in a back street where we were having a quiet night with a few drinks, in walks a werewolf couple. Now, I didn't know they were werewolves. I'm not sure if Samantha did either but we both knew they weren't human. Both their heads snapped towards us as they entered. They had smelled us, straight away.

It did not erupt into a savage bar room brawl with teeth and fur flying. One of them, a woman called Elena, approached and asked if they could buy us a drink while her friend, a redhead, had gone straight to the bar. We accepted and Elena joined her partner before returning with drinks. What had begun as a quiet, somewhat hungover evening, quickly became a raucous party across the streets of Amsterdam. They were wild. I'm not sure if it is a werewolf thing or just those two, but I saw some things I cannot unsee.

Isla seemed to be in charge, although she didn't say as much, somewhat like Samantha and I. Elena spoke a lot. She regaled us with the story of how they both met. Elena had been travelling the Scottish highlands with her boyfriend. They had parked up in a secluded spot only to find out it was the location of a werewolf bar.

Isla and a few other werewolves ran it but upon meeting Elena, she had gone back to their camper van and what started out as a threesome became the demise of Elena's partner, but Isla turned Elena. She had known as soon as she had seen her that she wanted her and so she had taken her.

Werewolves were under no obligation to stay with those that were turned but Elena had been mesmerized by Isla. While Isla had initially wanted them to stay at the bar and eventually get rid of the few male wolves that were there, Elena quickly grew bored of the place. She had finally given Isla an ultimatum to go travelling and have some adventures or she would go herself. Isla had given in, and they had been travelling together for two years.

Like us, they hunted, then moved on. Werewolves did not need to eat human flesh or hunt humans but they enjoyed it. They hunted less than vampires, but they still had to be careful.

We left the bar at the suggestion of Isla. We slowly walked the streets of Amsterdam, wandering further from the tourist parts, out into the cobbled streets where there were hardly any locals roaming at that time of the evening. We were in no rush. The night was mild, and Samantha and I walked hand in hand while Elena and Isla had their arms linked.

It was nice. It was normal. Well, as normal as two werewolves and two vampires going for an evening stroll ever could be. We came across an old tavern-style drinking establishment that had seen better days and decided we were due another refreshment. As we got inside, it was extremely dark and didn't look like the sort of place that had a lot of visitors, or maybe wanted them. The girls found a table and I went to the bar and ordered four beers and four tequilas.

I didn't expect the place to have an extensive menu of alcohols from around the world so stuck to the basics that you were pretty much guaranteed to get anywhere. The bartender was quite a gruff fellow and spoke more in growls and grunts than real words. I wasn't sure it was a language barrier. I was confident that anyone who wasn't a regular would be treated in a similar fashion.

Perspective

Back at the table, Elena was doing all the talking. Isla couldn't keep her eyes off her. She spent most of her time watching her the way a child watches an ice cream cone. We had a few more drinks and while the wolves seemed uninterested with anyone around them, apart from us to an extent, I could see Samantha peering into the dark corners of the bar.

She was always on alert, no matter where we went. What she was expecting to happen, I had no idea. I often thought she was likely keeping an eye out for a tasty snack but in reality, I think it was something more. On that particular evening, I would find out when we left that there was a group of four men who had been sitting in the darkened corner, sipping their drinks and watching us.

My eyesight wasn't quite good enough to see them, but Samantha's was. It turned out Elena and Isla had seen them, too, but were less than interested. When we left the bar, Samantha leaned into my ear and asked me to go down one of the side streets and just keep walking for a bit and let her walk on with Elena and Isla.

I did as she requested, knowing better than to cause an argument. She always had a good reason for doing anything she did. In that instance, she was confident that the group of men who had been watching us would be more likely to attack if it was just a group of what they perceived to be helpless women. She was right in the fact that they would have preferred us to break off into smaller fractions. She was wrong about them going after the women. Only a few minutes after leaving them, had I decided to turn back and slowly begin to make my way back to them.

That was when I was quickly surrounded by four men who stepped from the shadows. Although I hadn't seen them in the bar, I instinctively knew. Now, I knew I was tougher as a vampire and my fear factor had been diminishing over the past few months as I retrained my brain to realise I was somewhat immortal.

I wasn't one hundred percent yet on my limits, but I did think that although I may not die, I still might have some trouble handling the four men at once.

I didn't spend a massive amount of time wondering about how things would pan out as the two men at the front pulled out knives. I was working under the assumption that their main goal was to rob me, but pride wouldn't allow me to offer them my wallet.

Well, pride and the fact that I was a god damned blood sucking vampire of the night. I accept that I had maybe watched a few too many movies. Blade, I was not. I did however carry the usual male ego where I was happy to put myself in harm's way if it allowed me to feel more manly. I knew our fangs extended when we were about to feed.

I hadn't known until that point that they extended even further when we were threatened or about to enter battle. As I felt them slide over my lips, I gave them the classic vampire hiss, making sure the full extent of my fangs were on display. It did not have the desired effect.

The first guy lunged at me and tried to stab me in the stomach with his knife. They were not playing. As I stepped to the side, the knife just missing me, the other guy lunged. I wasn't quick enough this time and he managed to stab me right through my side. By fuck it hurt. I managed to crack him square in the nose and he went flying backwards, leaving the knife in me and smashed into the guy who was behind him.

They both went down like a ton of bricks. A third guy, who had been standing behind the first two—the one who hadn't gone arse over tits—had a moment of hesitation but he came for me. He had a short iron bar that he was swinging wildly as he came forward and the first guy who still had his knife was coming around the side of me. Feeling confident I wasn't going to bleed out, I pulled the knife from my side.

At least I then had a weapon to fight back with, other than my teeth that had been so far useless. It was at that point that the iron bar wielder literally disappeared from before my eyes. What I had failed to see due to the speed she had moved, was Samantha hitting him around the waist in a rugby tackle. They had crashed into the ground just behind me, but I was so focused on trying to keep the other guys in my line of sight that I had missed it.

Iron bar guy's throat had been torn out before I turned round. The other chap with the knife became a little distracted at that point. Not only did he, too, find the attack from Samantha to be shocking but it was at that point that Elena and Isla literally dropped from the sky onto the two on the ground. I had no idea how far away or where they jumped from, but they landed on top of the two men who were trying to untangle themselves.

Both of the women had fur sprouting from them at an alarming rate and their faces now had long dog-like snouts. The teeth that hung from their mouths, going at all angles, put my fangs to shame. The girls seemed to want to toy with their prey, though. The slashes of claws, while removing chunks from the men, were not meant to kill them. There were no bites at the throat. No death blows were flung. They were enjoying the sheer terror that was coming off the men in waves.

Realising I had gotten a little distracted, I turned back to the one man who remained standing. I could see he was ready to run but there was no way I could let that happen now. I pounced. As I landed on him, he managed to stab me in the other side. My fangs found his throat, and unlike the girls, I tore his throat out straight away. I stuck my face in the hole and gulped the blood as it covered me. By the time I was finished, Samantha was, too.

She had come over and casually sat beside me on the pavement. Her face was covered in claret and I'm not going to lie, the streetlights making it shine on her face just made her look cuter than she already was. Both wolves had the time of their lives. Elena tore the arm off one of the guys and threw it to Isla. Isla started clubbing the other guy in the face with it.

It was at that point that Elena tore the other guy's leg off. Their strength was incredible, but their wrath was beautiful. They enjoyed what they were doing. I'm not going to say it was the wolf in them because wolves don't do that, but I think they likely both had some psychopath genes in them before they were turned. Either way, they were well suited to each other.

As the men started to bleed out, the girls bit huge chunks from them and feasted on the meat. The four of us looked like we had been in a horror movie massacre. It was hard to believe so much blood could have come from just four men, especially when Samantha and I had drank a fair amount of it. Before we got to the serious work of disposing of the bodies, the last thing I can remember is the howls of laughter that came from Elena and Isla. Their faces had begun changing back to their feminine looks that I was used to, and the fur was receding.

"This is one of the best nights I have had in ages," was the last thing I can remember Elena saying that night. Isla and Samantha were quiet as always.

We dragged the bodies to the closest river and our new wolf friends tore them into shreds. We dumped the bodies and never looked back. That was the last evening we spent in Amsterdam. We decided to leave the next day and move on to Germany. The girls wanted to come with us. They had heard a million stories about how werewolves came from Germany and were planning on going anyway but we made our excuses.

We wanted to continue on our own adventure and while we liked them and hoped we would maybe meet them again, the journey was ours and ours alone. The girls came to the airport to see us off. We exchanged hugs and Elena shed a tear or two. She seemed to be the emotional one for what was otherwise a pair of brutal killers but who was I to judge.

They waved us off as we went through customs, and we were on our own again. We had both been looking forward to seeing Germany but neither of us had any idea what we were heading for.

Germany was amazing. There were so many different places to check out, the food was outstanding. It was so different to anything either of us had seen before and we enjoyed spending time alone again. We partied less than we had in Amsterdam but that was nice, too. There is a time and place for everything. It felt right in the Dam, but it wasn't the life either of us were looking to lead. I found myself thinking about the wolf girls and how they were getting on.

Not that I was worried about them. They were more than adequate at looking after themselves. I wondered if there were other supernaturals out there and if there were, what the likelihood of us meeting them would be.

Samantha and I had slowed the pace a little after what had been an exciting first year together. Although Samantha was quite stoic in her manner, she would open up to me and tell me about her past on the odd occasion. She hadn't had an easy life as a child and had grown into a toughened woman before she became a vampire. Her experience of being turned wasn't quite like mine. From what she could remember, she had gotten into an argument in a bar with another woman. They had gone outside to sort things out and she woke up the next day in a ditch. She had picked a fight with a vampire who she could only imagine had intended to kill her but the vampire must have been recently turned herself, and was either lazy or stupid, because she didn't finish her kill.

Perspective

Samantha had known something was up, but it wasn't until the urge to drink blood had got stronger that she started to suspect what had happened to her. When she woke in the ditch, she had been covered in a tremendous amount of blood and thought that no one could survive losing that much and live. She had also known that there was nobody next to her so the woman she had left the bar with had lived.

It was only when she was struggling to put things together and in the process smashed up her apartment, that her fangs started to come out, that she knew what had happened. That very evening she had gone to the bar. She had stayed outside in her car until she had seen the same woman go into the bar again. She waited outside until the end of the night and watched as the vampire left with an extremely drunk, unsuspecting male.

Samantha left her vehicle behind as they were travelling on foot and followed them. She knew nothing of vampires apart from what she had seen in movies. She had thought about fashioning something into a stake and taking a mallet but had decided to carry two knives and a small hatchet. She had used the blunt side of the hatchet to dunk the guy over the head. He had fallen easily into the brush. The female vampire was really all that was holding him up.

She had spun quickly, but she had only turned into the knife that Samantha buried in her chest. She quickly followed up with the second knife that she relentlessly plunged in and out of the vampire's stomach. The vamp had gone down to her knees and was bleeding out. While this wouldn't have caused death, it was enough to incapacitate the vampire. Samantha had dragged her into the bushes and used the hatchet to cut her head clean off her shoulders. It had taken a bit of time and some brute force, but her head had come off in the end.

Samantha had never bothered to get rid of that body. She left it in the bushes with the unconscious guy and she took the head with her. Some of you may be wondering why I didn't get out then but to me, it seemed fair. The vampire had tried to kill Samantha, had fucked it up and Samantha had got her revenge. Seemed fair to me.

A lot of people don't know how to stand up for themselves. I don't know how many quotes I have read about forgiveness and not holding on, but it seems to me that while people often don't act upon their desires of revenge, they also don't let go and it just eats away at them for the rest of their lives. I say go get what you need and live as happy a life as you can.

There will likely be time for regret on your deathbed. Vampires don't really have a death bed, though. I now work on the assumption that my death will likely be violent. When I go, I will most likely be taken out by a rival vamp or someone I cross who finds out I am a vampire and they come after me. I felt that by Samantha telling me the story, she had some faith in us going on together as a couple. She wasn't the type to overshare so her letting me in on that part of her was a big thing.

Weeks turned into months and Germany, while we did all the tours and saw all the sights, was to remain uneventful for the considerable future. We set up home there in a quiet town where most kept to themselves.

We took trips to other European countries such as Italy, Sweden, and France. We loved them all, but they were more holidays than anything else. Two weeks here and two weeks there. Our grand travel plans had gone out the window. We had become a more settled version of what we had started out as. We had become a couple. The partying had lost its appeal. Being wild wasn't fun anymore. We just enjoyed each other.

At first, I had wondered if we would become some infamous vampire couple. I had visions of us meeting multiple types of other supernaturals and for one reason or another, us living a life of infamy. I had watched too much TV. The wolf girls were the last we had met, and it seemed it would stay that way. That was until, of course, a corpse was left on our doorstep one night. Luckily, the smell of blood had alerted us to it, and we were able to get rid of it before anyone else saw it, but it had obviously been left there for a reason and we did not know what that was.

The next few days were filled with wild speculation and more and more crazy hypotheses. We had no clue who had done it, and there was nothing in the way of clues. We had searched the body and the clothes he had been wearing and there was nothing. We talked about leaving and travelling again but we were both happy in the life we had set up.

We also both wanted to know who it was and what they wanted from us. Curiosity killed the cat, as they say, but we both had to know. We took turns staying up at night and waiting for anyone approaching the door again. We knew if they brought another body, we would smell the blood quicker this time if we were awake and alert, but weeks passed with nothing else happening.

We began thinking that although someone had been fucking with us, that it had been a one-off incident. That was until we came home one evening after a date night and found an envelope sitting inside the door. It had been personally posted. We opened it up to find a single piece of paper. On it was simply an address. No time or date.

You can imagine the dilemma it posed. We weren't even one hundred percent sure that it was from whoever left the body. We were fairly confident it was, but it just offered more questions than answers. Was someone watching the house? Why the secrecy, and why leave a body first? Wouldn't an invite have been sufficient? First of all, we looked at where it was. It was a few hours away in the car. That shocked us, too.

We had assumed that someone local had been out to get us for one reason or another but it appeared someone from a distance had an issue with us. That just made it stranger. We both knew we would have to go. There was obviously the option to see it for what it was. A dangerous scenario that would likely be best avoided but neither of us wanted to run away.

What if bodies kept turning up? We were happy where we were and didn't want to have to move or risk having the police snooping around. Facing it head-on was the plan. An actual plan was much harder to come by though. How do you plan for something that you have no clue about? I'm sure there are a few people who would go in armed to the teeth, but we had no guns and had no idea where we could get any. Gun laws in Germany prevented the day-to-day person owning one and while there was most likely a black market, we didn't know how to access it.

Neither of us had any knowledge of accessing the dark net. We had only heard of it in books but doubted it was as simple as looking it up on a search engine. To summarize, we didn't know what we were walking into, weapons wise we could get some bread knives and any tools we wanted to carry from a local hardware store.

We spent a few days talking things over. We had gone back and forth on whether it would be beneficial contacting our werewolf friends and if we were putting them at risk. At first, we felt it was best to leave them out of what was most definitely our problem but in the end, we decided to err on the side of caution as much as we could and see if we could get some backup. We both knew it may be a decision we would regret if anything happened to either of them but we both knew they could handle themselves.

I had called Elena's mobile, and she had picked up quickly. She was more than excited to hear from us and was half holding a conversation with me and half excitedly telling Isla what was going on. She had agreed to come help before I had heard Isla having any real say in the matter, telling me it was ages since they had any real fun and that they couldn't wait to see us again. I gave her our address and she told us they would be there tomorrow and hung up before I could say anything else. Samantha and I were delighted to have the girls with us.

If someone intended to cause us any harm, I felt better knowing we were a small team of individuals who were more than capable of handling ourselves. The girls' claws and strength were the cherry on the cake.

We had no idea when the girls would arrive. I had sent Elena a text message asking her but had no response. I will admit that a little doubt crept in. Had Isla decided it was too risky and talked Elena out of it? Had something happened to them on their way to meet us? My thoughts raced, driven by anxiety. Samantha seemed calmer than me, even though we had decided that very night would be the night we went to the address, with or without the girls.

We needn't have worried, though. They arrived at our place late in the afternoon. Elena had literally pounced through the door, knocking me on my ass and planting a huge kiss on my forehead. She sprung up and was hugging and kissing Samantha before I could get to my feet. Isla was much calmer in her entrance and shook my hand, before moving onto Samantha and giving her a small hug.

We took them through to the living room and went over again what had happened. The whole time Elena was twitching with energy. She was like an excited puppy. It just goes to show how perception is personal. Samantha and I were worried even though we were vampires, Elena was buzzing as if she had just been offered the opportunity to go on the most exhilarating adventure of all time and Isla, as always, was stoic. She showed no signs of concern or enthusiasm. Just mild amusement at Elena's excitement.

Perspective

She rarely took her eyes off of Elena. She was infatuated with her. I wondered at the time if she was only there because Elena was. It seemed to me like Isla could have gone back to the werewolf bar in the Highlands of Scotland and spent the rest of her days there, but Elena would not be tamed. She had clearly had an excitable personality before she was turned and being a werewolf had done nothing but enhance it.

We spent a little more time talking, and then we got in the car and began the drive. We had picked up a few hatchets and some dangerous looking knives. The wolf girls weren't too bothered about weapons. They had their claws and teeth. Samantha and I had our weapons and our fangs, and we knew we weren't easy to kill.

I had no idea how difficult it was to kill a werewolf, but I could only imagine it would be difficult. It was never a subject that we had broached at that point. We were all tense. None of us had the faintest idea what type of danger we were walking into. When we got to the town that the address was in, we decided to hide the car just on the outskirts.

There was an old, dilapidated cottage. We hid the car around the back of it. The girls couldn't smell any trace of any humans being there recently and we couldn't see any footprints. We all hoped that we would be returning to the vehicle at some point.

We made sure to stick to dark alleyways and underpasses as much as we could and when we got to the street we were going to, we hung back and watched for a while. It was late in the evening, and it was a cold night. The streets were deserted. Not that the town looked like it was ever a thriving community, but we had expected to have to avoid at least a few individuals. From leaving the car to our planned destination and so far, we had passed a few cats. We all knew we could wait there forever, and nothing would happen. We had come this far, and we were a badass group of four tough cookies.

I could say monsters, but I don't think it gives a true representation of who we were. I believed then and I still believe now that we all had good hearts. Judge as you may.

We decided it was time. The four of us got up from our crouched position in the alleyway that was across from the address we had been given, and we strode in a confident fashion across the road. I'm sure we each felt like we were being watched. I certainly did but none of us could see anyone around. When we arrived on the other side of the street, we stood in front of a massive black double door. It was wooden and had iron bars running across it. It looked solid.

There was no knocker or letter box, so I stepped forward and knocked loudly, three times. The street was quiet, and we could hear no noises from inside the building. We stood there for about twenty seconds, just staring at each other but we were all on high alert and then the door swung inwards slowly. The hinges creaked, no doubt a sign of age and possibly lack of care.

When the door was fully open, it sat back against the wall but there was no one there. In front of us was a descending staircase. The walls were rough stone and there was nothing on them. There was literally nowhere to go but down. From the outside, the building hadn't seemed like much, and the door did seem a little large and out of place, but we had expected it to open into some sort of entranceway or room.

We had not expected a set of stairs leading downward. Samantha and I were at the front, as this was really our thing. We both leaned in and peered down the stairs. We could see nothing. Every so often there looked to be candles further down the stairs but they did not give off enough light to illuminate all that much. All they let us know was that the stairs seemed to go down further than the basement level of the property.

I decided to try and be chivalrous and go first, but Elena pushed past me. She said she would likely smell trouble before we saw it. It was a fair comment. The girls, Samantha and I all had better vision than a normal person, but Samantha and I had nowhere near the capabilities of the girls when it came to picking up scents.

The stairway looked like the kind of place that would reek of damp but there was no smell at all. We began our descent. Elena went first, then I went, followed by Samantha and Isla took up the rear. There were very few situations I could imagine feeling scared with my group, but I can remember thinking I would have been sweating if I still had the ability.

I could feel my fangs beginning to slide out over my lips. They had readied themselves in a feeding position. I can remember wondering how quickly they would be battle ready if I needed them. As we descended the stairs, it became warmer.

Perspective

I chalked it up to us now being inside and away from the wind. My experience of basements and lower levels in buildings had always been that they were colder, but the heat continued to build. As we passed each candle on the wall, it made no difference to our sight of the bottom of the staircase.

We would see as far as the next candle on the way down and it was darkness after that. As we walked, I realised we were going deeper into the ground than I could recall going in any other building I had been in. I found myself forgetting about the danger we may be in and wondering who dug this out, and when it had been done. You never saw people do stuff like this in modern day. It was always people from the past.

They seemed to have a thing for digging into the earth. These days we were more likely to stick up a new skyscraper. There was no chat that I can remember. What was there to say? We just kept going. We had come this far. There would be no turning back.

It must have taken us half an hour to get to the bottom of the steps. We were all shocked that they had gone on for so long. The last step, underwhelmingly, left us standing at the end of a tunnel that was the same dimensions as the staircase. We now had the pleasure of more steps, only this time we would be going forward rather than down.

I can remember thinking it was all a bit theatrical. Maybe it's just how my mind works but I kept wondering if whoever wanted to meet us could have just organized a room somewhere at ground level. We moved along the corridor, Samantha and I pulling out a knife and a hatchet each and I could see the girls' hands had turned to claws and both of their faces, while not in full wolf mode, had begun elongating into snouts.

Who would really want to fuck with us? Two wolves and two vampires. We weren't exactly an easy target. After about another ten minutes of walking along the seemingly endless tunnel, everything changed. We entered a massive room. It was decorated like a grand room in a mansion. Tapestries hung on the walls, the furniture looked exquisite, and there were old style torches burning in wall sconces, lending a lot more light to the situation.

There were no windows for obvious reasons but apart from that, we could have been in any above ground mansion where the owner had plenty of money and fantastic taste. I could see jewels encrusted in some of the furniture. Even some of the old books lying on tables looked to be ancient and not the sort of thing people had lying around in their normal homes. They would be from a collection, and they would have been pricey to procure unless they had always been in the family. That did make me wonder who owned this place.

The room was empty of life, other than us four. I could see the girls sniffing the air more than they looked around. Samantha and I were taking everything in with our eyes but the wolf girls were relying on scent. There were only two doorways in the room. The one we came in and one on the opposite end of the room.

The door on it was identical to the external door. Just when I was thinking we were going to have to go through the other door and likely walk for miles, it slowly swung open.

A hulking figure ducked down and came in through the doorway. The door swung shut behind him. He was close to seven feet tall and wore a black hooded robe. He strolled unhurriedly to a huge, dark, stained wood desk, pulled the chair out and sat. He swept his hand across the table at the chairs that lay on the other side of it.

There were exactly four. The desk was like everything else in the room. Expensive looking. We all glanced at each other and back to the desk before slowly making our way closer. We were all peering around, waiting for someone or something to jump out on us, but the room remained free of anyone other than us and the huge shrouded figure. As we got closer, we each stood behind a chair and continued to gaze around.

"Sit!"

The voice was like gravel under a work boot. The figure swept his hood back. His skin was grey. That was the first alarming thing. Not grey like someone who is sick but grey like stone. The second alarming thing was he had protrusions at the front of his cranium. I wouldn't say they were horns as they were much smaller and they were rounded off. Even under the robe, I could tell his muscle mass was at least three times that of the biggest body builders. There was no chance he was human, but I had no idea what he was.

"Sit," he repeated.

Not having a great deal of other options, we took our seats. It was over an hour back to the surface and god only knew what was through the other door. I looked along the line of the others. I had taken the left seat, then it was Samantha, Elena, and then Isla.

Perspective

Samantha and Isla had their eyes locked on the grey giant and looked all business. Elena was smirking at him. I swear, it was like she was watching an amusing movie, rather than living through a dangerous and strange situation. I guessed at that point, that if anyone was going to make it out alive, it would be her.

"Why did you invite us here?" Samantha asked.

"Well, little one, you have been invited because you are a monster. You and your partner. I see you have brought some little monster friends as well," the grey figure responded.

"And you would be?" Samantha enquired.

"I am Layzamon. I am King of the Underlands."

Elena giggled. In hindsight, I should have predicted it. She was not taking this seriously, which amazed me, but we are each our own person and who was I to judge her. I did think at that point that she may be the reason each of us would have our heads removed from our shoulders but once the giggle was released, what could any of us do?

"You find that amusing, cad?"

The hulk-like grey being's eyes bore into Elena's. She was, at least to the eye, unfazed.

"The ruler of the undergrounds. Could you not have worked on a better line than that when you were waiting on us?" She gave him one of those stroppy teen girl smiles that implied he was a moron.

"You think I am here to impress you? You are not here by invite, mongrel. The bloodsuckers were invited. You tagged along like the little whelp you are. You have merely been allowed to enter my domain. Not invited."

The big guy clearly didn't like Elena.

"Why did you invite us here?" Samantha repeated.

"I invited you and your partner here because I have a use for you. I am the ruler of an army of what you would most likely think of as demons. You and your associate are demons who walk the earth freely. There are many things you could do for me."

I found it amusing he called me her associate, but unlike Elena, I did not giggle.

"What makes you think either of us would be interested in working for someone."

I knew why I loved Samantha. She did not ask what kind of work or have any interest in what sort of Remuneration or rewards were available. She had no interest in such things. We may be vampires, but I knew from experience the real monsters lay within humanity. Well, humanity and the giant grey demon who sat in front of us. I knew it couldn't end well.

There were going to be no negotiations. There would be no back and forth. Samantha wasn't the type. It was as simple as that. She knew who she was, and she knew her values and she lived by them, making no excuses and never bending her will to please others or to meet social conventions. Admittedly, this was not the same thing, but she was the same woman, and I could have written down what was going to happen before it did.

The big grey guy had possibly been in a position where he didn't get told no often. From what we saw afterwards, he had his accolades, followers and slaves, but he did not have what he wanted. Us. Supernatural beings. He saw us as demons, and like most things in life, it's all about perspective. It reminds me of that old saying, What is normal for the spider is chaos for the fly. We were told we would now work for him.

Promises were made that no one had asked for and subtle threats were given. I started to loosen up a bit. It was just us and one other person. He was a beast and who knew what powers he had but Elena's smirk was infectious. She looked like she should have had popcorn for the show. Neither she nor Isla looked remotely wolf-like at that point. I did worry they had let their guard down. Isla gave nothing away in her expressionless beauty. She looked like a grade A student paying attention but not particularly moved by the subject matter.

"So you want us to be your lackeys? To run around and follow your orders? Do the things you can't seem to do for yourself? I think we will decline, and for future reference, if you want to speak to us, next time, you come to us, and secondly, if you leave any more bodies on our doorstep, I will come back for you, and it will not end well."

The response came from Samantha. The conversation, after all, was between those two, basically.

The beast's voice was inhuman enough, but his laugh was terrifying. I was waiting on the roof coming down.

"You have no choice, vampire. None of you do."

Elena full out laughed this time. Not a chuckle. Not a guffaw. A full-blown belly laugh.

I did still find it disconcerting that we were sitting in front of a demon. I hadn't truly believed in them until that evening.

Perspective

I expected the big guy to get up and flip the massive table, guessing it would be nothing to him, or should I say it? It was at this point the door behind him, the one he had come in through, opened. I watched as gorilla-like creatures filtered into the room. For the sake of complete transparency, they looked like the drawings I had seen of neanderthal men. There were eight of them in total. I know you should never judge a book by its cover, but they looked dumb.

They were obviously clever enough to understand at least basic instructions as they lined up, side by side a few feet behind the demon. I took my eyes off them for a second to look along the row of my companions. Each of them stared at the creatures. I could not read their faces. None looked fearful. I wasn't quite sure how I felt. My mind was running fast, and I was wondering what the end outcome of it would be. The demon obviously intended to strong-arm us. Would it be death or join his legions, or was there really a third option? I wasn't sure.

"Now, I will offer you one more chance. Accept my offer or you'll be dispatched."

If I had money and the time, I would have placed a bet on Elena laughing. She did. I wondered if she was doing it because she found everything so funny, had a nervous disposition in tough situations, or the most likely, she did not give a fuck, and wanted to annoy the monster. Whatever she was aiming for, she succeeded in pissing it off, intentional or not.

The demon slammed its huge fist down on the table and the monkey monsters all left their spot and flew for us. All four chairs shot back as we rose to our feet quickly. The wolf girls were already changing as the creatures got to us. Samantha's and my fangs shot out. They were not our feeding fangs. They were fangs designed to rip living things apart.

It was painful when they came in and when there were so many and they were larger, it was even worse. The adrenaline helped, though, and the absolute lack of time to think about it or dwell on it helped, too. As the first creature arrived in front of me and I smashed it in the face with my fist, another of them speared me from the side.

I crashed into the floor, and they were both on me. As I fought with the one who landed on top of me, I was able to peer around the room quickly. No one would be coming to my aid. The creatures had paired off so each of us had our own battle. I even managed to see the hulking demon sitting at his desk, pouring himself a glass of something from a decanter. He seemed uninterested in the battle.

As the second beast dropped on top of me, I heard growls and howls from the other side of the room. I could not tell if they came from the wolf girls or if they came from the gorilla-like monsters. I had no time to worry about things like that, though. I was swinging strong punches into the ribs and heads of both beasts while they were more interested in trying to grab hold of me.

Nothing was having much effect but when the one on top of me leaned in closer, I sank the mess of fangs that were hanging all way out of my mouth into its face and tore its cheek off. Brainless or not, it let out an inhuman squeal and fell backwards off me, bringing claw-like hands to its face. I managed to get up on one knee as the other crashed into me.

We rolled across the floor and by sheer luck, I landed on top of it. I started raining blows down on its distorted face and I let out a scream of rage at it before I quickly leant in and bit out the front of its throat. It made no noises. There was a gurgling sound coming from it as I rose to my feet and turned my back on its dying body, lying on the floor.

I looked back to the other one I had bitten first. It was standing a few feet away, face contorted in rage, blood leaking from the hole in its face, running down its neck. I risked a glance 'round to see if any of the others desperately needed my help or if they were doing okay. Isla stood over two dead bodies, one with its head missing and the other with a hole in its chest.

Samantha had also dispatched the two that had come for her. Elena was the only one still fighting. I saw all of this quickly but as I was looking, the beast I had bitten, crashed into me. It wasn't until I got on top of the second abomination and started choking it to death that I was able to glance back around. Samantha and Isla were not moving in to help Elena, but I quickly saw why. She was in full female form, apart from both arms and hands from the elbow down.

She jumped back and forth and was toying with two of the creatures at once. She was smiling. I was not. I leant my bodyweight into the choke I had around the monster's throat. I could have easily leaned in at that point and ended its life with a bite but rage had taken over. I wanted to watch its eyes go dull as the life drained from it.

The second it stopped fighting and took its last breath, I stood. Part of me wanted to jump in and help Elena, not that she needed it. She turned towards me as she danced between the two neanderthals, saw that they were all dead apart from her two, stepped in towards them and with two swipes of her claws, they hit the ground. It was clear as day that she could have slain them at any point. She had been having fun.

I felt a wave of admiration come over me. Not so much because of her skills, but more about how she looked at life and situations. She seemed to get the best from whatever was going on. She even looked over at me and gave me a fucking wink and a smile as the beasts crashed down.

I can remember looking at the demon, waiting for him to lose his rag. I expected we would now have time to fight him like some boss man at the end of the level in a computer game but that was not to be the case. He didn't even look up from his desk. He was now sipping from the glass of whatever he had poured and reading a book.

He could not have been more unfazed if he tried. As I was taking everything in, the door opened again. This was the reason he wasn't bothered. He was not done with us yet, and I surmised he was not the type to do things for himself. It was not to be more gorilla-like assailants, though. This time creatures who looked like smaller versions of him came through the door.

They were slightly taller than me and definitely more well-muscled. Unlike the big guy, their skin was red, and they had small back horns in place of the stubs that he had. They looked like so many pictures of the devil I had seen but it was clear they were not running the show. I wondered if people had seen these guys before and that's where stories of the devil had come from. It mattered not. They kept coming, and if I counted correctly, there were twenty-one of them.

I was not thinking our odds were good. By their eyes alone, I could tell they had an intelligence the others did not. They also looked stronger and whether I made it up in my mind or not, they looked like they cared more about killing us than the last lot did. I have no way of knowing if it was truly the case, but they were moving in an agitated fashion, and it seemed they were just waiting on the order to do their master's bidding.

Once again, I peered around the room. There were eight dead bodies, twenty-one red demons, their boss and us four. Isla had stayed in mostly wolf form but remained standing on two legs. Elena had gone back to full female mode, had righted her chair and sat back in it and Samantha was staring down the large grey demon.

Without looking up, the demon in charge, who was still reading his book and sipping from his glass said two words.

"Last chance."

Elena laughed.

Isla sprung at him. In midair, several of the red demons crashed into her. They all landed on and then rolled across the large table. This time the main demon did lose his temper. He roared. Fuck me, it was loud. The whole place shook. Being that it was carved out of the solid earth, I was both impressed and shat myself. Metaphorically of course, but it was terrifying. He was clearly angrier about his drink being spilled, or damage to his book than he was about the loss of his servants, or however he saw them.

Isla had gone full wolf as she flew through the air. As she had changed, she had grown much larger than any real wolf I had ever seen. She snapped and snarled at the three red figures that had each pulled knives from their belts. Belts were all they wore. I should likely have mentioned that. None of them had genitals either. I assume they were created rather than bred, but who knows how the devil, or in this case, a huge grey demon, works.

I would have most definitely jumped in, but the attack by Isla had started the full battle in motion. Elena had also turned but she, unlike Isla, remained on two feet. She was covered head to toe in thick fur, which did seem to help the girls avoid getting as many injuries, and her face had once again grown a large, ferocious-looking snout.

The claws seemed to be the first thing that sprung out each time, which I suppose made sense. They grew larger than her hands but retained a humanlike shape. The main difference was the claws that burst from her fingertips. They were not an extension of her nails. They were something else altogether. They looked like bone apart from the fact that they were dark grey. She was moving before Samantha or I had a chance.

She, too, leapt straight at the grey figure, but the exact same thing happened. A few of the red figures tackled her. Samantha and

I were on the move by that point. Neither of us went for the large demon, knowing it was pointless. We went for Isla and Elena and began attacking the red things that were already in the battle. Each and every one of them that weren't already involved, piled in. It was chaos. I was swinging fists, grabbing and pulling those that were on one of my friends, and biting whatever came near my maw.

The grey creature was standing as we battled. He had risen as soon as Isla had crashed across his table and he hadn't taken his seat again. We all raged around him. As I was fighting, I saw a group of the demons surround Samantha. I was just about to fight my way over to her when Isla dropped from above. I have no idea where she sprung from, but she landed right in front of Samantha, as I used one of the red demon's dropped daggers to stab another demon up through the underside of his chin, pushing the blade up into his brain.

As I moved forward, my shoulder knocked his standing corpse over. Isla growled. On all fours, she was the same height as Samantha. As I came around the side of them, I could see she had turned so she was back to back with the wolf. I picked another dagger up and noticed Samantha had one, too. The demons weren't as gung-ho as the neanderthals.

While they were clearly game for a fight, they weren't as quick to rush in at all costs. Isla sprung forward, her giant paws slamming into two of the ones in front of her. She leant down quickly and snatched one of their heads from their body with her giant muzzle. I was still watching her as I came in at the demons from the side.

She lifted her huge paw and smashed it downward, obliterating the other one's skull. It was an impressive sight. Samantha had engaged in a knife fight with the one in front of her as I came up behind one who was just about to attack her from the opening that had been left by Isla. I grabbed one of his horns from behind and dug the blade into the side of his neck. It was at that point there was another roar.

The carnage stopped for a moment as most of the people and demons in the room looked to where the roar came from. It was not from the huge demon this time. It was from Elena. She stood at least eight feet tall. She had grown more than I had ever seen. She was still standing on two legs and while she still looked like a wolf, there was something bear-like in her appearance, too.

Her body and muscles had thickened. Parts of her now weren't covered in fur. It was as if there was only so much fur to go around and there was no longer enough to cover her entirely. The parts that weren't covered in fur, showed just how muscular her werewolf body was. There were veins popping out all over her. Her neck was likely as thick, if not thicker than my waist. She looked both terrifying and glorious. She was taller than the largest demon. Not by much, and he was thicker-bodied and had a ridiculous amount of muscle on his inhuman frame.

He was watching her with what looked like admiration. It was then she swung her arm and backhanded two of the red demons across the room. She went straight for the grey demon. I am sure I saw him smile but at that exact point, the remaining red demons attacked Samantha, Isla, and me. Isla was still in the shape of an enormous but normal-shaped wolf and was tearing into them with her teeth.

I could see blood had matted fur at several different parts of her body. While she made quick work of the demons whom she fought, there were so many of them and they all had knives. She tore out the stomach of another of the smaller demons as two jumped on her back. Two of them dove on me at the same time. As I went down, I saw Samantha swing her knife downwards towards a demon's face with incredible speed.

It was then that I realised that although vampires had no truly supernatural powers, other than the hard-to-kill and a bit stronger and faster than the average Joe stuff, that I mentioned earlier, I realised I wasn't running out of steam. If anything, I was getting a bit stronger. It felt like the old days when I got a pump on at the gym and got into a routine.

I could go that bit harder and that bit longer. The same thing was happening. I knew as I had been biting the demons, I had swallowed a fair amount of their blood, too. I do not know if that helped or if it made no difference at all. I just know as I crashed to the ground with the two demons that it almost felt good. I let out my own roar and threw a hammer fist at the one who landed beside me. I felt bone crack under my hand.

I spun round to the other and bit down on his face. My fangs were the longest they had been. I wasn't sure if there were more, or if it was just the size, but my jaw was stretched out. I tore skin and cartilage from the monster. I swallowed it all. I clasped my two hands and started hammering both down into the thing's skull at once. It stopped moving quickly but I smashed it a few more times. I got up quickly and jumped two-footed onto the other's skull. I felt it crack beneath me. I slipped and landed on my ass.

As a hand grabbed my arm, I grabbed it back rapidly, ready to yank it towards me, when I heard Samantha's voice.

"More of them are coming through the door."

She pulled me to my feet. More of the red demons piled in and a few jet-black ones. They were so dark that it was almost impossible to make out any of their features. These guys were vantablack. They were slightly larger than the others, but it was mostly the fact that they looked like moving black holes that was disconcerting. Samantha picked up two knives and went for them. I followed.

As we ran into the fray, Isla was finishing off the remainder of the red demons from the first wave. I wondered if she and Elena were tiring. I could see that Samantha, like me, was only getting stronger. I wondered if it was a defensive thing that happened to vampires, or if Samantha had even known about it. I didn't have a great deal of thinking time before everything went berserk again.

Isla had gone flying over Samantha and my heads, landing among the demons like a bowling ball launched through the air at some bowling pins. She was biting, snarling, and ripping them apart before we had buried a knife in any of them. As the three of us fought for our lives, or maybe our freedom, I wasn't sure which, I once again heard Elena roar, followed directly by the leader of the demons' roar. The collision of the two monsters shook the room. I had seen the massive wooden desk, thrown across the vast room and smashed against the stone wall.

I could go on, breaking down the details of our part of the fight for a long time, but the salient facts are simple. Samantha, Isla, and I continued to war with the smaller demons. Very few of them were actually small, but they were not in the league of their master. The more of them we dispatched, the more came through the door.

You may be wondering why we didn't try and block it, but it wasn't like a zombie movie where you just grab some stuff and nail it shut. There was rarely a second passed without an attack coming from one side or the other. At times, Isla was doing a decent job of slowing the flow coming through, but it was impossible for her to just fight in a static position.

Her coat was matted with blood, and I remember hoping she would make it through. I had no idea how much blood a werewolf could lose, and I also had no knowledge of their regenerative powers. The fight raged on, but the real spectacle of the evening had to be the war of the giants. Elena was vicious. If you have ever seen a feral cat fight, you may have some idea of how she went into the hulking demon.

Her blows, however, did not cause the same sort of damage as they did to the smaller ones. The demon rained blows down on her and his seemed more devastating. Whether it was the sheer size and weight of his body, or he had an entirely different makeup, I do not know. I know nothing about demon physiology. Elena certainly didn't look like she was messing around anymore.

We were still fighting and slaughtering the red and vantablack demons, but we were taking punishment. It wasn't only Isla who was covered in blood. We were beginning to move backwards into the hall as more of the demons came through the door.

"We're losing," Samantha shouted over the noise. We had stayed fighting side by side as much as possible.

I didn't know if we were losing, but we weren't winning, and their numbers were growing. I don't think the large demon had known initially how much of a challenge we were going to be or he would have had the hall filled with demons from the start, but he had overestimated his persuasion powers. Either that or he had underestimated us.

"Any ideas?" I shouted back.

"Isla, go help Elena." Samantha screamed at the top of her lungs.

I didn't think Isla would have heard above the noise in the room, but her wolf-like ears picked it up. Her massive wolf head had peered around. She had clearly seen what Samantha did. We were not going to win by killing the weaker demons. She bit the head off a red demon, and bounded across the room, springing at the last moment and landing on the grey demon's back as

Elena swung claws at him from the front. He reached over his shoulder, grabbed a thick pelt of fur behind her neck, while she was snapping at his arm, and he threw her across the room. She wiped out several demons as she smashed into the stone floor, and she let out a whelp for the first time in the evening. Samantha spun and made a line for the demon, too. I followed by biting chunks out of demons and slashing them as I moved. I watched Samantha do the same. She was covered head to toe in blood, her fangs looked like they were almost half of her face. I had never seen her look so beautiful.

As we arrived at the big guy with a hoard of demons on our tail, Samantha put a knife in his side. It went into the hilt. He swung his hand back, but she was ready and locked onto his arm and started biting chunks out of it. I dove onto his back. Elena was still ripping into the front of him as he pummeled her with his giant fists. I did not want to get in the way of those claws. If anything could end me, it may be them.

I sank my enormous fangs into the back of his neck with the intention of chewing my way to his fucking spine. Isla, having recovered, had come around his back again and was going for his legs. Her own claws were nothing to be sneezed at, but that maw. Those teeth. It was a sight to see. She tore chunks from his legs.

The four of us continued to tear and rip at him as the smaller beasts tore, slashed and stabbed us. Blood poured from each of us. No mortal would have survived half as long, but none of us were mortal any longer. There was growling and snarling, the sound of fists on bone, and of skin tearing.

The red and the black demons were still attacking us, but Elena and Isla mostly ignored them now, and Samantha and I did what we could to bat them back without letting up on their master. It was beginning to seem like an impossible task to bring him down. He bled just like a human, but we all knew he was more.

The chunks we tore from him did not grow back but he did not seem to be fazed. Whether it was adrenaline or something else, he fought like a world champion fighter on his best night. We had slowly destroyed his body, though, and when it was just seeming like our only option would be to join him, he went down on one knee.

That was enough for the wolves. Elena went into a frenzy. I could barely see her arms swing as she tore strips of grey flesh from his face and body. Isla had moved up his back, pushing me aside as she tore into the hole I had already made at his neck. He faded fast at that point. The fight was gone from him. His huge upper body crashed forward onto the floor and the room fell to silence.

Elena let out an ear-splitting howl followed by Isla. The red and vantablack demons ran towards the door. None of us gave chase.

As the door slammed behind the last of them, the silence was deafening. I have no idea how long the battle lasted, but I do know that after it finished, that silence seemed wrong.

All four of us were covered from head to toe in blood. Isla started shrinking back to the size of a normal wolf before she changed back to human form. She stood in front of us naked, and for all the stab wounds she had taken during the fight, there were none left on her human body. It was hard to believe. Elena didn't change back, or at least, not right away. She stood there, in her full glorious werewolf form. Her chest rose and fell, the parts that were covered in fur were matted to her body. I got the feeling that she wasn't quite ready for the fight to be over.

I sat on the floor where I was. I had no thought of getting a chair and after sitting for several seconds, I lay back, my head resting on a dead demon's stomach and I laughed. I could still remember my life clearly before I knew vampires existed. That evening, though, took things to an entirely new level. Samantha came over and lay next to me, her on her side, me on my back and I pulled her in close.

With the danger gone and the room empty, our fangs began to retract into our mouths. I ran my tongue around my lips, expecting them to be split in multiple places but they weren't. I guess it's a bit like the werewolves, changing back to their normal form. I genuinely could have fallen asleep right there.

Isla went to Elena. She snuggled into her stomach, being over three feet smaller and Elena, still in bipedal wolf form, wrapped a giant claw, gently around her back. It was at that point she began to shrink in size and the hair began to recede. It didn't take too long until she was back at more or less the same height as the rest of us. Samantha and I got to our feet as well.

"So, big question. Do we go after them?" I asked the others.

Elena wanted to. Samantha and Isla felt we should at least check what was behind the other door and where it led. That would be as far as our journey underground would go, though. None of us could get the door to budge an inch. It was immovable. We did try for a while, but we got nowhere. The room we were in was destroyed, but we had a look around, anyway.

The thing I was most interested in was seeing what the demon was reading. I had imagined some ancient text that could maybe bring us luck or wealth but no matter how hard I looked, I couldn't find it. It was gone. One of the demons must have taken it when they were fleeing. There was nothing else of value that we could find. The demons never came back, and we had nothing to do but make the long walk back to the surface.

We spent weeks watching that doorway. We had gone home after the battle. As we drove away from the doorway, tiredness began to seep in. We got back to our place, and I think we slept for two days but after that, we went back. We watched for a while and then we decided to check the door.

I'm not sure if we planned to go back down to the underground room we had fought in, but it made no difference. The door was now locked, and we had no way of getting in, short of renting a JVC and tearing the door off. We all felt it was better that it stayed shut. Even though we couldn't get in, we stayed for a long time and watched to see if anyone or thing came or went.

They didn't.

Elena had got us a camper van so we could park fairly close, and we could sleep and eat in the camper. We grew a lot closer and dare I say, became a family in the weeks that followed the ordeal. Samantha and I could never repay them. We knew that, and they expected nothing. We told them that if they ever needed anything, we would also be there for them and they had hugged us and told us they knew, and that they felt the same.

After watching the place for weeks, we all knew we had to move on. We couldn't spend the rest of our lives living on top of each other in a camper van in case the door ever reopened. I knew we would all likely go back periodically and check, but we had to live our lives. The girls came and stayed with us for a while.

It was fun and it was much easier sharing a house rather than the camper, but eventually, even though she had a real love for us, Elena wanted to go travelling again. There was something in that girl's blood that would not let her settle anywhere for too long. It was truly sad saying goodbye to the girls, but I knew we would meet again. We had gone through too much together to just be acquaintances who never saw each other.

After the events of that night, and when the girls left, Samantha and I were a lot closer. It was more than a relationship now. Dare I say, it was more than a marriage. We were bonded. We decided the night the girls left that we wanted to do things differently moving forward. We both knew if we did eventually die, we may go to hell.

I know most people think vampires must automatically go to hell and that they are evil. I don't see things as being that black or white. There are grey areas in every element of life. I believe in no religion, but I do believe there is an afterlife. I've met demons face to face, but I am not entirely convinced they come from what is commonly believed to be hell. Maybe I am wrong.

We left it until the next evening before we went hunting. That was where our main changes lay. We hunted bad guys exclusively. We didn't see ourselves as the good guys, but it sure fucking felt good. We started out small and would just find guys who mugged old ladies, or thugs who ruined people's lives on the regular. It was so easy. The world is full of cunts, and we had nothing but time. We didn't hunt every night. As I said, we didn't need to, but as we got better at finding the people we wanted, we did hunt more often.

Sometimes we put a lot of research and money into finding larger groups that we wanted to go after. Sometimes we just tortured one bad guy to get the details of another. It's really easy to get bad guys to talk. It's not like the movies. They don't act tough for long. They are self-involved and have no love for others, so they give them up easily.

Only a fear of being found out as someone who talked is a barrier but when it's the option of dying there and then at our hands, or more likely teeth, or the option of being hunted down later, they are going to go on the run. They don't get the chance, though. We kill them all.

We have been getting bigger fish lately. Money talks and we now have a few good underground guys who bring us info. It has never been discussed but they clearly know we kill the people they get us details on. They will see that each and every one goes missing after they pass the info to us, but they don't care. They are in it for the money, and we are doing the world a service. You will find few who miss a bad guy.

Our last large group we got was exhilarating. After pressuring our sources for a bit, they had finally got us the details of a pedophile ring. That had been a good night. We had both celebrated when we got the folder with all the information inside. We made those men and women suffer. We kept them alive for days.

There were no quick kills. One fat fuck's heart gave out but when I saw the heart attack start, I beat the shit out of him while he died. I burnt others, stabbed and slashed them, poured battery acid over them. I set them on fire and put them out. I beat them with clubs. I even padded the clubs sometimes so I could beat them for longer without killing them. I broke bones then stood on the appendage that I had broken. Man, I fucked those guys up. Those are the best ones. Those are the ones we pay the most for and urge our info guys to get.

Money is easy to come by. We rob the homes of the people we kill. They don't need their stuff anymore. We don't live a lavish lifestyle, but we spend a lot of money on the info, traveling to get our targets and whatever stuff we need to rent or buy for our work.

It was Samantha who suggested I write all this down. I can't imagine anyone will ever get a chance to read it, but she said it would help with my mental clarity. She knows I was big on self-improvement when she met me and being a vampire is no different. We need to keep our minds on our side. It's more important than ever.

I can't even imagine being a vampire and going down a deep black hole. I went through bad times as a human, but I need to be stronger now. Who knows how I could end up if I choose the wrong path. I could be like one of those goons who worked for the big grey guy. I knew they were out there. I didn't know how they came about but I didn't want to end up like them.

Vampire or not. I wanted to be the hero in my own story. I had my princess. I had my morals. I have my quest. All I need to get through each day is a new bad guy to hunt and I can keep the demons at bay. The mental demons that is. I think those are the hardest ones to beat. The physical ones are all muscles and show but no real substance.

The demons in your head could bring down your whole world. All I know is two vampires and two werewolves stopped a small army of demons doing something bad. For now, that lets me sleep at night. Tomorrow, I will look for a new bad guy to punish.

Beneath Still Waters

Gord Rollo

Prologue

Red Spruce Gypsum Mine,
Beckley, Nova Scotia, Canada
May 16th, 2020

There's a fine line between prosperity and ruin for most small Canadian mining towns, especially a tiny dot on the map like Beckley, Nova Scotia. Wedged between the official treaty lands of the Mi'kmaq (pronounced Mic-mac) and the Her'maqon (pronounced Hair-mac-on) indigenous peoples, Beckley sat on a plateau of sparse Spruce forests and exposed bedrock that neither of the native communities seemed deeply concerned about claiming. At one point in their storied histories, the two indigenous nations had been enemies and had fought a terrible battle on this patch of land, and enough blood had been spilled to keep either group of surviving ancestors from wanting anything to do with the supposed cursed battleground. Thus, Beckley was born, founded by good men and women filled with hope and excitement for the future, but if anyone from the surrounding towns and cities were asked, the new town never had much of a chance right from the start. Barren land was barren, and cursed land was cursed.

What more did anyone need to know?

But that was before the rich vein of gypsum was discovered beneath the thin layer of topsoil in the late 1970s. Some might have thought fishing was the largest industry in Nova Scotia, or perhaps coal mining, but the reality was gypsum (a relatively soft white or sometimes gray mineral) was the undisputed true lifeblood of this small Canadian province. Mainly consisting of hydrated calcium sulfate, gypsum can be crushed down to make wallboard, or drywall, as it is usually known. In fact, by the early 2000s, about 80% of all drywall sold in North America was being produced from the rock mined throughout Nova Scotia. But those sales numbers came from much larger operations than the Red Spruce Gypsum Mine.

Opened in 1985, the mine struggled along year after year, holding its own for the most part, but the residents of Beckley never seemed to gain much traction. A few steps forward, a few steps back. The people were salt of the earth, hard working men and women, but nothing ever seemed to come easy for them, their destinies tied to the gypsum mine whether they liked it or not. With just shy of four thousand people registered on the last official census, it wouldn't take very much of either good fortune or bad luck to swing the pendulum of chance one way or the other.

Prosperity or ruin.

On May 16, 2020, fate finally made up its mind.

It had rained for two weeks straight. Hard rain. The kind that kept reasonable people indoors and made the unlucky ones, who had no choice but to venture out into the chilly, late Spring storm, curse and bundle up under thick layers of clothing. But on the night of the disaster, the dark clouds had blown off to the East during the afternoon, the wind had calmed to a slight breeze, and the temperature had actually climbed two or three degrees back to where the citizens of Beckley could start to dream about the approach of summer—those who weren't working in the mine that night, anyway. Those who were, didn't have the luxury of dreaming of summer, they just had to fill their lunch buckets, pull on their boots, grab their hardhats and respirators, and make their way to the entrance of Shaft 3, the same way they did every other night, rain or no rain.

Shaft 3 was quite an unusual and dangerous place to work. Most gypsum mining is done using surface mining, meaning they dig right from ground level and just keep expanding their work zone until you have a rock quarry that gets deeper and deeper. The mineral is dug using large excavating machines or powerful drills, and filled directly into giant trucks that drive the spoils right out of the pit and take the gypsum away to be processed elsewhere. Almost all the gypsum in Nova Scotia is mined this way, but the vein of gypsum at the Red Spruce Mine on the outskirts of Beckley wasn't nearly as rich as the owners of the mine had hoped, and after thirty years of steady work, there wasn't much left to dig. Their quarry was tapped out.

Truth be told, if they hadn't found a smaller, vertical vein of

Gypsum just to the east of the first surface quarry, the mine would have shut down three years earlier. But the owners needed the gypsum, and the citizens of Beckley certainly needed the jobs, so they decided to switch to underground mining, where they mined the precious remaining mineral from deep shafts and tunnels only accessible from open-caged elevators and steeply sloped rail cars.

The work was far more difficult and dangerous, the risks huge when you added in the hazards associated with underground gases that could explode, ever-present cancerous dust making it impossible to breathe, claustrophobia problems from working in tight spaces and oppressive darkness, and the constant fear of a shaft or tunnel collapsing. As such, some of the people of Beckley started to move away, to try and find work at other, safer mines throughout the region. Fewer men wanted to work in the underground shafts, and hardly any of them wanted to work the nightshifts, when a lot of the dynamiting and drilling was done in preparation for the dayshift labourers, who would bring the gypsum to the surface. The owners of the mine raised the wages for anyone willing to work the nightshift, but it was still a constant battle trying to fill a reliable roster to keep the mine in operation. Thankfully, there was a group of forty brave men and women from the nearby Her'maqon reservation who showed up week after week to do the dirty jobs no one else wanted to do. Unfortunately, it would be those poor souls who paid the biggest price, on the night of the big flood.

There were pumps working steadily at the mine, of course. They'd been working nonstop for years, keeping the shafts and underground tunnels as dry as possible, but with all the recent rains, they'd been taxed to their limits. Normally, the rain and underground water could easily be pumped west of Shaft 3 into the vast rock quarry that had been the site of the surface mining pit for the last three decades. The quarry was a huge rock-lined area that would hold an enormous amount of water, but on that fateful night, two things happened simultaneously that would seal the fate of the underground mine, as well as doom the poor miners who were trapped deep in the tunnels. At 10:15 PM the power went out. Just a temporary hiccup in the electrical system, or so they first thought, but it was enough to shut down the water pumps and plunge the entire underground network of shafts and tunnels into darkness.

There were backup power systems, of course, safety requirements mandatory under Canadian Mining Regulations, but on this night, they failed to turn on. Budget cutbacks and shoddy preventative maintenance procedures had left the back-up generators in poor repair and, on the night they were most needed, non-functional. Even this egregious safety issue in itself wouldn't have been devastating, as the miners could have slowly made their way to the surface using the ladders on the outside of the elevator cages and the sloped tunnels used by the rail cars. It would have taken them a few hours, and they'd have had to do it in the dark using whatever headlamps or flashlights they could find. They wouldn't have been happy about any of it, but they would have eventually made it out before the lower tunnels filled with too much water.

But at the same time the power went off, and the back-up generators failed, the workers were just setting off another round of blast charges in one of the mid-level tunnels. The massive explosion went off in the suddenly dark chamber, and it was more by the noise of the rushing water than actually seeing it happen, that the workers realized they'd hit some kind of underground stream. There was an incredible surge of water in the tunnel that filled the chamber the miners were working in and created a waterfall of death into the shaft behind them, flowing down into the tunnels farther below. With no pumps working, and no power to even try damming up the incoming rush of water, the men and women could do nothing other than try to get above the flood zone, and climb for the surface. Some were lucky and made it out, and some were not. Some were washed away with the rising water, forced into the shaft and dropped several hundred feet into the darkness far below. And even some of those unfortunate people would somehow survive the fall or find something to grab hold of and eventually find a way up and out of danger.

It was the people working in the lower tunnels who were truly doomed. All that water rushing from above was quickly filling the tunnels, but as the water rose, the walls and wooden structures of the tunnels began to come apart and dismantle. Men and women alike screamed in terror as the tunnels started to collapse around them, blocking their way from reaching the vertical shaft and the only way out of the mine from those levels.

In the end, the pumps never did get restarted, and the back-up generators and electrical systems never came online. The water continued to rise, the tunnels continued to collapse, and the trapped crew of workers continued to scream. But there was no one who could help them. They either made it out somehow on their own, or they didn't. It was as simple as that. Of the nearly one hundred miners who were working in Shaft 3 of the Red Spruce Gypsum Mine that terrible night, only thirty-two of them made it out of the pit alive. The official death count was stated as sixty-five people, and would go down as one of the worst mining disasters in Nova Scotia history.

The town of Beckley would never really recover from the disaster. The town would survive, of course, because what other choice did the people have? Most of its remaining work force found jobs in forestry or the fishing industries, but no one would ever forget what happened on the night of the underground flood, especially the proud people of the Her'maqon nation, who lost a staggering thirty-four men and four women to the dark waters that terrible night. Rescuers would eventually recover the bodies of fifty-six men and women but most of those had been found in the middle sections of the tunnels. With the stability of the entire underground network in question, and the lowest levels of the mine still blocked and submerged, the decision to call off the recovery mission was reluctantly made, leaving behind nine bodies to spend eternity in their watery grave.

The mine was never reopened.

One

Red Spruce Lake
Present Day
July 15th, 10:25 p.m.

No matter how many times Bob Leeman walked out of the wooded area to gaze out over the calm surface of the lake—and it happened a lot, seeing as he walked his dog nearly every night to this same spot—it never failed to impress and surprise him. One minute he and his Boston Terrier, Willy, would be walking on a needle-strewn path through the darkened Spruce Forest, smelling the orange-rind fragrance of Nova Scotia's most popular tree, Willie stopping every fifth trunk to squirt his doggie scent along the trail, and them *wham*, they walked out into a completely different moonlit world. They went from forest to beach, darkness to light, in one small step—literally. The spruce needle pathway jarringly ended on a little plateau of beach sand that the town had trucked in load after load, from destinations unknown, and dumped between the forest and the recently created lake.

The lake itself shouldn't have been there, much less the beach. Although, at least the town of Beckley had no say in the lake's existence. After the big flood at the mine, and without the constant water pumps doing their thing anymore, the entire Red Spruce Gypsum Mine quarry pit had filled with rising underground water as well as the rain falling from the sky. The huge quarry was lined with rock and after several months of constant flooding, had started to look more like a freshwater lake than any sort of mining operation. After the first year, and after the water level had finally found its zenith, the kids in town had discovered the abandoned mine was an excellent place to hang out or go swimming. The water was a bit murky, and always stayed a bit cooler than any of the natural lakes and rivers in the area, but it was hard to beat the thrill of leaping off the rocky cliff walls of the quarry to splash into water that was in some places up to twenty feet below. The town council had initially been resistant to letting their kids swim and play in an area that still held such sadness and pain for many residents in the county, but they eventually decided there was no real harm in any of it. That, and the fact the kids—and most of the adults in Beckley—would use the newly formed swimming hole whether the council approved it or not, so why not try to turn the darkest event in the town's history into at least something reasonably positive. With that in mind, and after seeking the blessing of both the local indigenous nations in the immediate area, the town cleared away some of the trees, installed some picnic tables and garbage cans, fenced off some of the more dangerous clifftop areas, and hauled in all that sand to form the beach at the shallower end of the quarry where a trucking road into the flooded mine created a perfect walk in spot. Beckley's mayor, Jim Talbot, would officially change the name of their newest recreational park from the Red Spruce Gypsum Mine to Red Spruce Lake on May 16, 2022, commemorating the second anniversary of the disaster.

The walk to the placid lake had become a nightly journey for Bob—and now too, for Willie—after Bob's wife of twenty-four years, Marlene, had passed away after a mercifully short battle with lung cancer. He'd walked the dark woods alone at first, using the solitude and the cover of the Spruce trees to cry as much as he needed to, to remember his beloved partner, but the months of mourning and pain had gradually started to recede, and the weight of his grief slowly lifted. It wasn't until his daughter, Patricia, who lived in Halifax, had purchased him a tiny puppy she'd named Willie (for no real reason other than she'd said he 'looked like a Willie') that he had found himself actually looking forward to his nightly walks. There were still thoughts of righteous anger and grief, but more often than enough, there were moments of fun now, of happiness, of renewed life that he'd never expected to find again, especially hanging on the leash of a silly little dog.

Standing on the beach, Bob shut off his flashlight and bent over to unhook the plastic leash from Willie's collar. He smiled as the black and white terrier exploded away as he always did to scratch and sniff and roll around in the cool sand. The poor little guy was a bit of a runt and the breeder had informed Patricia that she hadn't thought the pup was going to survive when he'd been born, but what Willie lacked in size and strength he certainly made up for with curiosity and an astonishing level of energy. He was a fighter, had been since day one, and as crazy as it seemed (especially to Bob himself) something in the little dog's tenacious spirit had brought Bob back to life and given him a reason to fight again, too.

As Willie trotted to the edge of the water to get a drink, a loud "*crack*" sound distracted Bob, the noise coming from somewhere in the nearby woods. Slightly startled, as he had assumed it was late enough at night that he would be out here at the lake alone, the way he preferred, he quickly scanned the treeline around him. Nothing moved, and the sound was not repeated. Wait, there it was again, softer but somehow closer this time. Bob was a fairly big man, standing 6'1" in height and clocking in at around 220 pounds, which meant he didn't frighten easily. Still, the noise bothered him in a way that was hard to explain. This was *his* private spot. *His* time to be alone. Another "*crack*" in the woods confirmed he wasn't.

"Who's there?" Bob said, loud enough to be heard, but there was no answer.

Just a few falling branches? Teens up late, maybe?

But then he let his mind consider what he was actually afraid of.

Coyotes?

In Nova Scotia, the Eastern Coyote was a dangerous predator. Larger than most other breeds of coyotes, perhaps from past breeding with wolves, the average Eastern Coyote weighed around forty pounds with the bigger males weighing up to sixty, or about the size of a German Sheperd. Luckily, they tended to live farther north, but that didn't mean they didn't stray into this area every now and then. When they did, they were lean and muscular, and incredibly nasty, and could attack in packs very much like their wolf brethren. If Bob was caught out here alone with a pack of coyotes, or even just one that was hungry, he might be in a lot of trouble. And so would Willie. The little terrier was exactly the type of easy prey the coyote would go after.

"Get over here, Willie," Bob said, turning his attention back to the lake, intent on putting the leash back on his puppy's collar, or even picking his pet up, in case he needed to make a beeline out of here in a hurry. But Willie was no longer standing at the water's edge, where he'd been mere seconds before. In fact, as Bob shifted his eyes to the right and to the left, the little dog was nowhere to be seen on the beach at all. Bob was about to shout again, louder this time, his heart in his throat, but then he heard splashing in the water farther out into the lake. When he looked, he could see something was out there, but couldn't quite make out what it was. *Willie? Couldn't be. He wasn't a swimmer. A duck or goose, maybe? The coyote?*

Clicking his flashlight back on to see better, Bob swung its bright light out onto the lake and sure enough, there was Willie swimming around way out over his head, his mostly black body nearly invisible in the dark water. His stumpy legs certainly couldn't touch bottom way out there and as Bob watched, his little friend started to struggle and go under for a moment. Most dogs were excellent swimmers, but Bob was thinking about how his pet had been the runt of the litter and hadn't fully developed like other terriers. Mostly full grown now, the poor little bugger still only weighed about twelve pounds, and as far as Bob was aware, he'd never been in the water for more than a few seconds comically paddling around trying his very best but looking like he might sink at any moment. The very real possibility that Bob might actually lose his new (and only) friend to drowning hit the old man like a punch in the gut, and he started screaming.

"Come here, boy. Swim this way. Willie! *Willy*!" Bob screamed, all thoughts of whatever might be prowling around in the woods gone now, his mind focused only on saving his dog. He couldn't bear the thought of losing someone else he loved. *No. No way*. Out in the water, Willie's body disappeared for a moment, then struggled his way to the top again.

"I'm coming, boy. Just keep swimming."

Bob tossed the flashlight and leash to the ground and ran for the water. He used the old trucking road to wade in up to his waist and then dove into the chilly water in the direction where Willie was battling to keep his head above the surface. Bob was admittedly not the best swimmer himself, but panic and his love for the little dog drove him forward at a faster than expected rate and within a minute he'd crossed to the part of the lake where he'd last spotted Willie.

Willie was no longer there.

Oh my God! Bob treaded water, frantically turning in circles.

Please . . . No!

And then Bob looked towards the beach and the light from the flashlight that was still turned on laying on the sand, and damned if he didn't see little Willie, looking like a drowned rat, walking out of the lake all on his own. The dog shook the water from his drenched coat, and then sat on the beach, peering around for his missing owner. The small dog looked exhausted, and perhaps a little frightened being alone, but was ultimately unharmed.

"Why, you little bastard . . . " Bob said, but even through his anger he couldn't help but smile. Willie had surprised him yet again and proven once more that he was stronger than anyone who looked at his frail body gave him credit for. "You'll pay for this one, pup. No treats for you for a month." Laughing at the predicament he found himself in, and feeling more than a little foolish that he'd soaked himself for absolutely no reason, Bob started swimming back towards shore.

And that was when something grabbed his leg and pulled him under.

Bob, having no idea what had just happened, tried swimming for the surface, but whatever had a hold of his left leg wasn't letting go and he was pulled even farther into the depths. Using his right leg, Bob desperately lashed out in the darkness, connected hard with *something*, broke free, and with his lungs already starting to burn for oxygen, thrashed his way upward. It wasn't until his face broke out of the water and he gulped down several mouthfuls of life-giving fresh air that the real panic and fear set in.

What could possibly be big enough . . . strong enough . . . to grab my leg like that?

Bob had no answer to his question and no desire to find out. He frantically swam for shore, concentrating on getting out of the water and as far away from this lake as he possibly could. But it wasn't going to happen. Within ten feet, he was attacked again, his body slammed hard, knocked with the force of a great white shark into deeper water and away from the safety of the beach. Before Bob could scream, he was pulled underwater again, down and down and down, until his eardrums felt like they were going to burst. He screamed anyway, wasting whatever meager seconds of air he had trapped in his lungs, his fists uselessly pounding away in the darkness at whatever was holding him tightly in its grasp.

And then Bob was suddenly face to face with the creature, just close enough to see some of its blurred features. Only it wasn't the giant eel-like, shark-finned monstrosity he was conjuring in his frightened, oxygen-deprived brain.

It was a man.

Or was it? At first glance, he thought so, but seconds later he wasn't sure.

By the meager dissipating light of the moon far above, Bob saw a black-haired, man-like creature with high cheekbones and large glassy eyes that reflected the light filtering from above to cast twin slivers of illumination on his swollen, disfigured face, and his wide-open mouth. His fleshy lips opened in a monstrous grin and Bob could see there were way too many teeth to fit inside of a normal human mouth. He had a quick glimpse of razor-sharp, jagged teeth, and a black tongue that slithered out from the back of the creature's raw, red throat and licked Bob on the side of his face. Bob tried to scream again, and break loose, but there was no air left in his lungs to scream with, and he sucked in his first gulp of cold lake water. The water flooded his lungs, and he began to choke and struggle, but whatever it was that masqueraded as a man continued to hold him tight. Bob felt light-headed and his chest burned, as if a fire had been ignited in his throat and chest. His entire body began to shiver and shake, his arms no longer having the strength to fight his attacker, so for a moment he simply drifted in the water, neither floating up nor sinking deeper, his lungs filling with liquid now. A sense of calmness came over him then, a warm feeling of peace and relative contentment as his brain used up the last oxygen in his system and his eyes began to close.

And that was when the monster in the lake made a final attack. It drew Bob's drowning body closer, clamping that grotesque, oversized mouth onto the center of the dying man's throat, below his Adam's Apple, and bit down. Bob felt no real pain. He was beyond that now. All he sensed was a brief pinch on his chilled skin, a rush of hot blood in his mouth, and the final vestiges of trapped air in his waterlogged lungs bubbling out of his body into the creature's hungry mouth . . .

And then Bob felt no more.

Back on the beach, Willie shivered as he waited for his master to return. He was cold and hungry, and kept nudging his plastic leash lying on the sand, hoping somehow this would make his friend reappear and take him to that special place where his warm bed and his bowl full of kibble waited. But his master never returned.

Someone else did, though.

Out of the Spruce Forest, an older indigenous man carefully crept onto the makeshift beach. He walked slowly, his steps measured and careful in the deep sand. The man wore an ill-fitting black suit jacket over faded blue jeans, and a wrinkled fedora perched on his head with a crow feather sticking out of the hat band. His long hair was mostly grey these days, with a few streaks of black that stubbornly remained from his youth. Anyone who looked upon him might think he was in his late seventies or even his eighties, but they'd be wrong. He'd turned sixty-seven just this past month, but years of manual labour, heavy drinking, and these last few, hard years of bitterness and grief had aged him prematurely.

He'd been hiding in the woods and watching the old man from town and his little dog for quite some time now. He'd stepped on a couple of fallen branches earlier and nearly given away his hiding spot, but in the end he hadn't been discovered. The native man walked over to the edge of the lake and peered out over the water, but there was nothing left to see. The horrifying show was over. The surface of the water had calmed back down, and the lake was like a mirrored sheet of glass once again.

Turning away from the lake, the man bent down and gathered the flashlight and the dog leash that the old man had tossed onto the sand earlier. He turned off the flashlight, put it away in his suit jacket pocket, then clipped the leash to the shivering puppy's collar. The man had heard the dog's name being called out several times while he'd hidden in the woods, so he knew the animal's name.

"Come, Willie. Let's go get you dried off."

Willie hesitated at first, whimpering, confused. But he was hungry and cold, and he'd been trained to be a good boy and do what he was told, so he followed the strange man wearing the feathered hat into the woods.

Two

Red Spruce Lake
Three Days Later
July 18th, 1:45 p.m.

Underwater. Everything was quiet and peaceful, save for the bubbles exhaled out of the port in Sara Palmer's regulator that expanded and exploded as they headed for the surface world above. There were also the slight swooshing noises of her boyfriend Tim's swim fins as he slowly kicked his way along the rocky bottom of the lake five feet ahead of her. Even at that close of a range, the visibility in the murky water wasn't great today, and Tim's fins and legs were about the extent of what Sara could see in the direction they were swimming. She sped up her own kicks, not wanting to lose sight of him. Although both divers were young, both in their mid-twenties, they were well aware of scuba diving's cardinal rule—to never dive alone, to always dive with a buddy, and never leave their side from the moment you both submerged, until you both made it safely back to the surface.

Not that Sara and Tim were diving very deep today, only to about twenty-five or thirty feet, but they were both experienced enough to understand you never broke the rules, no matter how shallow you stayed. Too many people had tried to take on lady luck on their own in the past, and unfortunately, many of them were no longer alive today to regret that decision.

Of the two, Sara was by far the more experienced diver, which was why she was letting Tim swim ahead of her. If anything went wrong, she wanted to make sure she kept him in view at all times. Some small-minded men might have had a problem with that, with women being in charge of things, but Tim Hanson was a better man than that. He walked his own path, not worrying what anyone else thought, and held his own beside Sara on probably every other aspect of their relationship, other than when it came to scuba diving. He was smart enough to understand people could easily die underwater, and he knew he still had a lot to learn before he considered himself even half her equal down below the surface. They'd been dating for nine months now, but he'd only been taking dive lessons for a little over two months. Sara had been diving for years, ever since the summer she'd graduated high school, before Red Spruce Lake even existed.

They were skimming near the bottom on the western side of the old quarry, beneath what was generally referred to as the *swimming zone* of the lake. People could swim anywhere they chose to, of course, but the way the old mine had been carved out of the rocky ground, the western side of the quarry was much shallower than the eastern half. The beach area had been located on that side for obvious reasons, so people could walk into the water on the old trucking road, and then drop off into the relatively shallow water. Here, on the western plateau, the drop only went down about twenty or twenty-five feet, but off to the east, in the older part of the mine, the depth plummeted to between seventy and eighty feet—maybe deeper in some parts, especially out towards where old Shaft 3 had been drilled.

At twenty-five feet deep, there were very few men or women who could swim to the bottom of the lake without an air tank, so anything that might get dropped out of people's hands or pockets would drop to the rocky bottom and just sit there. So close, but essentially unreachable for whoever dropped them to be able to recover the items. Which was where Sara and Tim entered the picture. Twice a week for the last month, Sara and Tim would suit up in their diving gear and swim a basic grid pattern on the upper shelf of the lake to see what they could find. Sometimes, an actual person who had dropped something valuable or important (like a wedding ring, or their car keys) would hire them to search for their missing item, but more times than not, it was just the two of them on their own, conducting a treasure hunt to see what they might find. Some dives were better than others, of course, but they rarely came back to the surface without finding something of value. Just two weeks ago, they'd found a silver neck chain, a *Timex* wristwatch (that was still working), and two ten dollar bills that were just randomly floating around about a foot off the bottom.

Sara could already tell that today wasn't going to be quite as productive, not with visibility being so bad. On a good day, she'd be able to scan left and right and see objects on the bottom as far out as twenty or thirty feet in whichever direction she looked, but she and Tim couldn't see anywhere near that distance now. In fact, it was hardly worth being down here today, other than it was giving Tim another dive under his belt that he could add to his logbook. In that light, any dive was a good dive, she supposed, but if the water started getting any murkier, she was going to have to call an end to the dive, regardless.

While she was still mulling her decision over, she felt something touch her left leg and it startled her enough to make her squeal into her respirator. She quickly spun around to see what it was. To her surprise, she saw another dive mask, and the bushy, brown beard of her friend, Eddy Champlain. Tim must have heard her cry out and turned around to investigate, because suddenly he was there, too. A few seconds later, a fourth diver, Xavier Pictou, joined them. Sara and Tim knew both the new divers. They were all around the same age and part of the same dive club, but it was still surprising to meet them underwater like this. Eddy was a great big bear of a man, while Xavier was lean and wiry with jet black hair, and was about half of Eddy's size. The two men were as close to polar opposites as you might find, one a large white dude, the other a thin indigenous man from the local Mi'kmaq community, but they had grown up together in Beckley, were dive buddies, and despite their differences were best of friends in or out of the water.

As the four divers faced each other, Eddy held up his massive right hand and pinched his forefinger down to meet his thumb in the universal dive sign that asked, '*Is everything okay?*' Sara flashed that she was okay, and waited until Tim and Xavier acknowledged they were fine, too, then spread her hands out and away from her body to try and ask, '*What the heck do you want?*' Her message was either understood, or expected, because Xavier was already reaching for his underwater tablet to start writing something. In a few more summers, Sara hoped to have full face masks with state-of-the-art dive communications built inside them, but for now they were all just hobby divers and none of them could afford expensive professional equipment like that. Writing tablets were simple and cheap, usually made with just a white slate of plastic of any size with a pencil secured to it. Many divers used those small pencils they gave people on golf or mini-putt courses, but Xavier liked to use carpenter pencils with the flat sides and larger carbon strip, claiming he could sharpen them with his dive knife without going to the surface.

He scribbled for a few seconds and then turned the tablet to face Sara and Tim, so they could both read:

HEADING FOR LIP
JOIN US?

The '*LIP*' was the edge of the western shelf, where the drop off into the deeper, more dangerous regions of the lake began. Tim had been bothering her to take him out there for several weeks now, but she'd kept him in the shallows until he had some more time under his belt. In all fairness, there was no reason he couldn't go there. The lip itself wasn't any more dangerous than where they were right now, as long as they didn't descend down into the more pressurized water below. She grabbed the writing tablet from Xavier, and he handed over his pencil. Sara wrote only one word beneath his invitation:

VISIBILITY?

Xavier took back the tablet and quickly wrote:

BETTER THAN HERE

Sara glanced over at her boyfriend, but he was already enthusiastically nodding. She checked her air gauge and found she still had 2200 pounds of air pressure in her tank. Tim showed her his gauge and he still had 2100 pounds of pressure, enough to keep them breathing for at least another thirty or forty minutes at this depth as long as they weren't exerting themselves too strenuously.

Why not?

They weren't finding anything in the shallows today anyway, and Tim would be thrilled knowing she finally felt confident enough in his diving skills to head out a little bit deeper.

Decision made, Sarah gave Tim and Xavier the '*okay*' sign and pointed to big Eddy to lead the way. Eddy nodded, checked his underwater compass, and started swimming in an easterly direction. Xavier took a moment to put away his writing tablet but was soon following his dive buddy into slightly deeper water. Tim fell in line next, without having to be told, leaving Sara to bring up the rear.

Two by two, they swam in murky water, heading east, and just as Xavier had suggested, the farther away from the area most people swam and splashed around in, the clearer the water became. By the time they'd fin-kicked a hundred feet, even though they'd only descended a few feet deeper to the thirty or thirty-two foot level, Sarah could clearly make out all three of her dive mates. Just ahead, she could make out the edge of the western plateau, and the mysterious darker water waiting for them over the lip of the drop off. She glanced over at Tim and felt a rush of excitement flow through her, knowing he'd never been here before and was about to experience one of the coolest feelings you could as a novice diver. She grabbed his hand and together they swam up to the rim . . . and beyond.

It was technically the exact same water, at the exact same depth, but there was nothing like the surge of adrenaline that pumped through a diver's veins when the rocky bottom they had been following suddenly vanishes and you can see down for what looks like forever. Tim would feel as if he were flying, an eagle souring out and away from the safety of the cliff and hovering in mid-air over miles of open space, the valley—or in this case—the bottom of the old surface mine far below. It was a magical, as well as terrifying feeling all at the same time, and when Tim finally dragged his gaze off the void below to look over at Sara, she saw that his eyes were wide and full of wonder, just as she'd hoped they would be.

The drop off wasn't a vertical wall straight down to the bottom; it dropped down several levels twelve or fifteen feet at a time, an old mining road sloping down between the levels until you reached the bottom farther east. The visibility wasn't good enough to see all the way to the lowest level, but it was remarkably clearer than it had been back in the swimming area. While Sara and Tim hung out together, enjoyed the feeling of flying over the drop off, Xavier and Eddy immediately swam down into deeper water.

Xavier paused for a moment at the depth of thirty-three feet to squeeze his nose through his dive mask and try to blow out. It was at this depth, and every thirty-three feet down they went from here, that the pressure of the water doubled on a human body. From ground level, all the way up into space, there was only one constant atmosphere of pressure but every thirty-three feet you travelled down under water, your body went through another atmosphere, doubling the pressure you feel on your body. This sometimes caused pain in a diver's ears as they struggled to equalize in the higher pressurized environment, so squeezing their nose and blowing out was one of a diver's tricks to help them equalize their ears so they could continue their descent.

Xavier hurried to catch up to his larger friend, who was pointing rather excitedly at something below. It wasn't until he caught up to Eddy that he saw him reaching for an old sneaker that was snagged by its lace on the jagged rock wall. Xavier could see it was white, had three stripes on the sides, and the Adidas logo on the heel, but all of that was lost on him once he noticed the other side of the runner was shredded in four parallel jagged cuts from the lace right through the sole of the shoe. Eddy turned to him and held up his four fingers, curled them into claws, then moved them in a slashing motion, across the damaged shoe, indicating exactly what Xavier was thinking—that some animal had mauled it. Worse still, when Eddy moved the Adidas around in his hand to look at it better, his fingers came away with a sticky reddish-black substance inside the shoe that clouded the water slightly.

Blood? That's not good.

Eddy tried to hand the shoe over to Xavier, but he pulled away, not wanting anything to do with it. He was about to swim back towards Sara and Tim hovering above them, but something caught his eye farther down the cliff wall, half hidden behind a large gypsum boulder. Something a lot bigger than a running shoe.

The hell is that?

Xavier motioned for Eddy, but the big man had spotted it, too. He stared into Eddy's eyes, and although they were partially hidden behind the plastic lenses in his mask, Xavier could see the shock in his friend's face. From their current location, they could just see what looked like the exposed bare foot and blue jean covered pant leg of what presumably was attached to the rest of a drowned man or woman. Whoever it was, the rest of their body was hidden behind the large rock. Xavier pointed downward several times, motioning that they should go have a look. Eddy at first shook his head no, but after looking back at the ruined running shoe he still held in his hand, he reluctantly nodded his head, *okay*.

Xavier made it to the body first, swimming around the boulder and settling down onto this level of the shelf on his knees near the head of the drowned person. The body was face down but from the stocky shape and short hair, Xavier could tell they were dealing with a man rather than a woman, but he still had no idea who it might be. He tried to haul on the body's shirt to raise him up and turn his face, but the body was jammed in behind the rock enough that it was proving hard to move. Eddy showed up to help him out, and together they pulled the body free from the boulder, flipped him over onto his back, and received the shock of their lives.

The man's throat had been savagely torn open and ripped away; his open-mouthed screaming head only attached to the rest of the body because of the clearly visible ivory-coloured spinal column keeping the pale, skin-covered skull from floating away on its own.

Xavier screamed around his regulator mouthpiece, stuck in place, trying to comprehend what could have possibly happened, unable to pull away from the horrific sight. He might have stayed there in that frozen place until he ran out of air, but he felt the strong hand of his friend grasp the top loop on his buoyancy compensator and start yanking him towards the surface, and as soon as he was moving again, he broke free of his stasis and swam for the surface, too. They swam without looking back, without looking down, and only paused for the merest of seconds as they raced past Sarah and Tim to enthusiastically motion for them to follow them up out of the dark water . . . and then they were gone.

Sara and Tim had been enjoying their time alone for the few minutes that Xavier and Eddy had left them to go exploring. Tim had wanted to follow them down deeper, but Sara had stopped him. He had never been below thirty-three feet before, never crossed the boundary into another atmosphere of pressure before, and she didn't want to move his training along too quickly. Just being out here, hovering above the drop off, was enough of a step for today, and she could tell that although he might be a little disappointed, he was still basking in the wonderful glow of '*flying*' away from the edge of the lip.

For today, that would have to be enough.

Then, without warning, Xavier and Eddy had shot up out of the darkness and raced right past them, slowing only a little to urge them to head for the surface. They moved fast so it was hard to tell what was going on, but Eddy was holding onto what looked like and old, tattered running shoe in one hand, and they had both looked scared. Sara has never seen either one of them look afraid of anything, which made things seem even worse. She peered down below her feet for a moment, unsure as to what might be down there beyond her field of vision that had spooked them, but staying here certainly wasn't going to provide an answer. Whatever it was, the last place she should be lingering around was down here with Tim in the water. She pulled her boyfriend close and pointed upward a few times to let him know her intentions. He nodded and they were soon on their way to meet their friends.

Sara surfaced in a splash of bubbles, her right hand gripping Tim's weight belt just so she could keep them together and help control his ascent. Xavier and Eddy were less than ten feet away from them, gasping for air and literally shaking in their neoprene wetsuits. They'd both torn off their dive goggles and were yelling back and forth at each other, but not making a lot of sense.

"Did you see that?" Eddy said.

"Holy crap!" Xavier answered back.

"And look at *this!*" Eddy said, holding up the tattered running shoe out of the water like it was some great prize or ancient artifact. "I kept hold of it. Didn't want to . . . but hell, ya know?"

"What's going on?" Tim said after spitting the respirator out of his mouth.

"A dead body," Xavier said. "Didn't you guys see it?"

"A *body*?" Sara asked. "You're kidding right?"

"Of course not." The thin, indigenous man pointed over to his bearded dive buddy for back-up. "Look . . . Eddy even has the poor guy's shoe. Show 'em, Ed."

Eddy held up the grisly torn Adidas runner again, so they could get a better look.

"Who was it?" Tim asked.

"No idea . . . some older dude," Xavier said.

"I know him," Eddy said. "It was Bob Leeman. I recognised him as soon as we turned him over. He used to work with my old man at the trucking company in Beckley. Been retired for a few years, I think. Well . . . he's dead now so I guess it doesn't matter. What an awful way to die though, man. You believe that shit, X?"

"I know, brother. No way for any man to go. It'll give me nightmares for years."

"Why? What happened? He didn't drown?" Sara asked.

"Not even close," Xavier said. "He was attacked by some kind of animal, I think, but this isn't the place to talk about it. Let's get the hell out of here, okay?"

"Totally agree," Eddy said. "We're gonna need to go see your father, Sara, but before we do that . . . I'm gonna need a cold beer."

Three

255 Satchell Road
Beckley Police Department
July 18th, 4:00 p.m.

As far as smalltown police offices went, Beckley's red-bricked, two-storey building on Satchell Road always seemed to be busier than most. With all the unemployment in town, the drinking problems, and the constant disputes between the two neighboring indigenous nations, the idea of a sleepy little police station where the officers drank coffee and ate donuts all day was nothing more than a pipe dream for Chief Palmer and his crew. Today, on the other hand, had actually been fairly quiet, and there was even talk of locking the doors early and letting everyone head on home at a decent hour for a change.

Had been quiet, that was, until Sara, Tim, Xavier, and Eddy ran up the front stairs and started yelling and screaming as soon as they were inside the door.

"Lord have mercy," Joyce Foster shouted above all the commotion. She was tall and blonde, an eight-year veteran on the force, currently sitting at the front desk when the team of divers walked in. "Settle down and tell me what you're all so fired up about. One person. You, Sara. Go."

"It's bad news, Mrs. Foster. Is my dad here?"

"He's in his office. What's up?"

"What's going on, Sara?" The question came from down the hallway, and when everyone looked around, they could see Bryan Palmer exiting his office and walking towards them. "I could hear you guys all the way in the back."

Chief Palmer, Sara's father, had been the boss around here for fifteen years, and he'd been an officer here in Beckley for six years before that. Bryan stood 6' 2" tall and had once been an extremely intimidating presence to be around, but the years had thinned and greyed his hair, slumped his shoulders a bit from always being tired, and expanded his belly a few inches from too many late nights of pizza and beer. That said, he was still a terrific cop, and the people of this small community knew they could depend on him for pretty much anything that might come along. Sara and her friends knew that too, which was why they were here.

"Sorry to bug you, Dad, but this is something you need to know."

"No worries. What's going on?"

"This might sound crazy, but we found a dead body at the lake today. Well . . . Eddy and X found him. He's laying at the bottom, but it's not a drowning. Tell them, Eddy."

"Yeah, okay. First off, I'm pretty sure it's Bob Leeman. Him and my dad used to be friends back in the day."

"Bob?" Officer Foster said. "That's interesting."

"Why?" Chief Palmer asked.

"My friend, Pauline, works down at the humane society, and she told me a small black and white terrier was tied to the door of their building when she showed up for work a few days ago. The dog didn't have a tag, but she thought it looked like Bob Leeman's puppy. They tried calling him but never got an answer. Maybe now we know why. Anyway, go on, Eddy."

"Sure. X and I presumed the man had been out swimming and somehow he'd drowned, but when we turned him over to look—"

"You touched the body?" Officer Foster interrupted again.

"Well, yeah. The body was wedged behind a large rock, and we had to tug on him a bit to set him free. Is there a problem with that?"

"Probably not, no. It's just you're not supposed to touch dead bodies in case we have to look for evidence and stuff, right?"

"Forget about it," Chief Palmer said, anxious to hear what they'd found. "It's not a big deal. Go on."

"Okay, like I was saying, once we turned him over, I instantly recognised who he was, but then I saw his throat and saw how he died and X and I both kind of freaked out."

"What was wrong with his throat?" Chief Palmer asked.

"It was . . . *gone*."

"Gone? What does that mean, Eddy?"

"It means his throat was torn out," Xavier answered for his

friend, joining the conversation. "It was horrible. The wound was so huge you could see straight through to his exposed spine. I nearly threw up into my regulator."

"Are you saying he had his throat slit. That he was *murdered*?"

"No. That wound wasn't done by a knife. Show him the shoe, Eddy."

Eddy reached into a paper bag he'd been carrying and pulled out the white Adidas running shoe with three blue stripes on the side. He flipped it around so the chief and Officer Foster could see the ripped grooves on the other side. "We found this shoe before we noticed the body. It was higher up on the cliff face. It kind of looks more like claw marks or maybe teeth marks from an animal. I'm no expert, obviously, but it looks like Bob was attacked by a bear, or maybe a coyote."

"Then why is he at the bottom of the lake?" Officer Foster asked.

"No idea, but there's no freakin' sharks in Red Spruce Lake. The town has tried stocking different kinds of fish in there, but that takes years. There's fish down there, but nothing that can do *that* kind of damage to a man, so we figure he must have been attacked in the forest, and either fell or jumped from the cliff to try to get away."

Officer Foster took the running shoe, as well as the paper bag, from Eddy and gave him another look that told him she didn't approve of him touching this evidence either. She handed the shoe over to her boss beside her. "What do you think, Bryan?"

Chief Palmer took a minute looking at the ruined shoe before answering.

"Had to have happened out of the water. Nobody goes swimming with their running shoes on. Other than that, I don't know. The only bears we have around here are Black Bears. I've seen some big ones in the woods, but I've never heard of them attacking or mauling anyone before. Doesn't mean it couldn't happen, though. The coyotes are more dangerous for sure, but they're smaller. I don't know if a bite from one of them could do the damage you're talking about. Did the neck wound look like claw marks, or teeth?"

Xavier and Eddy glanced at each other and shrugged.

"I don't know," Eddy said. "The shoe looks more like claw marks to me, and Bob's wound looked like a big bite, but what the heck do I know about those kinds of things? We only looked at him for a second, and then we high-tailed it out of there."

"Yeah, okay. We're gonna have to get a look at that body. We need to get Bob out of the lake, regardless, so he can be properly buried, but I wanna have Doc Turner have a good look at him first. He'll be able to tell us what killed him."

"We can go back down and get him, Dad," Sara said, volunteering without hesitation. "Eddy, X, and I are all experienced divers, and we already know where to find him."

"I'm coming, too," Tim said.

"Oh no you're not—" Sara started to say, but Chief Palmer put an end to the argument before it even got started.

"Forget it. None of you are going anywhere near that lake tonight. You've done more than enough already. I appreciate you letting us know what you found, but I know a couple of divers who specialize in this kind of thing, and they only live over in Gainsbourg. Joyce, I need you to call Doc Turner and have him ready to work late, then maybe stop by Bob Leeman's house just to check it out. I'll call the divers. The rest of you, get the heck out of here and leave all this nasty work to the experts. Get going."

Four

Red Spruce Lake
Alone In The Dark
July 18th, 9:10 p.m.

As the sun prepared to dip below the horizon, Tony Marchello held the cellphone to his ear, slightly irritated he'd needed to make this call in the first place. He was a big man, wide at the shoulders and still carried a lot of the natural muscle he'd been blessed with, but age and his unhealthy lifestyle were starting to catch up to him. He'd lived a hard life and the closely cropped grey hair on his head was only one of the outward signs that things weren't likely to get better anytime soon. His body still looked decent for a man on the wrong side of fifty years old, but inside, his bones and joints ached from laying around too much, from not working or staying active enough as the years had rolled by. Tonight he didn't feel too bad, other than trying to ignore the headache he felt, starting to pound inside his head while impatiently waiting five or six rings for someone to answer his call. A familiar voice finally answered.

"Chief Palmer here . . . "

"Hi Bryan," Tony said, making an honest effort to sound cheerier than he felt, because he needed this job. "It's Tony. Ian and I are here at the lake, ready to go to work, but there's no one else here yet. We kind of expected you and the medical examiner to be here when we showed up. You guys still coming?"

"Yeah, sorry about that. Some asshole threw a brick through the front window of the CIBC bank on Main Street, and I'm still here, cleaning up the mess and dealing with the pissed off bank manager. I'm picking up Doc Turner when I'm done, and we'll be out there as soon as we can. Probably another hour."

"An hour? Shit. We're ready to go now. Okay if we just go get it done? We can have the body up from the bottom and sitting on the beach by the time you guys get here. No sense waiting, right?"

"That's fine with me. You guys know the drill. You know where to look, right?"

"Yep. Your daughter said off the edge of the drop off, first or second step down. Don't worry, I've dived here before. I know exactly where we're going."

"Alright, you guys do your thing and I'll get my ass out there as fast as I can. I appreciate the help, brother."

"Anytime, Chief. See you in a bit."

Tony ended the call and tossed his cell into the waterproof dive bag at his feet. He'd already started to suit up and was almost ready to get into the water. He was wearing his black wetsuit and weight belt; his fins, mask, tank, and the rest of his diving gear were laid out at his feet, on the beach. He turned to see how his friend was making out. Ian Fitzgerald was sitting beside their small aluminum boat wearing the same denim shorts and AC/DC T-shirt he'd worn here on their drive over from Gainsbourg. He was drinking a tallboy of Molson Canadian and staring vacantly off to the west, watching the last rays of sunlight slowly fading away.

"What the hell ya doing, man?" Tony asked his friend of over thirty years. "You're supposed to be getting ready . . . and I told you to take it easy on the beers. Christ, you can't dive if you're plastered, Ian. Even you're smart enough to know that."

"I'm fine. It's not like you're an angel either, my friend. You were tossing a few brews back earlier today, too."

"Of course I was, but that was *before* we knew we had a job tonight. I haven't had anything since. Look at you, though. You can hardly stand up, I'll bet. What good you going to be to me like that?"

"You worry too much. I'm fine. Besides, you told me we had to wait until Chief Palmer showed up and I don't see anyone racing to get here yet."

"He's hung up for a while. We're going in now, and if we get lucky, and you don't manage to screw things up, we'll be down and back on shore before they show up. Maybe a dip in the cold water will sober you up."

Ian Fitzgerald was younger than Tony by a few years, but it would be hard to guess that by looking at him. He was of Irish decent, and his thick red hair was mostly grey now, and you could see much more of his forehead than you used to be able to. He had always been strong and lean, but now that the majority of his meals and free time were dedicated to drinking, he was looking more frail than lean. He slowly climbed to his feet, stumbling a bit, but managing to pull on his wetsuit without too much trouble. He'd much prefer to just sit here on the beach and drink another few beers, but deep down he knew Tony was right. They had work to do, and both of them needed the money. Not that he would ever admit that to his friend.

"Hold your horses, old pal. I'll be right with you . . . "

It was 9:30 PM by the time the two friends had shoved their gear into the boat and started paddling away from the small beach out towards the deeper area of the lake. The sunlight was gone now, which was a shame. Tony had hoped to get into the water early enough that they wouldn't need their underwater lights. The body was supposedly down on the second shelf of the drop off. From experience, Tony knew the drop off started at a depth of about thirty feet, and then stepped down fifteen feet at a time from there. That meant their dive tonight would take them no more than sixty feet down. If they'd gotten here a little earlier, or if Ian hadn't insisted they stop to grab a six-pack of beer, they'd have been able to pull it off without lights. No sense complaining about any of that now, though. It was what it was—a night dive.

Tony Marchello and Ian Fitzgerald were both extremely experienced scuba divers and had spent more than twenty years plying their trade in both the Canadian Armed Forces, as well as in the commercial dive industry after they retired from the navy. Chief Palmer had known both men for more than a decade now, and what he'd said about them specializing in body recovery had been true. The only facts he hadn't shared with his daughter and her friends were that Tony and Ian hadn't exactly retired from the navy on their own accord. Their escalating drinking habit was putting them and others in unacceptable danger, so they'd been gently nudged towards early retirement with a promise of an honourable discharge as long as they left quietly.

They had found work as commercial divers easy enough, but without the procedures and regimented duties they'd had in the forces to keep them relatively under control, the two friends' addiction had become steadily worse. Especially now that the economy was going into the crapper again, and they could find less and less decent work. So when Bryan Palmer had called, they were happy to suit up and help the chief out with the body recovery in the flooded old mine. A quick dip to the bottom, tie a rope to the deceased man, pull him to the top, deliver him to Chief Palmer on the shore, and Tony and Ian would be back home with cash in their pockets in time to make last call at the pub if they hurried up and got moving.

That was the plan, anyway.

"I think that's far enough," Tony said. "That big Spruce tree up on the cliff is the marker I always use. If you stand up there during the day, you can look down and see the different colour water on the shallow side of the lake from the deep. The drop off should be right below us."

"Whatever you s . . . say, boss?" Ian said, slurring his words slightly.

"Shit, Ian. You're in no shape to go diving tonight. It's not all that deep, but still. I don't feel comfortable about it. Maybe you ought to stay on the boat."

"I told you already . . . I'm fine. You think you're a better diver than me?"

"That's not what I'm saying, and you know it. I'm just trying to do this as fast as we can. I could use you up here in the boat, that's all. I'll go down, tie a rope around the guy, and you can pull him up and into the boat for us. Easy-Peezy, right? No need for us both to go down there."

Both men were well aware divers should never swim alone—especially in the dark—but Tony was just trying to help out his intoxicated friend and Ian was too drunk to care.

"I guess you're right," Ian said, starting to warm to the idea of staying dry. Why should both of them get wet if they didn't need to. "I'll be ready when you need me. When you give the rope a good yank, I'll start pulling him up. Deal?"

"Deal," Tony said, his poker face firmly in place. "Help me get my shit together, then. We've wasted more than enough time already. Let's get this done."

Ian helped get his partner's buoyancy compensator on and his tank hooked up to his regulator, nearly falling out of the boat doing so, but within a few minutes Tony was sitting on the edge of the boat and falling backwards into the water to start his dive. He grabbed the end of the long line of thin yellow rope they'd brought out with them, gave Ian one last '*okay*' sign with his forefinger and thumb, and quietly disappeared under the surface. Ian watched for his friend's bubbles for another few minutes to make sure Tony wasn't having any obvious issues, but that got boring in a hurry. Sitting alone in the boat, holding onto the far end of the yellow rope until he was needed, he reached into his dive bag and pulled out another can of Canadian. He cracked the beer open and took a large swig.

Then settled down to wait . . .

Tony descended the first twenty feet in darkness, letting the cool water embrace him, enjoying the feeling of freedom that diving had always given him. Taking a big, calming breath through his mouthpiece, he adjusted his mask slightly to make it more comfortable, and then turned on his headlamp. He was carrying a small hand-held flashlight as well, attached to his left wrist by a thin strap, but the visibility was quite good tonight, and his headlamp would likely end up being all that he needed. He could see about twenty-five feet in any direction, which should be more than enough to get the job done.

As expected, the lip of the western swimming plateau was directly below him, down another ten feet, the drop off into the deeper areas of the lake just off to his right. He readjusted his grip on the rope, making sure he wasn't going to get himself tangled up in it as he descended, then inverted his body to start swimming down. He veered over the lip and dove headfirst down the wall. Chief Palmer's daughter hadn't been able to say exactly where the body might be found, but it should be a simple matter of dropping down to the second shelf and then searching either left or right. Hopefully he'd get lucky and pick the right direction on the first try.

Feeling his ears *'pop'* as they equalized to the new atmosphere of pressure, he knew he'd crossed the thirty-three-foot mark. Wasting no time on sightseeing, he kicked his fins harder, speeding his decent towards the sloped bottom of the first shelf, and continuing over the next lip to keep heading down. This was where the Adidas running shoe had been found, as far as he knew; somewhere on this section of wall, although it could have been anywhere within one hundred feet on either side of him. Tony was still hoping to get lucky, though, and could envision dropping another ten feet to land on the second shelf within headlamp distance of the dead body.

Unfortunately, it wasn't meant to be. Tony added a few puffs of air into his buoyancy compensator to slow his decent and soon found himself standing upright on the rocky bottom of the second shelf. There was nothing to see. No dead body. No fish. No anything. And for the first time, Tony started to realize how creepy it was down here in the dark all by himself. Drunk or not, if something went wrong, at least Ian would have been here beside him to help him out. Now if something went south, he was completely on his own.

Not exactly a calming thought.

Tony shook his head to shake off the negative vibes. Turning his head in both directions, there was no way of knowing which way to swim, so he went with his gut instinct. He set out in a northerly direction. If he didn't find what he was looking for in a few minutes, or if he ran out of rope, he'd turn around and start coming back in the opposite direction. Luck was on his side, though, and after swimming only forty or fifty feet, the dark silhouette of a prone body started to come into view, Tony's headlamp illuminating the man's feet first, then his legs, waist, and upper body last. Tony intentionally didn't want to look any farther than that, having been told the man had suffered a grievous injury to his neck and throat area somehow. Not that Tony was squeamish, and he'd seen many dead bodies in the water before, but hey, if he could avoid being grossed out tonight, he'd much prefer it.

Approaching the body, which was floating freely on the bottom—not jammed behind a large boulder like he'd been told it might be—his attention was glued to the task at hand. Now that he'd found the body quite quickly, all he had to do was wrap the yellow rope around the deceased man's waist and give Ian the signal to start pulling him up to the boat. He was starting to think they just might make last call at the pub after all, the way things were going.

But then Tony felt a wave of water pressure wash over him from the right side, and when he turned his head to look, he saw the shadow of something moving out of the range of his light. He had no idea what it had been, but by the pressure wave that had hit him, he knew it was something large and moving really fast.

What the fuck? He had time to think, but before Tony had time to do anything else, he was under attack.

Something came out of the darkness behind him while his head was facing the other way. Tony felt the presence approaching in some primitive, instinctive way and managed to half roll over onto his left side before it was fully upon him. Tony watched in horror as a huge, clawed hand grabbed him by the top valve of his air tank to hold him in place, and the bloated face of an enraged man-beast swam into view. Its face and body clearly belonged to a man, but Tony could see several slits in the creature's neck opening and closing like fish gills, how it somehow appeared to be breathing through. The man or monster—whatever this thing was—opened his gaping mouth and snarled at him, revealing a cavern of long, pointed fangs. Tony tried to shake free, afraid he was going to be bitten, but instead the creature did something that in the moment scared Tony even worse.

His assailant used the curled claws on his other misshapen hand to slice through the rubber hose that ran from Tony's air tank to the regulator clutched firmly in his mouth. Bubbles began hissing out of the cut tube, the compressed life-giving air rushing out of the tank without anything to hold it in place. Tony sucked in a breath on his regulator, out of habit, but received only a mouthful of cold water for his efforts. The fear hit him then—a fear even more terrifying for him, than the knowledge he was being attacked by something not of this world—that without an air supply, he was going to drown down here in the dark. He'd been a diver in one capacity or another for most of his life, but his deepest secret was that he'd always feared this was the way his life would eventually end.

With a strength born of sheer panic, he lashed out, striking his attacker in the eye with his fist. He rocked the man-creature's head back with the powerful blow, but he could already feel his need to breathe zapping his strength and resolve to fight. He went after the beast's eyes again, anyway, hoping to scratch and claw them out of their oversized sockets, but the thing that looked like it had once been a man, latched onto his free hand and pulled it away. The creature let go of the air tank valve and tore the mask and headlamp free from Tony's face, taking away his ability to see, but sparing him the final horror of watching the man's mutated mouth expanding longer and wider than any human mouth should ever be capable of stretching. Tony was drifting in and out of consciousness now, alone in the dark, his lungs flooding with cold water. The part of his brain that was still consciously aware of what was happening was praying the end would come soon, and that it would be painless.

His dying wish would go unanswered.

The creature savagely bit into the tender flesh of Tony's throat and began feasting.

Ian Fitzgerald was fast asleep in the aluminum boat when he felt a small tug on the yellow rope he'd haphazardly tied around his wrist. He'd been nodding off for the past fifteen minutes and hadn't wanted the rope to fall into the water, so he'd looped it around his left wrist and tied it in a knot just in case. The first few pulls merely stirred him back to consciousness, but the third tug nearly yanked him clear out of the boat and into the water.

"Son of a *bitch*!" he screamed, his heart thudding in his chest as he tried to regain his balance. "Alright already. Relax. I got the message. Loud and fucking clear . . . Jesus!"

Ian sat back down and began reeling in the rope as fast as he could. It was hard at first, as he'd expected with the weight of a fully grown man's body on the other end, but once he got the weight moving, it became much easier. If Tony was keeping up, he'd be able to help steer the body towards the surface as well. The only hard part might be trying to pull the deceased man out of the water and into the small boat, but they'd figure it out. Probably wasn't worth the bother. They could just tie the body to the boat and simply drag him into shore.

Ian tried to coil the incoming yellow rope into neat, concentric loops at his feet on the bottom of the boat, but he had a headache, his hands were shaking, and his coordination was shot, so he ended up tangling the wet rope into a big, knotted mess.

Who gives a damn? As long as we get the poor bastard topside.

Eventually, he felt another yank on the rope and figured that meant Tony was telling him the body was close to the surface now. Ian slowed his pace and prepared to see the body popping up beside the boat at any second. He hoped the man hadn't been underwater for too long and wasn't all bloated and rotting like some waterlogged corpses could get. And then he felt and heard a solid *'thunk'* underneath where he was sitting, on the hull of the boat.

"Oops," Ian said, a smile on his weathered face. "Sorry about that, my friend."

He pulled the rope to the side to drag the dead man out from beneath him and then gave it one last mighty pull as he saw a shape rising out of the dark lake. The dead man came out of the water right beside where Ian was sitting, and as the momentum drove the body up, Ian found himself looking straight into the blank, glassy eyes of his best friend. The yellow rope was wrapped around Tony's ravaged throat and under both his arms.

Ian half screamed, half gagged, and he threw up a bellyful of stale beer directly onto his friend's lifeless face. Horrified (at what he'd seen as well as what he'd just done) he dropped the yellow rope and let Tony's body slide back down beneath the surface. Momentarily stunned, Ian sat there like a statue, unable to move, unable to breathe, unable to react.

What just happened? he wondered, his intoxicated mind racing. *What do I do now?*

While his brain tried unsuccessfully to connect the dots and figure out some logical pathway of events that could lead to Tony's ghastly death, the yellow rope started to move again. At first Ian thought it was Tony's body still sinking, but no, the rope was being dragged away from the boat, moving in a direction that didn't seem possible. Unless Tony was still alive somehow and trying to swim for shore, but there was no chance of that. Even drunk, there was no way Ian was buying that his friend had somehow survived a sickening wound like that. He was dead and gone.

Then who's pulling on the rope?

As if someone had heard his thought, the rope started moving faster, the slack being peeled off the rowboat at a furious pace. At this rate, the entire length of rope would be back in the water in no time . . . and it was still tied in a knot around Ian's wrist. Stifling another scream, he instinctively grasped the rope with both hands trying to stop it from being taken overboard. Whoever (*or whatever*) was on the other end, was far stronger than Ian, though, and the rope continued to rush out. Skin and blood flayed off in equal measure onto the side of the boat and spraying onto the surface of the lake, the thin rope carving a deep groove in the palm of each of his injured hands.

His pain was accomplishing nothing, so he dropped the rope and clumsily tried to undo the knot on his wrist. Even with his hands ruined, he almost had it undone when the rope snapped tight, and he ran out of time. Ian was pulled out of his seat with a force strong enough to nearly yank his left shoulder out of its socket, his body going airborne for ten feet before crashing belly first into the cold water of the lake. He was dragged across the surface for fifty feet, trying to scream but every time he unclenched his teeth, he gulped in mouthfuls of dark, churning water. And then, just as suddenly as it had begun, the rope stopped moving and Ian sank into an upright position. He was still wearing his wetsuit, so he didn't sink—he just hovered there in the center of the deepest part of the lake.

Ian had his wits about him enough to finally loosen the knot around his wrist and toss the end of the yellow rope as far away from him as he could throw it. Then he clenched both hands into fists and started taking deep breaths. His damaged hands hurt like hell, but the cold water and pain had sobered him enough now to understand the predicament he found himself in. Tony was dead and whoever had killed him was coming for him next. He may have been an alcoholic, but the one thing Ian wasn't, was a coward. He could try swimming for shore, but he knew he'd never make it there. Whatever was going to happen, it was going to happen out here in the center of the lake. He turned around and around in a slow circle, fists raised, ready for whatever was coming. Man or beast, he would fight. He knew his chances of success were slim to none, but what other choice did he have? Thankfully, there was enough light from the moon above to see the entire surface of the lake, so no one was going to sneak up on him. Not without him seeing them coming.

Unless, of course, the attack came from below.

Ian felt two powerful hands clamp onto his ankles and he cried out in despair and anger, mad at himself for not expecting this was the way it would happen. The moment he was pulled underwater, he knew he was in big trouble. He managed one last half-breath before his head submerged, and although he tried to punch and flail and kick as best he could, nothing he did was going to save him. Still, he fought anyway, getting at least a few licks in. All too soon, his lungs were burning for air, his strength already fading. He didn't accept his fate, but knew it was inevitable. Ian gave up struggling and gazed towards the surface. He watched the moonlight slowly fading to black and the pressure on his body steadily building, knowing he was being dragged down deeper and deeper and deeper to a place he wasn't coming back from. He screamed, one last guttural shriek of shock and pain and rage into the icy darkness, and then he closed his eyes and was gone.

From shore, hidden deep in the shadows of the Spruce trees, the older indigenous man with the feather in his hat had silently watched the events that transpired out in the deeper areas of the flooded old mine. He'd been there when the two divers from out of town had pulled in with their pick-up truck, and he'd been there to watch them both die at the hands of the man living at the bottom of the lake. He hadn't said a word, hadn't moved a muscle, but he'd been there this whole time . . . waiting, watching, as he always did.

Five

275 Rathburn Avenue,
Bryan Palmer's Residence
July 19th, 11:50 a.m.

The front door crashing shut woke Bryan out of a deep, dreamless sleep. He'd finally made it home and into bed at around 6:30 AM that morning, and he was still exhausted from last night's endless craziness. He'd managed to deal with the broken window situation at the bank in decent time, but then Joyce Foster had called to let him know there was indeed, no sign of Bob Leeman over at his small house. Chief Palmer had driven over there to meet her, and together they'd decided they had sufficient reason to break the lock on the side door and go inside to have a look. No one had been home—including the Boston Terrier puppy—but there was also no indication of damage, or any other mischief having taken place on the property. Bryan had eventually sent Joyce home for the night, and he'd moved on to pick up Doc Turner at the medical clinic, so they could make their way out to Red Spruce Lake to meet up with Tony Marchello and Ian Fitzgerald.

That was when Chief Palmer's night had truly turned bizarre.

It had to be pushing midnight by the time Bryan and Doc Turner made it to the end of the tree-lined road from town, and finally arrived at the lake. Tony and Ian's Ford 150 pick-up truck had been parked in the gravel area near the entrance gates, but neither of the hired divers from Gainsbourg were anywhere to be found. Bryan had been expecting to see his friends back on shore with the deceased body in tow, with Ian bitching and complaining about how long they'd been sitting there waiting. Instead, the entire parking lot, beach, and lake beyond had been eerily silent and as still as a graveyard. Leaving his Bronco running and aiming the headlights out over the water, Bryan had seen a small aluminum boat floating around at the eastern end of the lake, but from that distance he hadn't been able to tell if there was anyone in the boat or not.

Bryan had yelled out across the lake, but there had been no reply.

He and Doc Turner had decided the divers must have still been down under the water, retrieving the body, so they'd settle in to wait for them to resurface. They'd waited for almost another hour. By then, although neither were scuba divers, they'd known that something was wrong. Tony and Ian had to come up when they ran out of air in their tanks. Even if they had more tanks in the boat, they'd still have had to come topside to switch the tanks, and no matter how long they'd waited, there hadn't been so much as a ripple in the water.

Then Bryan had found two empty beer cans on the beach, and their feelings of dread had gone from bad to worst. So they'd walked around the lake, they'd searched for any signs of what might have happened, and they'd called in back-up from town to help them, but several hours later they were still no closer to finding Tony Marchello and Ian Fitzgerald, or figuring out what the heck had happened. It had turned into a long and frustrating night.

There was a loud knock on Bryan's bedroom door, bringing him back to the present. He was still so tired and desperately wanted to drift back to sleep, but the chief struggled into a sitting position and said, "This better be good. Who the hell is it?"

The door slowly opened, and Byran was relieved to see it was only his daughter, Sara, standing in the hallway with a confused, slightly angry look on her face.

"What the heck is going on?" Sara said, her voice louder than it needed to be.

"I'm trying to sleep, what does it look like is going on?"

"Not here, Dad. At the lake? Tim and I were headed out there for a swim this morning and the entrance gates are padlocked shut. There was a line up of other cars and everyone's pissed off. People were asking me what was going on, but what do I know? There's a sign on the gate saying the lake is closed and off limits pending a police investigation. Something about you calling a meeting at the town hall tonight, too. What's going on?"

"Oh that . . . yeah, well, I would have told you this morning but you were still asleep when I finally made it home. And to be honest, I was so tired all I wanted to do was crash and forget all about last night. Figured I could tell you once I got some sleep. What time is it, anyway?"

"Nearly noon."

"Shit . . . is that all? Well, I guess I'm up now. What do you wanna know? I closed the beach. I didn't have any choice."

"Why? What happened. Couldn't your dive buddies find Mr. Leeman's body? I told you to let me and Eddy and—"

"We don't know if they found the body," Bryan said, interrupting. "There's bigger issues than that now."

"Why? What happened?"

"Doc Turner and I went to the lake last night and no one was there. Tony and Ian's truck, boat, and some of their dive gear were all still there, but they were nowhere to be found. As far as I can tell, they went into the water to recover Bob's body, but neither one of them came back up again."

"Oh my god!" Sara said. "That's awful. Are you sure?"

"No. Not really, and that's just it. No one knows what happened. We don't know if it's actually Bob Leeman's body that your friends found at the bottom. We're not sure if Tony and Ian's bodies are now down there beside him. We're not sure of *anything*."

"So you're closing the beach until the bodies are all recovered?"

"Yes. Well . . . yes and no. There's more to it than that. Bob, Tony, and Ian may not be the only people missing. I shouldn't tell you this, but we've had at least three other people reported missing in the last few months. I know the standing joke around town is everyone keeps leaving Beckley to find work somewhere else, but that's not funny anymore. Especially when all three of these missing people were reportedly last seen headed for a swim at Red Spruce Lake."

"*Really?* You don't think they all drowned in the lake, do you? But Bob didn't drown. He was mauled or attacked by something, and . . . oh *Jesus*, you're not thinking—" Sara cut herself off, not liking the direction that question was taking her.

"We don't know anything, Sara. But we can't presume everything is okay out there. Not anymore. There's a chance they were attacked. Some of them, anyway. Maybe a few did leave town.

No one can say for sure. But as the Chief of Police in Beckley, I have to do something, so we've shut down the lake until we can figure out what the hell is happening to people out there. I've called a town hall meeting for 5:00 PM tonight to let everyone know. I haven't figured out what to tell everyone yet, or even what I *should* tell them, but I have to keep that area clear for a while. And that goes double for you, too, young lady. No sunbathing, no swimming, and for God's sake . . . no scuba diving. Got it?"

Six

100 Main Street,
Beckley Town Hall
July 19th, 4:45 p.m.

Tom Cassidy stood quietly on the front stairs of the town hall dressed in his police auxiliary officer uniform, while the citizens of Beckley entered the building. He'd been told to keep an eye out for '*troublemakers*', as Chief Palmer had put it. Being a twenty-year-old man born and raised here in Nova Scotia, Tom had no concrete idea of what constituted being a troublemaker, but he had his sights set on joining the police force for real as soon as he was able, and planned on doing everything he could to please the chief tonight. Thankfully, he was a tall, muscular kid, with broad shoulders and close-cropped brown hair that made him look older than he really was. There weren't too many people who wanted any part of getting Tom angry, so, young or not, he was as good a selection as possible for the routine task of keeping any hoodlums from disrupting the meeting tonight.

Not that there had been any problems, so far at least.

It was Tom's nose that sensed trouble, before his eyes did. He'd been following the progress of a pretty young lady named Chrissy MacIver as she walked past him, his eyes getting stuck on her backside for a tad longer than they probably should have. But then he smelled something rotten that brought him back to attention, and he turned to see an old, dishevelled man approaching the bottom of the stairs.

Oh man . . . here we go.

From the familiar colour of the skin on the man's weathered face, Tom could tell the man was from one of the local indigenous communities, but his filthy clothes and the stench coming off him told the volunteer officer that the man was probably homeless. He was wearing a baggy, black suit jacket over ripped blue jeans, and a wrinkled fedora perched on his head with a crow feather sticking out of the hat band. His long, grey hair was greasy and clumped with spruce needles, telling Tom the man slept out in the woods more often than not, using the ground as his bed. The old man stumbled on the first stair, reaching for the railing to steady himself. His awkward movements had Tom wondering if on top of being dirty and smelly, perhaps he might also be drunk.

What it all added up to had Tom thinking only one thing: *Troublemaker*. Tom took two steps down from the doorway and met the old man with his large right hand raised up high like a stop sign. "Hold it right there, mister. What do you think you're doing here?"

The older man was immediately intimidated and stepped back down onto the sidewalk. "I . . . I'm just here for the meeting. I was gonna . . . gonna talk to the chief about—"

"No, you're not," Tom said in a matter-of-fact voice, interrupting the native man. "I can't let you go in there smelling like that, friend. Sorry. If you go down to the truck stop, they might let you take a shower and you can come back."

"But I need to see Chief Palmer. He knows me. My name's Stanley Blackmore, but most people just call me Steamboat Stan. I've been living out in the woods by Red Spruce Lake, and I've seen what's been going on out there. I think he'll wanna talk to me. Please."

"Sorry, pops. It's not happening tonight. Maybe you can go see him at the station tomorrow . . . after you clean yourself up a little, you know?"

"No, that's not good enough. I need to tell him what I know tonight. Right now. I can be in and gone before the meeting even starts. Just let me by so I can . . . "

The older man tried to walk up the stairs and push his way past Tom to enter the building, but there was no way in hell the auxiliary officer was going to let that happen. He grabbed the man around by the neck and dragged him back down onto the sidewalk in a semi-headlock. The old man didn't put up much of a fight, half-falling, half-thrown down onto his knees at the bottom of the stairs. His feathered hat flew off and landed out on Main Street.

"Sorry, pops," Tom said, meaning it. "I don't wanna rough you up. Things are tough for you, I get it. But we don't want you here right now. Chief Palmer has a big problem on his hands and I'm here to make sure everything goes smoothly tonight. Do us both a favor and just go back to where you came from. You hear me?"

The man called Steamboat Stan lowered his head in shame and slowly climbed back to his feet. He retrieved his feathered hat and turned for one last look inside of the town hall where people would be talking and making guesses about things he already knew. But the young policeman was probably right. The people of Beckley didn't want him here. None of them gave a damn about him or the things he cared about, so why even bother? With a sigh of regret, Stan turned away and started walking down Main Street, shuffling in the direction of the woods, headed back home.

Seven

Red Spruce Lake,
Two Days Later
July 21st, 9:50 p.m.

Throughout the day, the small creatures of the forest had the run of the place, the squirrels, rabbits, and mice scurried around the trees and rocks with a sense of reckless abandon. While the sun shone brightly in the sky overhead, they truly seemed care-free and blessed, foraging here and there, gathering their nuts or their seeds, darting around wherever they wanted to go with nothing to fear or give them reason for caution. But the small animals' time in the spotlight was limited, the hours numbered, and as the sun continued its journey westward, the shadows in the forest began to lengthen and the temperatures started to drop. Soon the light would begin to fade, and instinctively the weaker animals would understand it was time to go into hiding again. Time to settle into their burrow or their nests, or wherever it was they hunkered down in when the darkness came.

Night was the time for predators.

When darkness descended on the forest, it was time for the Great Horned Owls, the Eastern Coyotes, and even the Black Bears to take the main stage. The bears tended to only hunt for several hours after dusk, and then find a place to bed down for the night, but that was only if they'd been lucky enough to fill their bellies first. Hunger was what drove the nocturnal hunters to prowl the night in search of prey. If they didn't feast, they would die.

But the carnivores of the forest weren't the only predator hungry tonight. Another beast, one stranger and far more dangerous than whatever else roamed this isolated area of Nova Scotia, could no longer stand to wait for sustenance to come to him the way he had before. The men in uniforms with badges and guns had closed down the lake two days ago, chained up the front gates, so that no one from town could go swimming or jump into the lake from the cliffs above. By doing so, they'd unknowingly, yet effectively, cut the creature off from the supply of readily available humans he'd gotten used to over the last several months after awakening from a long dormancy. He didn't need to feed every single day—or at least hadn't needed to in the past—but the more he fed, the greater his hunger seemed to be growing. And tonight, the beast was ravenous.

If the prey wasn't coming to the creature . . . then he had to go to the prey.

The man-monster surfaced in the shallows on the west end of the quarry, near where the makeshift beach had been created. He paused long enough to ensure the last of the sun's rays were gone, and that no one was watching him from the shadows. Seeing that all was quiet, the creature crept up the incline of the old mining road until he was fully out of the water for the first time in years. His legs, powerful as they were for swimming, were a little unsteady on dry land, and he took a few tentative steps to make sure he was balanced. His muscular body was naked, covered in a carapace of fish-like scales that hadn't been there the last time he'd walked upright like this. Five long slits of flesh opened and closed on both sides of his neck, and he had to concentrate in order to stop trying to draw oxygen in through his gills and breathe slowly and steadily by sucking in air through his enlarged mouth. The flesh on his throat stopped moving and he began to breathe a little easier.

The creature raised his taloned hands to his face to feel how much his features had changed, but other than his eyes feeling like they were bulging slightly out of their sockets, his transformation hadn't affected his head and face as much as other areas of his body. His mouth and teeth had grown monstrous in size, but the rest of his nose and facial features were still basically humanoid in appearance. His hair was long enough that he could see it was jet black in colour, but where his ears had once been on the sides of his head, there were nothing but two small circular openings covered by a thin membrane of flesh.

Satisfied with his new body, the man-monster dropped his hands to his sides and started walking away from the lake. He was forced to skirt around the entrance gates using a trail that took him through a pathway in the forest. Eventually the trail exited the trees and he found himself standing back on the road that would lead him into town. He raised his nose in the air and could smell the scent of humans getting closer with every step he took.

As the creature from the lake walked, his hunger grew.

Eight

113 Brelus Drive,
Travis And Margo Peterson's Residence
July 21st, 11:30 p.m.

Tonight was Travis and Margo Peterson's second wedding anniversary. They were young, fit, and attractive, both of them having the same dark hair and green eyes which made them look quite similar to one another. Both had recently turned twenty-six years old, and being a young couple constantly struggling for money, they'd both had to work today. That was fine; there was nothing much they could do about that, but it had meant celebrating their special day had to wait until after they both finally made it home. Travis had made dinner reservations for 7:00 PM at a decent Italian restaurant in town named *The Tuscany Market*, and together they'd spent two wonderful hours drinking wine and slowly savoring the pasta and fresh baked bread they were given. It was a real pleasure not having to rush or have anyone bothering them, and they could simply enjoy each other's company and talk about their future plans together.

Travis was a factory worker at *Miller's Fishery*, but he'd recently been promoted to manager and things were looking better now that he didn't have to stand on the canning line for eight hours every day. The money was a bit better, too, which obviously helped. Margo was a stylist who worked at *Express Yourself*, a local beauty salon that took care of the hair, nails, and make-up for women of all ages. Unfortunately, in Beckley, that mostly meant older women who came in every three weeks like clockwork for a dye job and a perm. Margo was happy enough, but someday she hoped to open her own salon, maybe in a bigger city where fashion and style trended more to the younger crowd.

After supper, the happy couple returned home and did what

most people did on their anniversaries—or at least the ones who still cared about each other—they grab-assed their way to their bedroom, laughing and giggling the way young lovers tended to do, and had really good sex several times over the next few hours. By 11:30 PM Travis and Margo were sweaty and tired and perfectly content with the way their anniversary had turned out. And had it not been for Margo playfully elbowing him in the ribs to get his attention, Travis would have drifted off into a blissful sleep within minutes.

But Margo wasn't quite ready to have their special day end so soon. She turned to Travis and said, "Hey . . . wake up, mister. Let's go for a swim."

Half asleep, Travis yawned and said, "Really? You sure? The pool gets pretty cold at night, you know?"

The house they were renting had a concrete swimming pool in the backyard, but there was no gas or electric heater to warm up the water and at night the temperature tended to drop several degrees along with the air temperature. During the hottest part of the day, the cool water was refreshing, but at night . . .

"Oh don't be such an old fuddy-duddy. You sound like my dad. It'll be fun and will wash some of that sweat off you."

"It's not me I'm worried about . . . it's you, but hey, I'm up for it if you are? Turn on the light so I can find my swim trunks."

"For god's sake, Travis. It's our anniversary and there's no one here to see us. We don't *need* swimsuits. You know what I'm saying?"

Margo ran for the sliding glass door in their bedroom, yanked it open, and ran giggling out into the backyard stark naked. "Last one in is a rotten egg!" she shouted as she ran.

Damn girl's crazy.

He laughed and chased after his wife all the same. He nearly caught up to her on the concrete pool deck, but Margo didn't hesitate, leaping into the shallow end of the pool. He splashed into the water beside her and took some measure of victory in the fact that the pool water was just as cold as he'd warned her it would be.

"*Yikes!* It's freezing in here . . . and you forgot to turn on the lights. I can barely see you." Travis, reached for his wife, intending to pull her to him for some body heat, but she squirmed out of his grasp. She used her hands to splash him away and started swimming for the deep end.

"Oh no. You'll have to work harder than that, *boyo*. Catch me if you can . . . "

Travis grinned. He gave Margo a head start, and then started swimming after her. It wasn't like she had anywhere to go to get away from him. The inground pool was big, but it wasn't *that* big. Within twenty strokes they'd both made it to the far end, reaching up to hold onto the diving board so they wouldn't sink and could still talk. With his one free hand, Travis curled it around Margo's slim waist and pulled her close to him. This time she didn't put up a fight, and by the light of the moon, their lips met, and they kissed. For both of them, it might have been the most romantic kiss of their entire marriage. Neither knew that it would also be their last.

Death was lying in wait for them at the bottom of the pool.

The creature was on his back in the deepest part of the pool, with the feet of the two naked humans less than four feet above him. They were so close he could almost reach out and touch them, but he restrained the urges in his primitive mind—for now—waiting for the right time to make his presence known. Although he was capable of surviving out of water, the beast was far more comfortable within its soothing, cool embrace. So when he'd stumbled across this backyard oasis it only made sense to submerge himself and regain his strength after his taxing walk into town. As luck would have it, two humans had decided to join him.

"See . . . the water's not so bad now, is it?" Margo said, her soft voice purring in her partner's ear. "If *someone* was to go get me another glass of wine, it might go a long way towards convincing me to show an appropriate level of appreciation. I'm just sayin' . . . "

"Be right back," Travis said, making a comedic show of swimming as fast as he could for the shallow end closest to the house. He hopped out of the water, running naked back into their bedroom through the sliding glass door, and headed for the kitchen to pour a few glasses of wine.

Margo laughed as he entered the house, the sight of his lily-white ass running in the moonlight putting a smile on her face and making her realize how truly lucky they were to have found each other. Anniversary or not, she loved Travis with all her heart no matter what day the calendar said it was, and she was thankful they were still together, their relationship stronger than ever.

Margo felt something brush against her right foot.

She disregarded it, her mind still wrapped up in happy thoughts, but then she felt it again. More of a nudge this time, more forceful and impossible to ignore. Instinctively, she kicked out with her leg, but there was nothing there. She tried peering down into the water, but it was too dark to see much farther down than her belly or waist. She tried to reassure herself.

It's nothing, right?

But then she felt the unmistakeable touch of a rough-skinned hand caressing her right knee, slowly moving up her naked thigh . . .

Margo tried to scream, but before she could open her mouth and let any sound out, someone grabbed hold of both her legs, ripped her free from the diving board she'd been loosely holding onto, and dragged her head underwater. She didn't even have time to suck in a breath. Seconds later, a beastly man's face appeared before her as she struggled to free herself. Not just a regular man, though. Even in the dim lighting conditions she could see it was the swollen, disfigured face of someone straight out of a horror movie, making it impossible for her to recognise or guess who it might be. Panic-stricken, she wondered, *What is this . . . thing? It can't be a man, can it?* Margo lashed out with her fists to strike her attacker, but her blows were ineffective, bouncing off the man-monster with little to no effect.

Spots began to appear in her eyes, blurring the edges of her vision. Her need for oxygen was so great, she couldn't resist the urge to suck in a gulp of water, even though she knew it would only make her situation worse. She gagged on the chlorine-treated water, retching underwater, sucking in more of the chemical-laced liquid in the process. *Help me, Travis . . .* was her last rational thought as her attacker moved in for the kill. Margo saw the creature open its monstrous mouth and she saw a quick glimpse of the rows of jagged teeth within, just as the beast lunged for her throat and started tearing at the tender flesh of her neck. She was drifting away to a warmer place now, but still she felt the monster start sucking on the wound it had created, sucking the blood from her neck, sucking the last air from her lungs, sucking the life from her frail body, sucking . . .

Travis jammed the cork back into the top of the bottle as best he could and put the rest of the white wine back into the refrigerator. With a filled glass in each hand, he hurried back to Margo, retracing his steps through the bedroom and the sliding glass door out into the backyard and across to the concrete deck surrounding the shallow end of the pool.

"Sorry it took me so long," Travis said, squinting into the darkness as his eyes tried to readjust from the bright lights inside of the house. There was no reply. "Margo . . . ? I sure as hell hope you're not mad. It took me forever to get the damn cork out of the bottle."

When there was still no response, Travis did what they should have done back when they'd first came outside—he walked over and flicked on the pool lights. There was only one light, a big circular one beneath the diving board in the deep end, but as soon as the underwater light flashed on, Travis began to scream. Margo was lying face up at the bottom of the deep end, his view of her body slightly blurred by the copious amount of blood that had been spilled in the water. Even from this end of the pool, though, Travis could see the hideous wound in his beautiful wife's throat, and instantly knew she was dead. He screamed a second time, dropping the wine glasses, where they shattered on the concrete walkway at his feet.

And then something grabbed hold of him around his ankles.

Travis looked down, his mind partially frozen from seeing Margo at the bottom of the pool, and he wasn't sure what he was even seeing at first. There was a wild, dark-haired man—or something that looked like a man—standing naked in the water below him, his muscles bulging and tense, his belly and chest covered in what looked like some kind of aquatic animal scales. The creature made a hissing sound unlike anything he had ever heard in his life, and when it opened its impossibly large mouth, Travis could still see bits and pieces of what he knew must have been Margo's ruined throat. The monster's teeth and tongue were painted crimson, still saturated in his poor wife's spilled blood.

The beast gripped harder on Travis' ankles, yanking his feet out from under him in an attempt to pull him into the pool. Travis fell hard, his head bouncing off the concrete decking violently enough to crack his skull in several places. Blood began running in the cracks on the decking under his head and he was instantly knocked unconscious. In the end it was a blessing, and Travis had no knowledge or awareness of being roughly dragged into the water. He'd eventually join his wife at the bottom of the deep end, but for that grisly reunion, he would have to wait.

The creature was still hungry . . .

Nine

Red Spruce Lake
Recognition And Respect
July 22nd, 5:59 a.m.

The sun was a sliver on the eastern horizon, the sky turning from black to grey to orange. Most of Red Spruce Lake was still shrouded in darkness, though, the trees and the walls of the cliff surrounding it dutifully, holding back the daylight like vigilant guards protecting the battlements of some medieval castle.

Steamboat Stan took a deep breath and stepped out from his hiding spot in the forest the moment he saw the creature returning from town and walking back onto the sandy beach. Blood and saliva trickled from the creatures gaping mouth, dripping down onto his pale belly with every plodding step. The beast was clearly headed back into the water to wherever it called home down in the darkness, but Stan felt he had to at least try and communicate with the monster whom he knew had once been a man.

Maybe I can still put a stop to this . . . before it's too late.

With more confidence than he felt, understanding that he could be heading towards a gruesome death, Stan walked as near as he dared to the transformed, naked man and tried to find the words to speak that might make some kind of difference and put an end to all this death and unnecessary madness. While he thought of what to say, Stan removed his wrinkled fedora with the crow feather from his head and slowly bowed towards the creature in a show of recognition and respect.

The creature was surprised to see the indigenous man, and even with all his strength, teeth, and claws, part of his brooding mind feared this skinny old man for some unfathomable reason. He raised his nose to the wind and smelled the foul stench of the man's clothes and body, snorting in disgust and turning away. He had some scattered memories, but those memories were buried deep within him. Not completely forgotten but hidden far enough away that the monster couldn't remember who this stranger was. The beast moved farther away from the dishevelled man, only wishing to return to the lake and rest from his successful hunting trip. He should have been back here hours ago, but he'd been so satiated from killing the husband and wife in town that the creature had fallen asleep at the bottom of his victims' pool. He'd only recently woken up and was struggling to get back home to the comforting, fresh water of the lake.

Stan spoke in an old dialect of his native Her'maqon tongue, slowly and clearly, to the creature who was refusing to even look in his direction.

"Pune a Ge' nnu'-gluli," he said. *Stop and talk with me.*

The water monster stopped moving, confused as to why the man was speaking to him. Stranger still, he understood the ancient words being said. He turned his face towards his dirty visitor and paused to hear more.

Stan continued on, speaking in the ancient language of his forefathers.

"This has to stop. You know it as well as I do. I understand why you felt you had to do what you did, but it was never meant to be like this. I can help if you'll let me. But not here. This land . . . this forest . . . this lake is cursed. Come with me to the sacred land of our fathers and your soul can still be redeemed. It's not too late. Please . . . "

The creature stood as still as a rock for nearly half a minute, listening, thinking, wondering, but a ray of sunlight crested over the trees to the east and covered his mutated body in its amber glow. Almost instantly, steam started to rise from the beast's scaly belly and fleshy arms, and his exposed skin started to bubble and turn black. The monster screamed in rage and pain, unsure what was happening. Urged by instincts he didn't even know he had, the beast ran for the cool water of the lake, all thoughts of the stranger's calming words now gone, his single focus now only to submerge himself in the life-sustaining water and swimming into the blessed darkness of the deepest area of the lake.

"No . . . *wait*!" Stan said, feeling that he'd actually been getting through to the creature. But it was too late. The beast dove into the shallow waters off the beach, his blackened skin making an audible *'Hisssss'* when he plunged below the surface.

The creature splashed his way into deeper water, and then as suddenly as he'd appeared on the road from town, he was gone. There were ripples in the water that moved outward in concentric circles all the way until they reached shore, but soon those were gone, too, and the surface of Red Spruce Lake was as still as glass.

Stan stood where he was for nearly an hour, troubled by what he'd just seen, unsure what to do next. The sun continued its eternal journey, rising higher and higher, moving above the canopy of the Red Spruce Forest into a beautiful robin's egg blue coloured sky.

Ten

77 Dawson Crescent, Apt. 3
Sara Palmer's Apartment
July 23rd, 2:50 a.m.

Someone pounding on the front door of her apartment woke Sara out of a restless sleep. She rolled over, still tired, not at all happy to have been woken up. She and Tim had argued last night, and she'd gone to bed early, feeling mentally and physically exhausted from all the negative crap that had been going on lately. Tim wanted to move their relationship to the next level, asking her to let him move in with her, but Sara—as much as she truly cared for him—wasn't quite ready to do that. After living under her father's fairly strict roof her entire life, she loved having a place all to herself and cherished the privacy and peace that her apartment afforded her. Tim could visit anytime he wanted to and stay over several nights a week like he was already doing, but as far as him living here permanently—24/7—Sara felt she needed to say no to that. At least for now.

The banging on the front door continued, forcing Sara to jump out of bed to go see what was going on. Dressed only in a white T-shirt and panties, she grabbed her furry pink robe off of the hook on her bedroom door and tossed it on. It had to be Tim coming back for round two of their fight, and Sara had a bad feeling that it wasn't going to end well. She hoped she was wrong, but who the hell else would be knocking on her door like a lunatic in the middle of the night?

It was Tim, of course, but before Sara could even start to tell him his smartest move would be to go home and leave her alone for a few days, she was shocked to see Xavier walk into her apartment right behind him. Even stranger, big Eddy pushed through the doorway into her kitchen, too, holding onto a four foot long, black suitcase Sara had never seen before.

"What on earth are you guys doing here?" Sara asked, not particularly happy to see her three closest friends. "Do you have any idea what time it is?"

"Sorry, Sara," Tim said, "We wouldn't be here . . . *I* wouldn't be here bugging you, but this is really important, and we didn't want to wait until morning. Have you heard from your father in the last few hours?"

"No, why would I? What's going on?"

Tim shrugged, tears welling in his eyes. "Tell her, X. I can't do it."

Now, Sara's alarm bells were really ringing. She couldn't remember ever seeing her boyfriend cry before. Something major must have happened.

"It's Travis and Margo," Xavier said. "They're gone. *Dead.* Killed by that motherfucker in Red Spruce Lake."

"What? Travis and Margo are dead? When did this happen?"

"I don't know. Maybe last night, maybe the day before. All I know is their bodies were found about midnight by Jack Taylor. Travis was supposed to be at a poker game last night at Jack's house, but he didn't show. I guess no one has seen either of them since their wedding anniversary. Anyway, Jack's party broke up around 11:45, and he'd been trying to call Travis for hours. At that time of night, he figured someone should be home, but there was no answer. So Jack went over to see if everything was okay. It wasn't. Jack found Travis and Margo floating face up in their swimming pool. Both were dead. Both of them had their throats torn out, the same way Bob Leeman was left at the lake."

"Oh my god . . . " Sara said, tears springing to her eyes as well. Travis and Margo were close friends to all of them. They'd all grown up together in Beckley, and Travis and Margo had been the first of their age group to get married. Sara had even been one of Margo's bridesmaids at their wedding. "Jack called you to tell you all this?"

Xavier nodded. "Just about an hour ago. I called Eddy, then we grabbed Tim and here we are. We thought you needed to know."

"I take it my dad already knows? Jack called the police?"

"Yeah, he's already over at their house," Tim said. "Doc Turner is there, too. They'll probably be tied up for a while, but we've already talked about this and made up our minds. We're not waiting for him."

"Wait for him for *what*?" Sara asked.

"We're taking this freakshow out of the picture," Eddy said, his voice deep and angry. "We're not waiting for *anyone's* help. Not anymore. Not after this."

"Who are you talking about, exactly. We don't know who's doing any of this."

"The hell we don't. Maybe not his name, but we all know where to find him. Everything bad that has happened in this town lately is connected to Red Spruce Lake, and we're going out there to find that rotten bastard and make him pay for what he's done. Whether he's a man or a monster . . . I don't care. We're taking him out."

"And you want *my* blessing? *Jesus*. Do you even have a plan?" Sara asked, looking down at the black suitcase Eddy was still gripping in his tightly clenched fist. "What's that thing?"

"It's a little something I like to call . . . *payback*." Eddy said, setting the case down on the kitchen table and opening the two latches on the side.

Inside the foam-lined case was a three-foot-long silver aluminum cylinder with what looked like a black plastic handgun grip on the one end. There were also three, thin metal arrows that looked as if they would fit into a small opening at the other end of the weapon. It didn't take Sara long to realize what she was looking at.

"You have a spear fishing gun?"

"Nope," Eddie said with a grin. "I've got *two* of them. The other one's still in the trunk of the car. Both use compressed air cylinders to fire the bolts, which means they're way more powerful than the cheap ones that use a rubber sling."

"*Holy crap*! And you're going to go down to the bottom of the lake searching for something you don't even know is there."

"Oh . . . he's there. The police searched the woods. There's no place else he can hide."

"Bullshit. You're letting your imagination get the best of you. You really think there's a monster there that can not only breath underwater, but can walk out onto dry land any time it wants? Did you ever consider it could just be a normal man. You said yourself Bob Leeman might have been attacked up on the cliff and then jumped or fell into the water. A killer could have thrown him off the cliff just as easily."

"Maybe. Yesterday I could have still believed that, but not

anymore. X and I saw the damage that . . . *thing* did to Bob's throat. You didn't. And now Jack is telling us that Travis and Margo's heads were nearly bitten clean off. *Bitten,* Sarah. Normal men . . . even psychos, don't bite people's heads off. I told you before, I don't know what *he* or *it* is, but they deserve to die."

"Are these legal?" Sara said, tentatively running her hand along the shaft of the dangerous looking spear gun.

"Not for freshwater fishing . . . no, but we're not going fishing. The cheap guns with the rubber slings that only shoot fifteen feet are allowed in freshwater lakes, but these beauties will kill at double that range."

"Which means you might get arrested?"

"Which *means* we don't have to get as close to the monster with big teeth and claws."

"Which is also why we're not waiting until morning," Xavier said, closing the speargun case and ending the argument. "We're going now because we might be able to catch this fucker sleeping. We wait until morning, and we lose the element of surprise."

"You have lights with you?" Sarah asked.

"Of course," Tim said, stepping in to grab his girlfriend's hand. "Four sets of fully charged headlamps ready to go. The tanks are all filled and ready to roll too."

"*Four sets* . . . ?" Sara said, finally understanding the real reason they were here.

"One for each of us. This madness has to end. Somebody has to stop this creature from murdering any more innocent people, and like it or not, we're the best chance this town has to stop it. And you're our best diver and by far the fastest swimmer. Travis and Margo were your friends, too, Sara. We're not here asking for your *permission* . . . we're asking for your help."

Eleven

Red Spruce Lake
Stranger On The Beach
July 23rd, 3:45 a.m.

The ride from town was a quiet one.

Tim rode with Sara in her Honda Civic, and Xavier and Eddy followed close behind them in Eddy's beat up Chrysler 200. Normally they would have piled into Xavier's Chevy Silverado Crew Cab, which seated all of them comfortably up front, and had loads of room for their gear in the back. For such a small man, Xavier drove the biggest pick-up truck in Beckley, but it was in the shop getting new brakes, so they'd had to split up into two vehicles tonight.

They pulled their cars as close to the locked gates at the entrance to the lake as they could. Xavier climbed out of Eddy's car and walked past Tim and Sara without stopping to speak with them. He was carrying a bolt cutter and went straight to the padlock and chain holding the entrance gates together. With one quick squeeze, the bolt cutter easily broke the hasp on the lock. Xavier unwrapped the chain, tossed it and the broken lock into the ditch beside the road, and swung open both sides of the fence. He motioned Sara to drive through the gate, which she did, and watched in her rearview mirror as Eddy did the same, stopping only to let Xavier climb back into the car.

Even after they'd parked the vehicles and started gathering their things, no one seemed eager to break the silence with any of their usual witty conversations and friendly chit chat. Each of them was lost in their own private thoughts and fears, perhaps wondering if they were getting themselves into something way over their heads that they knew they shouldn't, but none of them knowing how to back out of this insanity before it was too late.

"Let's get all this crap to the beach," Eddy finally said.

It had taken them longer to get here than planned, having decided to stop uptown at the dive shop and '*borrow*' four large dive knives from the back room of the store. Steve Gaither, the owner of the dive shop was a good friend, and had given Sara a key to the back door of the shop over a year ago, in case she ever needed to fill her talks or pick up any supplies when Steve wasn't around. She always kept track of anything she or her friends took so they could pay for it later on, and tonight had been no different. They all had dive knives already, of course. It was a standard item in any serious scuba diver's kit, but most knives were small and used only to cut fishing line or whatever other small task was required. These knives had ten-inch blades on them and were used by commercial divers, designed for heavy duty underwater work.

Like monster hunting . . . Sara sarcastically thought, taking the blade out of its plastic wrapper and loading it into her bag along with her other dive gear.

It was a warm, clear night and the light of the moon illuminated the entire park. As the group of divers headed for the beach, all their eyes were riveted on the surface of the lake, searching for any telltale ripples or splashes that might reveal their adversary was aware of their arrival and already watching them. The water was calm, though.

Dead calm.

Not exactly a comforting phrase under the circumstances.

Each of the divers dropped their gear bags and tanks near each other on the sandy beach, and rather than talking, immediately started to get ready. Sara was in her wetsuit and strapping her new knife to the outside of her left thigh when she noticed they were no longer alone. A dark shadow was walking towards them from out of the forest.

"Hey g . . . guys," she said, fear causing her voice to crack. "Who the hell is that?"

All eyes turned in the direction she was pointing, and more than one hand moved towards their knives until the visitor exited out of the shadows and they could all see who it was. It was just an old homeless man, an indigenous drifter with a ragged, black suit jacket and a crow feather stuck in his dirty hat.

"Stop right there, mister," Eddy shouted, not knowing who this person was and not about to let a dishevelled stranger get any closer to them. "Whoever the fuck you are . . . turn around and get lost. We don't have any food or money to give you so go beg somewhere else."

"I'm not here to beg," the indigenous man said in a soft voice.

"We don't care what you want . . . fuck off."

"Relax, Eddy," Sara said. He's harmless. I've seen him talking with my dad over the years." And then to the visitor, she said, "They call you Steamboat, don't they?"

"Yes, ma'am. Steamboat Stan. Your father has been good to me . . . for the most part, anyway. I'm not here to cause any trouble. I'm here to help."

"With what?" Tim asked.

"With the reason you're all here . . . the *Sabawaelnu*."

"The Saba . . . *what*?" Eddy asked.

"Sabawaelnu," Xavier said. "It an old native word. It means water demon or water devil. Are you Mi'kmaq, friend?"

"No. I grew up on proud Her'maqon land, but hated being corralled onto a reservation, so I live free among the trees and the animal spirts now."

Xavier nodded, understanding more than his friends the stranger's resentment for being forced to live on a reservation. He'd grown up with similar angry thoughts. "The Her'maqon people and the Mi'kmaq may have differing opinions, but we share many words in our language and culture. I respect your decision to live free, but I'm not sure how you can help us with the creature in the lake? How do you even know about any of this?"

"I've been watching this unfold right from the start . . . back from when the monster, as I'm sure you all call him, was a hard working, decent man."

"You know who he is?" Sara asked.

"I do. His name is . . . *was* . . . Jonathan Blackmore. He's my brother."

"Your *brother*? For real?" Tim asked, stunned by what he was hearing.

"What happened to him?" Sara asked, ignoring her boyfriend's rhetorical jab. Obviously, the old native man was serious and had no reason to lie.

Stan took a moment to compose himself, removing his fedora and sitting cross-legged in the sand. He waited for the others to sit, too, but it was only the girl who chose to kneel beside him and urged him to speak his mind.

"Only one of you, the skinny one with skin like mine, will understand the native traditions and legends, but all of you will remember the disaster at the gypsum mine back in 2020. The power went out, the pumps stopped working, the drillers set off explosives that opened a massive underground water stream, and the mine and everyone trapped in it was washed away in minutes. Some people made it out . . . and a lot of people didn't.

"There was a large group of Her'maqon men and women working in the lowest part of Shaft 3 that night, including my brother. I was there, too, but I was working one level up when the lights went out and water started pouring in. I knew it was bad . . . everyone did, and people started screaming and crying for help. There was no help coming, though, and people soon realized they were on their own if they wanted to get out of the mine alive. I was just as scared as the rest of the workers, but I wanted to save Jonathan and the others from my village. Try to, at least.

"So I turned on my headlamp and went down the ladder, not up, but when I reached the lower level the water was already waist deep and rising. I was shouting for my brother, and I didn't understand why none of them were coming to the ladder. I walked around the bend in the tunnel and that was when I saw that the ceiling had collapsed. I could see a group of workers through a small opening in the fallen rocks, begging me to help them, but what could I possibly do? Through the gap I saw Jonathan wave to me and smile. And then he started to pray. I knew right then that he'd accepted his fate, and I thought he was praying to *Kisulkwe*, the great creator of our world, preparing himself for his journey into the afterlife. But I was wrong.

"Even among the screams for help, and the wails of despair, I clearly heard my brother shouting to the water demon, *Sabawaelnu*, and just before I ran for the ladder to save myself, I saw a huge, black, shadow beast rise from the water below Jonathan and enclose around his body like a ghostly cocoon or protective shield, saving him from the incoming flood. I knew in my heart what a terrible thing he had just done. I also knew this would only be the beginning . . . not the end. That was the last time I ever saw my brother alive and still a human being, but as we now know, it wouldn't be the last time that I, or other less fortunate people, would see him."

"I thought they recovered all the bodies who drowned that

night?" Eddy said, his voice less angry than before, but still sceptical of what he was hearing.

"Not all of them, no. They made an honest effort to recover everyone, but there were nine workers, mostly Her'maqon men and women, who were never found at the very bottom of Shaft 3. My brother was one of them, but he didn't drown with the rest of his people behind that collapsed ceiling. He survived . . . and *changed.*"

"Changed into what?" Tim asked.

"I'm getting to that," Stan said, taking a deep breath to settle his already frayed nerves. It wasn't easy for him to tell this story. "Like I said, I knew what my brother had done, and that there would be no denying the demon he'd foolishly summoned that night. The *Sabawaelnu* had been banished from the Mi'kmaq and Her'maqon lands a millennium ago, exiled from our hallowed ground and forced into the wilds where it could cause no more harm. Or so our elders thought. But as your friend can tell you, the Mi'kmaq and Her'maqon nations haven't always lived in peace. A great battle was fought on the land the gypsum mine and now this flooded lake stand on. It was a savage war, a pointless, bloody confrontation fought only for greed and senseless pride on both sides. The war nearly decimated my people, and the Mi'kmaq suffered incredible losses as well. By the time calmer heads prevailed, neither side wanted anything to do with this cursed area. Too much blood had been spilled . . . too much senseless death.

"But it was the perfect place for the *Sabawaelnu,* so I moved into the woods and kept watch, knowing someday my brother would eventually come back. His change took a lot longer than I thought—years longer, in fact—but signs of his evil presence began to show about six or seven months ago. Animals were the first to go missing, snatched while trying to drink from the lake. One moment a deer or a coyote would be there . . . the next they were gone. And then the humans started to disappear. People swimming, people fishing, people jumping into the lake from the cliffs. They'd dive under and just never come back up. I knew that Jonathan . . . or whatever he had become, had finally returned."

"If you knew who was killing all the people, why didn't you tell someone before now?" Tim said. "You should have gone to the police."

"I tried to. I was at Chief Palmer's town hall meeting and I was planning to tell him everything I just told you, but they wouldn't let me. Some young officer at the door didn't like the way I looked and smelled, and he threw me down in the street and made me go away."

"I want to know something," Eddie said, still trying to understand what was going on. "Let's just give you the benefit of the doubt for a moment and say that this ancient demon, whatever it's called, has taken over your brother's body and is killing people in Beckley . . . why is it only eating their throats? A creature that size needs sustenance to survive. A lot of food . . . so why wouldn't it eat more of the victim's bodies? There's not much meat in a boney neck."

"The answer to that is simple," Stan said. "The *Sabawaelnu* doesn't survive on meat. It's not *eating* anything. Tearing out their throats is just a means to an end."

"You mean it's drinking their blood?" Tim asked. "Like some kind of vampire?"

"Kind of like that, yeah. The Her'maqon people believe when a man or an animal dies, they cross over to the spirit world and become one with nature again. On a man's dying breath they release their spirit . . . their souls, exhaling them out of their bodies so they can join their ancestors in the realm of the great spirits. So when you say my brother is eating their throats, he's actually stealing their souls.

"The beast drags the victim down underwater to drown them, but as they're dying, he bites into their throat . . . much like your vampire legends, but rather than biting into their carotid artery to suck out their blood, the *Sabawaelnu* bites into the victim's windpipe to suck out and inhale their dying breath. The demon survives by feasting on their souls."

There was silence for a moment, everyone absorbing what they'd just heard.

"If all this is true," Xavier said, "and from the stories my grandfather told me as a kid, I actually believe you . . . sort of, this gives us twice the reason we had before to kill the monster. This isn't just a mindless animal killing at random to survive. This is a demon stealing not only the lives of our friends and neighbours, but by eating their souls it's robbing them of any chance of an afterlife too. We have to stop it before it destroys anyone else."

"I agree. The demon must be destroyed. But there still may be a way for us to save all of the victim's souls. Even my brother's, potentially, if you're willing to consider it."

"How?" Sara asked.

"Remember that this is cursed ground beneath our feet. If the creature dies here, my brother's soul, along with all the others, will be forfeited along with it. But if you can lure the beast to the surface and we can find a way to take him to hallowed ground, it's not too late to save them. The *Sabawaelnu* cannot survive on Her'maqon land. The demon's spirit was banished from there long ago, and the power of that decree is still bound by powerful magic to this very day. If we push, carry, drive, or drag the beast onto my people's land, the demon's spirit will be cast out of Jonathan's body into the wilds again. If that happens on hallowed ground, the souls of its victims will all be set free."

"That's not true," Xavier said, shaking his head. "I was taught that native magic only protects native people. It might save your brother's soul, but the rest are already lost."

"You may be right, young man, but you also might be wrong. I won't lie and tell you I know for sure. I was taught that Her'maqon magic protects all of us."

"Either way, your brother won't survive the demon being cast out," Xavier said. "He's not walking away from this alive."

"I know he won't. But he can die a free man . . . his spirit able to resume its journey, to join his ancestors the way it should have on that terrible night inside the old mine. I want the killings to stop as badly as all of you do. I'm just trying to find a way to release all the victims and save my brother's soul, too."

"It's a great story, old man," Eddy said. "But I don't see how we can help you. We'll be lucky to kill this monster without it tearing out our throats, too. How the hell are we supposed to get it out of the lake and move it what . . . ten kilometers to the Her'maqon reservation?"

"I have something that may help," Stan said, reaching into his wrinkled, jacket pocket and bringing out a glass amulet on a gold chain. The charm was in the shape of a tree, with a trunk and a full canopy of leaves above it.

"What is it?" Sara asked, moving closer to get a better look.

"The tree of life. It's not magic or anything, it's just a necklace that's been in my family for generations. If there's any part of Jonathan left inside the beast . . . and I believe there is, he'll recognise this and come after it. He's wanted it his whole life. It's his by birthright, but when he disappeared, it was passed down to me, instead. Use it to lure him into the shallows, and maybe even out of the water onto the beach."

"And then what?" Tim asked. "I agree with Eddy. We're a hell of a long way away from your sacred land. We're wasting time here."

"There might be a way," Sara said, her mind spinning. "Stan, you need to take my car to town and get my dad and Doc Turner. The keys are in it. Tell them what you told us and tell Doc to bring something strong enough to knock your brother on his ass for a while. The strongest drug he has. Meet us back here and we'll see what we can do. No promises. We're going to defend ourselves if we have to, but if we can figure something out, be ready with the needle when we get back. Maybe some ropes or chains, too. We knock out the demon, put him in the back of my dad's police Bronco, and then drive as fast as we can onto Her'maqon land."

"That'll never work, Sara, and you damn well know it," Eddy said. "It's a fantasy. We came here to kill the son of a bitch who murdered our friends, and I'm not risking my life . . . *any* of our lives, for some fucked up story about native magic and underwater vampires. It's all bullshit and even if it's not, it's not my problem. I just want the bastard dead."

"I hear you, son," Stan said, nodding his head in agreement. "My brother deserves no sympathy. I won't blame any of you for defending yourselves. I'm only saying that if somehow there's a chance to get what he's become back here on dry land, please consider it. Maybe it doesn't work, but at least I'll know we tried. I can live with that. You better get going, though. You have to be back here before sunrise."

"Why?" Xavier asked.

"Because *Nakuset*, the sun god, was placed in the sky by the creator to destroy darkness and evil. The sun will burn the demon to death before we can get him into the chief's car. I've seen proof of it. I watched my brother return from town early yesterday morning and when the sun's rays crested the trees and touched his exposed skin, he began to blister and burn."

"Holy shit," Eddy said. "You're saying this demon really is a fucking vampire. They can't walk in the sun either. This gets creepier by the minute, man."

"It makes sense, though," Xavier said. "All myths and legends usually spring from the same places, and there's some level of truth hidden in all of them, regardless of which culture they came from. The legends of *Sabawaelnu* and vampires probably come from the same source material, and both are probably true. The creature in the lake is proof of that."

"So let's go find us an underwater vampire," Eddy said. "Or maybe we should call it an *aqua*pire. That has a good ring to it, right?"

No one seemed sure what to say for a moment.

"I'm kidding. I don't care what the fuck you call this nightmare, I just want it gone. Vampire, Native Demon, or just some lunatic with a hidden air supply, a speargun stake through their heart ought to slow them down, whoever or *whatever* they are, don't you think? We'll try it your way first, Sara, but the second things go south and one of us is in trouble, I'm killing the motherfucker. Deal?"

Sara looked over at Stan, and he nodded. "Deal."

"Good. Let's get moving, then."

The group gathered their tanks and weapons, and headed for the water. Sara was the last to follow, and she turned to face Stan one last time. "Check Travis Peterson's house on Brelus Drive first. That's where Doc Turner and my dad probably are. If somehow we get lucky, you better be ready for us."

"We will be," Stan said, handing Sara the glass amulet.

She hung the charm around her neck and walked away to join her friends. Speaking over her shoulder without looking back, Sara said, "If you know any special prayers you can say to those ancient gods of yours, Stan . . . this would be a pretty good time to start saying them. We're going to need all the help we can get."

Twelve

Red Spruce Lake
Beneath Still Waters
July 23rd, 4:25 a.m.

When Sara entered the lake, the water felt colder than usual. She'd been on night dives before, but the water felt chillier than she could ever remember for this time of year. Or perhaps it was only her imagination acting up, her body's last-ditch effort to convince her this was a really bad idea and she should turn around right now and go back home. A part of her wanted to do exactly that, but Tim had spoken the truth back at her apartment when he'd said the four of them were Beckley's best chance at stopping the demon and ending the gruesome deaths. He'd been right, so no matter how afraid or unsure she was that they were going to accomplish anything other than getting themselves killed, Sara was determined to see this through. Helping Stan reclaim his brother's soul was a whole different matter entirely, and deep down she knew the chances of pulling that off were slim to none, but she'd cross that bridge when—*if*—they ever got there. First, they had to stay alive.

Together they waded out into deeper water, then swam on the surface out towards the middle of the lake. Conserving their air supply might end up being crucial to their success, and there was no need to start using up their limited supply until they were hovering over the drop off. It had been determined that Eddy and Tim would carry the spearguns. While it was true that Tim was the least experienced diver of the foursome, he was by far the most experienced hunter in the group, and his years practicing with both firearms and bow and arrows made him the best choice to carry one of the spearguns. Eddy was keeping the other one, simply because the weapons belonged to him, and he was the only other diver who knew how to shoot them.

When the group reached the approximate starting spot, Xavier held up his hand and quietly spoke. "We should be right over the lip, guys. Try to stick together if possible, but if we have to split up, I'll go with Eddy, and Sara can stay near Tim."

"Yeah . . . and I know we just said we'd try help out the homeless guy," Eddy said, "but I'm killing this thing if we find it. No offence, but Stan's living in fantasyland, and he's not one of us. Even if his story's true, we're not dying to save whatever's left of his brother. He's the bad guy here . . . not us. We hit this fucker hard and fast and get out. Got it?"

Everyone nodded.

"Good. We'll go first, X. See you two at the bottom."

Eddy and Xavier released air from their buoyancy compensator and sank out of view. Seconds later, Sara and Tim saw two lights below their feet and knew their friends had switched on their headlamps as they were descending.

"You ready?" Tim asked.

"As ready as I ever will be, I guess. Listen . . . I'm sorry we had that stupid fight earlier tonight. You know I care about you, right?"

"I know, Sara. Don't worry about that. Now's not the time, you know?"

"I know. Okay. I just needed to say it. Down to business, then. You've never been as deep as we're going so keep your breathing as shallow and calm as you can. The air in your tank compresses as the pressure in the water increases. If a full tank lasts over an hour in shallow water, you'll only get thirty-five or forty minutes at the depth we're going. Maybe less. Keep an eye on your gauge and let me know if your air's running low."

"I'll be fine. We'll *both* be fine. Come on . . . we gotta go. I don't want to leave Eddie and X down there on their own."

There was nothing left to say, so Sara said nothing at all. They stared into each other's eyes as they hit the button on their buoyancy compensators, and slowly sank into darkness.

Sara waited to switch on her headlamp until she was sure Tim had turned his on first. She knew she needed to stop acting like his girlfriend—or even his dive instructor—but old habits died hard, and she couldn't seem to shake her feelings of fear and worry for him. Deep diving was a dangerous challenge all on its own, never mind strapping a spear gun to his wrist and weighing his conscience down knowing he was supposed to help protect the group from a monster waiting somewhere in the murky water below. Sara was worried about her own safety, too, of course, and the safety of Eddy and Xavier as well. How could anyone *not* be afraid? She had put on a show of courage on the beach, but she was well aware underestimating the grave danger they were all in would be naïve and incredibly foolish.

Visibility wasn't too bad—at least twenty-five feet—and seemed to be getting better as they sank deeper. Sara could see the lip of the shallow western plateau off to Tim's right—her left—but they didn't stop their descent the way they had last time. She adjusted her mouthpiece, her ears equalizing as they crossed into the second atmosphere of pressure and continued down. Tim had a bit more trouble equalizing, but he finally must have got it because he quickly flashed her the '*okay*' sign and turned his eyes back to the dark water below their feet.

He's afraid . . .

She didn't blame him for a second.

Out of the gloom, two lights appeared below them as they continued to drop. They were approaching their friends at the bottom of the old quarry. She tapped Tim on the arm to get his attention and showed him that she was about to pump some air into her BC to slow her rate of descent. Tim understood, mirroring her moves, and together they sank to a controlled landing on the rocky bed of the lake. Eddy and Xavier were nodding their heads to greet them and immediately set off swimming farther west into the heart of the deepest section of the lake. Sara motioned Tim to go next, so that she could take up her usual position behind him, but he shook his head *no*, pointing at the spear gun to let her know he wanted to take up the rear this time. It made sense, and Sara swam off on the heels of Xavier.

In less than a minute, their headlamps started to reveal something huge straight in front of them, and out of the darkness, a full size, enormous rock truck was revealed, complete with eight-foot tall, solid rubber tires. The machine had once been used to haul massive loads of crushed gypsum up and out of the quarry using the sloped mining roads, but it, too, had become a victim of the mine disaster and had been left down here parked for eternity in the deepest part of the lake. Sarah, Eddy, and Xavier had visited the sunken relic many times in the past, but Tim had never seen the abandoned Rock Truck before, and by the wide-eyed look on his face through his dive mask, Sara could tell he was impressed. Unfortunately, this wasn't a sightseeing dive, so Eddy quickly swam the group around the front wheels and headed towards the eastern end of the quarry, where a sheer rock face rose straight from here all the way to the surface. Sarah knew exactly where Eddy was going, and it filled her heart with dread, knowing that whatever was going to happen, it was probably going to happen soon.

Eddy paused, hovering about six feet above the bottom, and pointed at what appeared to be two black holes in the face of the rock wall. They were old tunnels that sloped even farther into the earth, connecting the surface pit they were in now with Shaft 3, where the disaster had happened. It was these same tunnels that many of the trapped miners had used to climb to safety on that awful night in 2020, and it was inside one of them that Eddy felt they had the best chance of finding the creature's underwater lair.

Eddy aimed two fingers at himself and Xavier, and pointed to the tunnel on the right, and then shot his fingers at Sara and Tim and pointed at the tunnel on the left.

He wants to split up!

That wasn't what they'd agreed on.

No way, she indicated by violently shaking her hear side to side. She brought her hands together, hoping he'd understand she wanted them all to stay together. There was obvious safety in numbers, and going their separate ways might be a really bad idea.

Eddy shook his head, too, and tapped first his regulator in his mouth, and then his dive watch with his finger. Sarah immediately understood he meant they didn't have time to search both tunnels together. Air tanks empty fast at increased pressure depths, and as much as she hated to admit it, her large friend was probably right. If they chose the wrong tunnel to search, and found nothing, they might run out of air before they would have time to search the second cave. At least if they separated, one of the teams should be the lucky—or unlucky—ones who find the monster and try to flush it out.

Sara checked her air pressure gauge, saw it was already down lower than she'd hoped, and knew there was no time left to argue. She nodded her head, and waved Eddy and Xavier to get moving. She and Tim split off to the left. Each group had a speargun, three metal bolts to load the gun with, and their brand-new dive knives strapped to each of their legs. On the beach it had seemed like they had enough weapons to face the man-monster together as a foursome, but now that their numbers had been cut in half, and the encounter was imminent, it felt like they were woefully unprepared. Sara watched as Eddy and Xavier disappeared into their tunnel, and then before she had a chance to change her mind, she pointed at Tim to get moving.

Tim swam into the tunnel on the left, speargun loaded and leading the way . . .

The tunnel was in the shape of a half circle, a flat rock floor with an arched roof. From the floor of the lake, the tunnel angled down and away from them into an inky blackness their headlamps had a hard time penetrating. The opening was approximately twelve feet wide and less than that high, leaving enough room for Sara and Tim to swim side by side. Sara hung back a little, just in case Tim had to quickly swing his speargun to the left or right to fire off a shot. She had her dive knife out and ready, in case they were attacked from behind. The visibility was instantly worse as soon as they crossed the threshold into the old mining tunnel, and the murky water combined with the walls of the chamber being so close, heightened claustrophobic fears she hadn't been aware she had until that moment. Every fibre in her being wanted to grab Tim by the arm and yank him out of this awful place, but they kept on going, anyway.

A hundred feet into the tunnel and the weight of the rocks around them metaphorically weighed heavily on Sara's mind. She wasn't sure she was going to be able to do this for much longer, and the more her anxiety grew, the faster she was breathing, using up more of the precious supply of air in her tank. Tim, for his part, seemed to be doing okay, concentrating on the ten feet of tunnel they could see ahead of them.

And then out of nowhere there was a man standing in front of them.

Tim, being a trained hunter, fired his speargun without hesitation and the razor-sharp metal bolt flew deeper into the tunnel with an audible '*HISS*', finding its target dead centre in the man's exposed chest. Hope ignited a fire within Sara's chest, but then their progress illuminated the man's entire body, and they could see the hideous wound that had already been on the man's ruined neck.

He's already dead. One of the creature's recent victims.

She knew the man hadn't been in the water for too long. He was definitely showing signs of decomposition, especially his abdomen which was starting to bloat, but it wasn't as bad as Sara expected it to be if the dead man corpse had been here in this tunnel for weeks. As bodies decompose, their organs start to produce gas which make the dead body start to swell, eventually floating their remains to the surface. In cold water like this, that process took a lot longer, but still, this man couldn't have been down here more than a week or so. Sara saw that the dead man was only wearing one running shoe and figured this had to be Bob Leeman. How and why his body had been moved all the way into this deep tunnel was anyone's guess, but she figured the monster must have brought him here to perhaps hide him. Whatever the reason, more importantly it meant the creature might be nearby, lying in wait.

Tim reloaded the speargun with his second bolt, and they reluctantly swam on . . .

The visibility in Eddy and Xavier's tunnel was no better. In fact, it might have been worse. To make matters even more dire, Eddy's headlamp kept flickering on and off, taking away half their light for several tense seconds before finally coming back on. They moved along the descending tunnel, praying the light would stay on, but knowing there was nothing they could do about it, either way.

They passed a side tunnel, heading to the right, but the opening was much narrower with debris that had fallen, calling into question how stable the walls and roof might be. Xavier pointed for them to stay in the main tunnel and keep heading in the direction they were going. Eddy agreed and kept moving. In the end, it would be a bad decision. Less than fifty feet farther into the tunnel, Xavier felt a small wave of water pressure on his back, and he turned just in time to see the beast swimming rapidly out of the darkness towards him. The creature had probably been waiting in the side tunnel for them to pass, but none of that mattered now. Xavier screamed into his mouthpiece, hoping Eddy would hear the noise, and he took a swipe at the approaching monster with his dive knife. The knife missed the underwater vampire's chest and heart but sank a few inches into its collarbone area. The creature howled in pain but kept on coming.

Eddy heard both his friend and the creature scream, spinning around in time to see Xavier lose hold of his knife and it falling to the floor below. The creature spun Xavier and grabbed him around the throat in a headlock motion, dragging the smaller indigenous man backwards towards the entrance to the tunnel. Eddy lined up his speargun and had a perfect shot at point blank range, but he likely would have hit his best friend, too, firing the metal bolt straight through both of them with one shot. He saw a bit of the creature's deformed—but still recognisably human face and head—over Xavier's shoulder and he desperately wanted to pull the trigger, but he just couldn't take the chance. Accuracy with a speargun isn't very good, and he'd only fired the weapon a few times under practice conditions—not while his friend's life was on the line. Eddy hesitated, and then it was too late. The creature dragged Xavier out of sight.

Cursing himself for not taking the shot, Eddy swam after them . . .

Tim led Sara deeper into the tunnel. They'd had to squeeze past Bob Leeman's dead body, and for a brief moment, Tim considered trying to pull the speargun bolt free of the dead man's ribcage. He'd decided against it—not wanting to touch the corpse—and instead motioned Sara to stay close to him before moving forward. Together they swam another thirty feet into the tunnel and like last time, their headlamps illuminated another man floating near the ceiling, blocking their path. Only this man was wearing a wetsuit and was practically missing his head. Whoever he was—likely one of the ex-navy divers Chief Palmer had hired to retrieve Bob

Leeman's body—his mask and respirator were torn from his face and his neck had been so savagely bitten, that the skull was flopped over backwards barely held in place by his spine. The man's eyes were still open, his final scream silently frozen on his open mouth. Unlike last time, Tim refrained from pulling the trigger on his weapon and senselessly shooting another dead body. Barely.

Their lights also revealed the second navy diver floating a few more feet beyond the first. He, too, was wearing a wetsuit, but curiously, there was no sign of a buoyancy compensator or an air tank anywhere to be found. This man's throat was also destroyed, but at least his face was undamaged, and it looked like he'd died a somewhat more peaceful death than his nearby friend. But what the hell did Tim know? He was no doctor, and one torn out throat was probably just as horrifying a way of dying as the next.

Sara tapped him on his shoulder, and he almost fired the speargun into the wall of the tunnel beside him. Tim thought she had spotted the monster, but what she was pointing at was farther into the tunnel where it looked like the ceiling had completely collapsed. They moved closer but it was obvious that this was the end of the line. There was nowhere else to go except back the way they had come. Tim felt a measure of relief wash over him, happy their tunnel had ended up being nothing more than a dead end, but they certainly weren't out of danger yet. He pointed back towards the exit, ready to get the hell out of this tunnel. Sara quickly agreed, and together they started making their way out.

Wonder if Eddy and X are having better luck?

Eddy was swimming as fast as he could. He knew Xavier was a dead man unless he could catch up to the water demon quickly, before it found a place to hide. The light from his friend's headlamp was no longer in view, and no matter how hard Eddy kicked his fins, he didn't seem able to make up any ground on the creature. And then to make things a hundred times worse, Eddy's headlamp began malfunctioning again, flashing off and then back on, randomly flickering at the worst possible time.

And then the light turned off . . . and stayed off.

Eddy was plunged into total darkness. Very few people have experienced pitch-black conditions in their lives—there's always some residual light source around them, even if it's extremely faint—but deep inside the tunnel, a hundred feet below the surface of the lake, with dawn still an hour or so away, Eddy may as well have been in deep outer space. A sudden wave of panic and fear stopped him in his tracks for a moment, and instead of swimming, he was forced to inch along the tunnel, feeling his way on the uneven, rocky wall. Worse than the darkness, were the blood-filled images his mind kept conjuring up of the attack he was convinced would be coming at any second. The underwater vampire would come for him now . . . or now . . . or wait, maybe *now*. The suspense of waiting for a painful death was horrendous, and every second that passed took its toll on the big man.

Hold it together. This isn't over yet.

And then Eddy saw a soft glow in the distance, and as dim as it was, it still caused a surge of hope and adrenaline to course through his body. *It's gotta be X* . . . The tiniest glow of light was enough to get Eddy moving fast again, throwing caution to the side, and swimming as fast as his legs could move.

I'm coming, brother. Hang in there just a little bit longer.

As he swam, the light grew larger, and fifteen feet farther, Eddy could make out his surroundings better. Fifteen more feet and finally, there his friend was, lying face down on the bottom of the tunnel. The creature was nowhere in sight.

Please . . . please . . . please . . .

Eddy swam to Xavier's side and pulled his body upward using the loop on his friend's buoyancy compensator. It wasn't until they were face-to-face that Eddy could see the shocking damage done to his best friend sometime in the last few minutes while they'd been separated.

The creature hadn't had time to feast on his neck like it had with the other victims, so perhaps out of sheer spite it had quickly torn Xavier's lower jawbone completely free of his face. Eddy could see where its claws had slashed into Xavier's throat and ripped upward, leaving a huge gaping hole in his friend's face. Xavier must have died in agony, all alone, perhaps clinging to the hope that Eddy might come and save him. His eyes were still wide open, accusing Eddy through his dive mask—in the big man's mind, at least—letting him know how much Eddy had failed him. None of that was true, of course, but the guilt Eddy felt made his blood begin to boil with a need for revenge.

Eddy only waited long enough to take the headlamp off his friend to replace his own faulty one, and swear to Xavier he'd come back for him when he could, before moving fast in the direction of the tunnel entrance. His fear was gone now, his panic forgotten, leaving behind only his growing rage. Eddy let his speargun lead the way along the tunnel, only one thing on his mind now.

I'm coming for you . . . motherfucker!

Sara sighed with relief when she and Tim finally exited the claustrophobic tunnel, returning to the main area of the lake. They had no way of knowing how Eddy and Xavier were making out, but as they weren't floating out here in plain sight, Sara had to presume they were still inside their tunnel. At least she hoped that was why they weren't out here waiting to meet them. She wasn't sure what to do next, but she and Tim weren't leaving without their friends until the very last breath of air had been sucked from their tanks. With that in mind, Sara checked her air pressure gauge and had Tim show her his, too. Tim was running lower than she was, but both of them would be fine for a few more minutes. Hopefully their friends would show up by then with good news, and they could all head for the surface together.

She figured the best place to wait might be over by the huge, abandoned Rock Truck. It was sitting in a central location, where Eddy and Xavier would look for them first. She pointed Tim in the right direction, in case he wasn't sure, and followed close behind. In forty feet, their headlamps started to illuminate the behemoth mining machine out of the darkness, and Tim headed straight for the truck's rusty front grill.

Before he made it there, Sara saw a shadow move behind one of the truck's massive rubber wheels, and before she could warn Tim, the creature was swimming straight for him. Tim noticed the beast at the last second and fired off another metal bolt from the speargun, but he'd had no time to aim, and the shot sailed harmlessly wide. He tried to reload his weapon, but the monster was already upon him, grabbing Tim around the waist and dragging him upward. Sara had her dive knife at the ready, but by the time she'd moved the ten feet to close the gap between them, Tim and the creature were soaring towards the surface and moving out of her range of visibility. One moment Tim had been directly in front of her, the next he was gone.

Seconds later, before she had time to react, Tim's headlamp and dive mask drifted slowly back down into Sara's view, landing on the bottom of the lake, almost within arm's reach of where she was floating.

Oh fuck . . . !

Her heart jumped into her throat.

"Leave him alone, you bastard," she uselessly screamed into her regulator mouthpiece, swimming for the surface to try and help her boyfriend. But it was already too late. She saw what at first she thought was a number of giant worms or fleshy-coloured eels dropping out of the darkness above her, but with growing horror she realized it wasn't any kind of animal at all. It was the contents of Tim's body cavity, his entrails ripped out and sinking, still attached to his disembowelled body trailing out from below his rib cage and eviscerated open torso that descended soon after. Most of Tim's body and wetsuit had been torn away. His upper torso, left arm, and head sank down through the murky blood-tainted water, landing right on the hood of the Rock Truck's cab in a pile of his own intestines. There was a considerable amount of blood and viscera in the water, but of Tim's lower body, it was nowhere to be seen. His legs, waist, and right arm were missing. In Sara's traumatized condition, she actually looked up to see if any more of her boyfriend's body parts were going to start raining down on top of her, but none did. The rest of the person she'd grown to love was simply *gone*.

Sara could barely move. All the terrible events of the past week had finally caught up to her and now poor Tim had paid for her stupidity with his life. Why had she ever agreed to let her friends talk her into this madness? And how could she have even thought about letting Tim, with almost no underwater experience, come down here with them. She should have called her father, and they could have called in the Army or the National Guard or somebody else to deal with the creature. *Anybody* but poor, sweet Tim. She felt nauseous, hopeless, and totally bone weary—tears freely flowing down her cheeks and starting to fill up the air pocket at the bottom of her rubber dive mask.

Tim . . . I'm so sorry.

She sobbed so hard it was difficult to breathe.

The creature came at her from behind, and she wasn't aware it was there until it struck her in the back, driving her forward into the front grill of the Rock Truck. She turned and swung at the beast's throat with her knife, but the man-monster was far quicker than her, and it grabbed hold of her wrist with its big, clawed hand. Its talons were still covered in gore that hadn't fully washed away yet, and Sara screamed as it squeezed her wrist until she felt something inside '*SNAP*'. Her dive knife fell out of her grasp as her left hand and wrist both went numb, falling to the bottom of the lake and out of her reach. Sara kneed the creature in the groin and hit it hard enough that she heard the beast groan in pain, releasing its grip on her for a moment. With no time to waste, Sara swam upward, hoping to put some distance between them, but the man-monster recovered quickly and caught her within seven or eight feet. It drove Sara down onto her back on top of the massive truck's front hood, and she found herself pinned less than two feet from Tim's pile of innards, his severed torso, and head. From this close, she could see that Tim's eyes were closed, and for whatever reason that image gave her some peace.

At least he doesn't have to watch me die, too.

Her mind spun, and not at all thinking clearly anymore.

The beast hovered over her, seemingly enjoying the look of terror in Sara's eyes. It opened its deformed mouth and let her have a good look at the rows of jagged teeth inside. And then, the underwater vampire tilted Sara's chin up and away from him and started moving in close to her, ready to bite her throat. This was the end, and Sara knew it. She closed her eyes and prepared for the sting of the creatures razor sharp fangs.

But nothing happened.

Sara opened her eyes. The creature still had her pinned to the hood of the giant truck, but its mouth was closed again and it seemed to be distracted by something on her chest.

The glass amulet. Stan was right. Whatever's left of Jonathan's mind and memories, he still recognises the family heirloom.

Not that it was going to do Sara any good. She was trapped under the strength of the vampire demon's hand and the weight of its powerful body and could hardly move a muscle to wiggle around—never mind trying to escape. The creature shook its head, looking confused and frustrated for a moment, but then its eyes narrowed and focused in on Sara's throat again. Its mouth started to open again, and the creature sat up straight for a moment, preparing to attack.

And then Sara heard a distinctive '*HISS*' sound nearby and was surprised to see the razor tip of a metal speargun bolt burst a hole in the center of the creature's scaly chest. The metal bolt exited a foot out of the front of its body in a spray of cloudy red water, coming to a stop mere inches from Sara's own belly. The creature howled in agony and spit out a mouthful of thick blood and vomit onto Sara's face. She squealed partly in disgust, but also in delight because she knew what must have just happened. Sure enough, when she looked past the creature's bulky shoulders, Sara could just make out Eddy hovering about fifteen feet away, still aiming his speargun at the demon's exposed back. Sara pushed with all her strength, and managed to roll the beast off her, and by the time she'd managed to pull herself free of it, Eddy had reloaded his next bolt and was taking aim once again.

Kill the son of a bitch!

Sara felt no guilt whatsoever.

Eddy pulled the trigger a second time and the bolt whizzed through the dark water, striking the vampire creature high in the throat. It was a glancing blow but tore a good-sized chunk of flesh from the left side of the monster's neck. Sara was staring straight into the eyes of the demon when the second bolt had struck and there was no real response in the creature's face and body, other than another gush of syrupy blood mixing with the lake water. Its eyes just rolled back in its head, and its body went limp. The creature slowly sunk to the bottom of the lake, but it never moved again.

Sara finally turned to acknowledge her friend, and she swam over to give Eddy a big underwater hug, or as best she could anyway, with all their dive gear on.

"You did it!" she screamed into her regulator mouthpiece, not knowing if Eddy could understand her, but not caring. Eddy looked happy for a moment, but then he seemed to freeze, his eyes locking on something behind Sara's back. When she turned to look, she realized he was just now seeing Tim's destroyed body for the first time, torn virtually in half, lying on the hood of the abandoned Rock Truck. Sara turned Eddy's face away from the terrible sight and made sure he stayed focused on her. She removed her mouthpiece for a moment, put her mouth as close to the big man's ear as she could get, and loudly asked, "Xavier?"

Eddy just shook his head.

Nothing more needed said. Sara knew exactly what that meant and she was smart enough to know that this wasn't the time to dwell on both of their losses.

Sara used the index finger on her uninjured hand, repeatedly pointing towards the surface. *Let's go up,* the gesture meant. Eddy certainly didn't need to be told twice. He nodded and together they pumped a little air into the buoyancy compensators to start floating back towards the real world far above. They stopped once at twenty feet for a decompression safety stop, because they'd been down at depth for a decent length of time and it was a smart way of avoiding any chance of getting decompression sickness, or '*The Bends*' as it is often called. In a best-case scenario, they would have stayed at their safety stop for five minutes but neither Sara nor Eddy had enough air left in their tanks to stay down that long. Besides that, neither one of them wanted to spend another second in this cursed lake if they could avoid it.

Not this morning, anyway. Maybe never again.

Together, they surfaced under the blessed light of the moon, spitting out their mouthpieces and gulping down their first real breath of fresh air in what felt like forever.

Thirteen

Red Spruce Lake
Back On The Beach
July 23rd, 5:15 a.m.

It was Sara's dad, Bryan, who spotted the divers first, but Doc Turner, Steamboat Stan, and Mick Sullivan—another Beckley police officer—all joined in, shouting and urging them to swim towards where they waited on the beach. At first, their response was on the cheery side of things, happy to see Sara and Eddy swimming in their direction, but then the mood suddenly changed as they noticed that not all the divers were present and accounted for. Chief Palmer knew something bad must have happened straight away, but didn't want to say it out loud, for fear his voice would make his dark thoughts true.

Oh shit. Where's Xavier and Tim?

Stan was stunned into silence for his own reasons. The reality of what he was seeing was finally hitting him, and the hope he'd carried for years, of releasing his brother's soul from the *Sabawaelnu* water demon was now all but lost. Surly, the presence of the chief's daughter and her large friend meant that Jonathan, and the vampire creature he'd become, was dead. He quietly waited for the divers to return to shore, feathered hat in hand, taking some solace in the fact that he'd at least tried his best. He could find a way to live with that. And despite his personal loss, in his heart he knew the most important thing to focus on was that the terrible killings would now stop.

Sara helped Eddy stand when they reached shallow enough water, and together they removed their swim fins so they could walk the last ten feet up and out of the lake. Officer Sullivan and Doc Turner were there to help them take off their dive tanks and weight belts and carry them away from the shoreline.

"You okay?" Doc Turner asked Sara, seeing her cradling her left wrist.

"I'll live," Sara said, but then burst into tears when her thoughts returned to what had just happened to Tim. Xavier, too, even though she still had no idea what had actually happened to him. She tried to hold it together and stay strong, but her emotions got the best of her when she finally came eye to eye with her father. "*Oh, Dad . . .* " she said, wanting nothing more than to run and throw her arms around his neck like she'd done when she'd been a child and something had upset her. She started moving towards him, her arms open wide—

"Watch out, Sara!" Eddy screamed.

When Sara turned around, she was shocked to see the hulking, scaly body of the vampire creature splashing out of the shallow water, knocking Officer Sullivan out if its way, and charging straight towards her. She backpedaled away from the beast, but it was moving too fast, catching up to her and driving her down onto her back on the cold sand before she could do anything about it.

How can it still be alive? I saw its eyes roll back. I watched it die.

The man-monster opened its huge mouth and shrieked in triumph to the sky above, blood still freely flowing from its own deep wounds on its neck and near the centre of its chest. Then it stared back down into Sara's eyes and she saw the rage reflected in its still mostly-human eyes, and she was sure this time her luck had ran out—she was about to die. But the creature did another strange thing, it reached for her throat. Not with its jagged teeth but with it's clawed right hand, seemingly still driven with a singular purpose of obtaining Jonathan's family heirloom hanging around Sara's neck.

"Help me!" she screamed, trying to fight the beast off with her one good hand.

Her father and Officer Sullivan would both be armed with their Glock service guns, but surprisingly it was Stan, the frail-looking homeless man who came to her aid first. The indigenous man stepped in behind the beast who had once been his brother, and clobbered the creature with a hefty log he must have picked up somewhere nearby on the beach. The thick wooden timber impacted on the side of the creature's head, right in the temple area, with an audible '*crack*' sound that echoed across the lake and rebounded off the cliff face beyond. The water demon crumpled to the ground unconscious, landing on, but then rolling off Sara onto its back in the sand beside her. Its eyes were closed, but everyone could see its chest was moving up and down, still breathing.

Sara sprang to her feet and started shouting at the startled group of people around her.

"Quick. Tie it down, or chain it. Whatever you guys brought. And Doc . . . I hope you brought the knock-out drug?"

"I . . . I did," the flustered doctor said, obviously in over his head seeing the man-monster lying on the sand at their feet. He fumbled in his jacket pocket for something, and when his trembling hand came back out, he was holding a large syringe. "You sure about this, Bryan?"

The chief nodded. "Do it."

While the doctor bent and administered the drug into the muscular arm of the creature, Officer Sullivan and Eddy ran to gather the ropes, spikes, and hammers that had been brought from town in the chief's Bronco. Within a minute, people were scrambling, tying ropes around the creature's arms and legs, stretching them tightly out away from its unconscious body, and pounding metal spikes into the ground to secure the beast in place in the chance that it somehow woke up.

"No, no, *no* . . . " Stan started shouting, being ignored by everyone except Sara, so he tried pleading his case with her. "Stop this. There's no need for ropes. We're wasting time. The *Sabawaelnu* is unconscious . . . the demon sleeps. All we have to do is carry it to the chief's vehicle and drive to sacred ground on the Her'maqon people's land. There's still time to save my brother's soul before the sun comes up. Please . . . you have to help. You promised me."

Sara looked like she didn't know what to say. She was in obvious pain and looked exhausted. "I didn't promise anything. I said we'd *try*. I'm sorry, Stan. It's too dangerous and there isn't enough time."

"No . . . *no*, don't say that. You promised. I just saved your life. You can't turn your back on me and my family now. My brother needs you. *I need you!*"

"Forget it, old man," Eddy said, no sympathy whatsoever in his voice. "We listened to your story earlier, but none of that matters anymore. That son of a bitch practically tore my best friend's face off, so fuck your brother and fuck your legends. I say let him burn."

"Easy, son," Chief Palmer said. "Whatever happened to Xavier isn't Steamboat's fault. You can't blame him for any of this. That said, I agree with you. I don't think moving this . . . *thing*, is worth the risk. It's just too dangerous."

Stan glanced back and forth between Eddie, Chief Palmer, and Sara, not believing what he was hearing. He didn't trust many people in this world, and had a lifetime of reasons why, but he'd been sure these people would try and help, but here they were talking about the eternal damnation of his brother's soul as if it were nothing at all. Deep down he should have expected this. Treachery and lies were nothing new to the Her'maqon people. No one from Beckley had ever helped him or his family before, so why would they start now?

"Please, Sara," Stan said, desperately hoping the lone woman in the group might have a softer heart than the others and understand how important this was. "I'm begging you. Don't let them do this. You'll regret it for the rest of your life."

"I'd help if I could," Sara said. "I don't know . . . maybe we—"

"No way," Eddy said, interrupting his friend. "Maybe *nothing*. Remember what that abomination did to Tim down there. You think he deserved to suffer like that? We got one chance to make it pay for what it did . . . and we're taking it."

Sara had tears in her eyes again, but she nodded—decision made.

"Eddy's right. Your brother made his own choice, and now we're making ours. The creature has to pay for what it did to our friends, and to the people of this town. I'm sorry."

"*Noooo . . .* " Stan screamed, and without thinking he charged at Sara, his frustration, sadness, and anger directed at the person he was the most disappointed in. "I saved your life, you . . . you *bitch*!"

Before Stan could reach her, Officer Sullivan and Chief Palmer were on him, wrestling him to the ground. "Let go of me," the homeless man said. "You've got no right. He's my brother. My flesh and blood. I wish he'd killed all of you *bastards*!"

Chief Palmer helped drag the smaller man back onto his feet and said, "Get him out of here, Mick. You and Doc Turner go back to town and lock his raggedy ass up in the drunk tank at the station. Maybe a night or two in a cell will make him see things a bit more clearly. Take the Bronco and get moving."

Officer Sullivan was a big man, and when he was fired up, he wasn't the kind of man to mess with. Once he had Stan firmly in his grasp, the homeless man was going with him whether he liked it or not. He started dragging Stan backwards towards the police SUV. Doc Turner stopped to pick up the homeless man's feathered hat, and followed along, looking more than happy to finally be leaving this place.

"You'll pay for this, Chief," Stan screamed as he was being dragged into the parking lot and stuffed into the back of the Bronco. "All of you will . . . "

But then Officer Sullivan slammed the door in Stan's face and the people on the beach could no longer hear his angry voice. Behind the glass, his face was still contorted with rage, tears running down his cheeks from his wild, bloodshot eyes. It wasn't until the Bronco drove out through the park gates that everyone relaxed and managed to take a deep breath.

"Jesus," Chief Palmer said. "What a shit show."

"Yeah, and it's not over yet," Eddy said, nodding to the heavily restrained body of the creature from the lake lying completely still less than ten feet away.

Sara and her father both turned to look.

"What do we do now?" Bryan said.

Sara looked to see if there was any hint of light on the eastern horizon yet. There wasn't, but she knew it wouldn't stay that way for much longer. She took a deep breath and said, "The only thing we can do . . . we wait."

Fourteen

Red Spruce Lake
Sunrise
July 23rd, 5:58 a.m.

Sara sat on the cool sand, wrapped in her father's police jacket. It was a thin, summer jacket with the Beckley Police logo stitched onto it and not really designed for warmth, but for the moment it was all she had to keep the chills at bay. Eddy and her father stood chatting quietly nearby, both of them stealing glances in her direction every few minutes, checking to see if she was still holding things together. The creature was tightly bound closer to the shoreline where they'd left it, breathing heavily and still fast asleep.

A flicker of colour caught Sara's attention and she peered up to see the first hint of dawn breaking above the horizon in the east. It wasn't exactly light yet, but definitely a soft glow that hadn't been there a few minutes before when she'd last checked. In a perfect world—or maybe in one of those alternate universe superhero movies she'd grown up watching—the water demon would have been drugged so deeply that it continued sleeping peacefully straight through whatever awful thing was about to happen. But multiverses were only in the comics, and Sara Palmer's world was far from perfect.

The creature coughed once, then again, and opened its eyes.

"Oh crap," Sara said, jumping to her feet. "Guys . . . *it's waking up.*"

Bryan and Eddie were by her side in a heartbeat, and Sara was slightly taken aback, seeing her father with his Glock drawn from its holster, pointing it at the creature's chest.

"*Wait* . . . what are you doing, Dad?"

"It's too risky letting that thing wake up. If it gets free, we're in a lot of trouble."

"I hear you, but I think we need to let this run it's course naturally."

"Why? Why can't I kill it right here and now and be done with it?"

"Maybe you can, but Steamboat Stan said the creator of the world put the sun in the sky to destroy darkness and evil. He might be a bit of a crack pot, but this creature is pretty much the definition of darkness and evil. Stan's been right about most of this stuff so far. I just think we should listen to him and do this the right way."

"You really believe all that native demon and vampire stuff?" Eddy asked. "You think sunlight is actually gonna fry this son of a bitch?"

"I have no idea . . . but there's only one way to find out."

The creature was rolling its head back and forth now, reacting to the sound of their voices. It was opening and closing its deformed mouth, slowly regaining consciousness. Its eyes were wide open, too, but they looked glazed and unable to focus. Whatever drug Doc Turner had given the beast, it was obviously not fully out of its system yet.

"Okay, I guess," Chief Palmer said. "But just so you know, if that beast fully wakes up and starts cutting itself loose with those claws, I'm unloading this clip into it's head and chest."

"Fair enough," Sara said, hoping it wouldn't come to that.

To the east, looking just above the canopy of Spruce trees that surrounded the lake, the soft glow in the sky had become pink in colour, and even as she watched the hues changed again and the first hints of red and orange were peeking over the horizon. Sara peeked over at the creature, and it was sniffing the air, a deep growling noise starting to come from its mouth, but so far its body lay relatively motionless. For now.

Come on, sun. Hurry up for Christ's sake!

The morning sky was noticeably lighter now, the darkness seemingly running to hide from night's eternal enemy upon its unstoppable approach. Sara could easily see how the indigenous peoples of this land would believe the sun was a god, and Stan's tale of it being placed in the heavens to protect the Her'maqon people seemed all the more real to her now. The circular shape of the sun could be fully seen now, its rays still filtered through and blocked by the heavy foliage of the trees, but within minutes it would rise high enough to start chasing the shadows away on Red Spruce Lake.

Perhaps sensing the approaching danger, the creature's arms and legs began to twitch and shake. The ropes that bound it were strong and tight, but the demon was more than capable of using its razor-sharp talons and teeth to cut and chew itself free. The creature flexed its back, the ropes straining against its unnatural strength, but they held. Frustrated, the creature let loose a demonic scream, starting to thrash back and forth against the ropes holding it in place. It hadn't thought to try cutting itself loose yet, but as the seconds passed, the hold the drug had over its mind was diminishing and it seemed to be regaining its senses more and more.

The first rays of direct sunlight finally crested the trees, touching the water beyond the shaded area of the eastern forest, out closer to the center of the lake, and slowly spreading across the placid surface towards where Sara and the others waited on the sandy beach. And as the sun rose higher in the sky, the speed of the golden light on the water sped up, too, a visible wall of blazing colour racing towards them. Within seconds it would be upon them.

The creature bellowed in rage, whipping its arms and legs in a frenzy, trying to break free. Almost by accident, one of its sharp claws snagged on a rope and immediately sliced straight through it, the web of ropes just as vulnerable as Sara and her father had feared. The creature sensed its opening and began hacking and biting into the ropes still holding it in place. One rope after the other separated and flew apart. The creature managed to sit up, only its legs still fastened to the ground. It turned to look directly at Sara, and let out a bloodthirsty, high-pitched scream of triumph.

But the water demon was too late.

Sunrise had finally arrived on the beach, the sunlight a weapon of the gods just like Steamboat Stan had said it would be. The sun's rays washed over the creature while it was still flailing at the last few ropes tied around his legs, and the effect was immediate and devastating. Its exposed skin began to smoulder and char. The oils in its skin boiled and blackened, producing a cloying smoke that was released into the air, smelling both sickly-sweet and rancid at the same time.

The creature's howls of rage turned to screams of agony, its muscular arms swiping at and clawing the air around it, trying to strike back at whatever invisible enemy was causing it such terrible pain. The long black hair on its head suddenly burst into flames, the creatures face engulfed in fire, attacking its eyes and mouth. Both of its eyes boiled and burst from the heat, one right after the other, the gooey mess spraying down its scalded cheeks. Within half a minute, the entire creature was burning, the scaly skin of its belly peeling off to show a glimpse of the man's human stomach beneath for a moment, until that skin, too, was consumed by the fire. The creature continued to shriek in agony far longer than anyone thought possible, its guttural wails still present until its ribcage burst apart when its blackened lungs finally exploded. After that, the carcass of the beast intensely burned in silence. Even the bones burned away to powder and dust, the body entirely destroyed within minutes.

Sara had watched all of this happen with a strange sense of detachment, and a feeling that there was a power at work here—a presence—that she and the others watching the vampire creature burn that morning were never meant to understand. It somehow felt like primal justice had been delivered, a vicious wrong that had finally been made right again. By who, or for what reasons, Sara had absolutely no idea. In the end, all that was left as evidence that anything had happened out here at Red Spruce Lake, was a large, charred stain somewhat in the shape of a body in the middle of the sandy beach.

The monster, who had once been a man, was completely gone.

Fifteen

Beckley, Nova Scotia
One Week Later
July 30th, 9:00 a.m.

The past week had been one of sadness and confusion for the citizens of Beckley, Nova Scotia. Most of the people had no real idea why they were attending so many *'closed casket'* funerals of friends and neighbors, but like the fine Canadians they were, they soldiered on, bringing hot casserole dishes and Alexander Keith's IPA to the family members' houses, supporting those who had lost loved ones as best they could in these trying times. The people were tough, though, and Beckley would survive. It had been through bad times before and it would struggle through these dark days as well.

Sara Palmer, Eddy Champlain, Chief Bryan Palmer, Officer Joyce Foster, Officer Mick Sullivan, and Doc Turner had gathered on the same day the creature had been burned out of existence for a closed-door meeting at Chief Palmer's house. There was always the law to think about, of course, but there was an argument to be made that proper justice and punishment had duly been handed out and the cases of the mysterious disappearances and deaths—the ones they actually knew about, at least—could now be officially closed. They all agreed the best course of action was to bury the truth about what had actually happened out at Red Spruce Lake, and the underwater vampire they had successfully (some would say *luckily*) managed to destroy. No good could come from telling the truth. Rumors were going to spread anyway, there was no way to stop that from happening, but they could always deny any knowledge of the facts, or of having participated in any of it. Some people would believe them. A lot wouldn't. Some probably didn't really care. Either way, it was the smartest course of action to take.

Eddy had been adamant that he was going back underwater to collect his best friend's body, and no one in the room had been able to talk him out of it. The very next day he'd joined a small discrete team of divers from the Maritime Forces Atlantic, who had been called in to help quietly retrieve the bloated bodies of Xavier Pictou, Bob Leeman, Ian Fitzgerald, and Tony Marchello. Eddy had also helped retrieve what they could find of Tim Hanson off the hood of the submerged Rock Truck, and then searched the rest of the area until they eventually found Sara's boyfriend's lower half. These bodies, along with the mutilated corpses of Travis and Margo Peterson, who'd been found in the deep end of their backyard pool, would make up the list of hastily planned closed casket funerals that the good people of Beckley would attend over the next several days.

Sara had spent most of the last week over at her father's house. She was relatively fine at the start, but once Tim's remains had been brought back to Doc Turner's medical center—in two separate body bags—reality had hit her pretty hard. She avoided the funerals and chose to grieve in her own way. She'd recover, but it was going to take her a very long time. For at least the immediate future, Sara had no plans of ever scuba diving again.

The one person everyone had forgotten about in this tragic mess was Steamboat Stan. Chief Palmer had left him in one of the small holding cells in the basement of the Beckley Police Station, unsure as to what to do with him. Stan had been cooling his heels in the cell ever since the early morning of the 23rd, when Officer Sullivan had thrown him in there and told him to "*settle the fuck down.*" There had never been any real thought of charging the homeless man with any crimes. None of what had happened had been Stan's fault, and the chief knew the indigenous man's curses and threats, as he'd been getting dragged away from the beach, had been nothing more than frustration, anger, and sadness over what had become of his brother.

Chief Palmer could have released him the next morning, or certainly the day after, but he decided it might be best for everyone involved if he kept Stan off the streets for a few extra days. Stan hadn't agreed to keep the truth hidden like the rest of them had. He was a loose cannon in all this but seeing as Stan had barely said a word in the last week to anyone inside the station, the chief was reasonably convinced the man wouldn't have too much to say about the matter once he was released either. The truth was, his brother had been the one at fault here and he was the reason all of these people had been killed, so what would Stan or his family stand to gain by letting the cat out of the bag, so to speak?

While Stan silently sat brooding in his holding cell, Chief Palmer bought him a new set of clothes. Palmer had picked up for him some socks and underwear, a leather belt, a new pair of Levi blue jeans, and a white, button-up dress shirt that he knew Steamboat liked to wear. He also had the homeless man's black suit jacket professionally cleaned, as well as his trademark feathered hat. Stan had been given access to the shower room and had shaved and washed his long hair twice since he'd been detained. At the very least, the homeless man could walk out of the station clean and smelling decent for the first time in a while. What Stan did after that was up to him, but Chief Palmer hoped he'd see they'd had no choice in what they'd done that morning and let the whole terrible matter just drop.

Stanley Blackmore was released from police custody at 9:00 AM on July 30, refusing to speak with Chief Palmer or any of the other officers on his way out. He only wanted to be left alone, the way he'd grown used to over the years. He was wearing all his fancy new clothes that the chief had either bought or had cleaned for him, but none of that material stuff mattered to Stan. Never had, obviously, but worldly possessions meant even less to him now.

Besides, he didn't plan to live long enough to need any of them.

Stan had given up on life. While he'd been on guard at Red Spruce Lake waiting for the inevitable return of his brother, he'd at least had some purpose to wake up to, some meaning to his daily struggle. But now that his brother had been brutally destroyed and Stan was truly alone in this awful world, he couldn't think of a single reason left to keep living life like this. Why bother? Would tomorrow miraculously be any better than today, or yesterday had been? The answer, at least in his angry, depressed mind, was '*no*'.

Stan walked with his head down through the center of Beckley one last time, not speaking to or acknowledging a single person along his route. Once outside of town, he turned onto Regional Road #3 which would lead him directly past Red Spruce Lake. There were a few vehicles that passed him as he walked, but he didn't bother trying to hail any of them down to bum a ride. He was finished asking for handouts from anyone anymore, but especially any white people cruising by in their expensive cars. Stan had experienced a lifetime of racism aimed at himself and the indigenous people of this area, but up until last week, he'd never held any hatred in his heart for anyone. That was before Chief Palmer, his daughter, and their little group of cruel vigilantes had decided their friends and families had more worth than Jonathan did. They'd made the decision to condemn his soul like he was as important as a tiny bug.

Stan understood why they had done what they did—they were afraid of something they couldn't comprehend—but that didn't mean he had to accept their decision, or not acknowledge the flames of rage their actions fanned in his confused mind. When he'd said to Chief Palmer that he had wished Jonathan had killed all of them, he'd meant it.

And he still did.

Hatred hardens even the purest of hearts.

It was something his father had often said, and the truth in those cryptic words weren't lost on him. In fact, today they made more sense to him than ever.

Stan eventually turned off onto the gravel road that led to the beach parking lot. His makeshift home was just off to the left in the forest surrounding the lake, but he had no reason to go there anymore so he just kept on walking. After entering the park though the open metal gates, he was pleased to see that there were no cars in the parking lot and no one else around who might have walked or ridden their bike. For the time being, Stan had the entire lake all to himself.

It didn't take long for Stan to find the charred-black area on the sandy beach, where his brother had been destroyed by sunlight while staked down to the ground. No one from the chief's office had even taken the time to rake the sand to hide where the underwater vampire had met its fiery end, and something about that bothered Stan even more. He walked over and knelt in the sand near the discoloured area, and removed his feathered hat. He prayed for his brother's soul, tears streaming down both sides of his face by the time he was done.

After Stan had said everything he could think to say, he stood back up and dusted off the damp sand from his knees. He placed his hat with the crow feather in the center of the charred area, said one more goodbye to Jonathan, and started walking towards the lake. He'd never been a great swimmer and his plan was to simply walk out into the water until it was over his head and start swimming until he couldn't keep himself afloat any longer. After that, he'd sink into the cool, clear water and let the lake claim his body the way it probably should have back when the gypsum mine had flooded. Stan reached the shore and began walking in.

"Esgipa'tl . . . Gwi's" a familiar voice said from behind him, speaking in the old tongue of his forefathers. *Wait . . . little brother*, the words meant.

Stan stopped in his tracks, water up to his knees.

When he turned to look back at the beach, his brother was standing on the dark sand that Stan had just walked away from. Jonathan was in his human form that Stan remembered, not the beast he had become, and he was wearing Stan's hat upon his head.

"Jonathan . . . is it really you?" Stan asked, but deep down he knew there was no way that was possible. His real brother was dead and gone.

"I am whoever you need me to be, Stanley."

Stan was close enough to shore that he could see the eyes of the thing pretending to be his lost brother. They were black as coal with no iris in the center. Stan knew immediately who it was who stood before him, but instead of fear he felt an odd sense of excitement.

"What do you want with me, *Sabawaelnu*?"

The demon on the beach smiled and laughed. "It may not be what *I* want with *you* . . . it may be more of what *you* might want with *me*."

"I don't understand," Stan said, but he thought he actually did.

"Revenge, boy. *Vengeance*," the creature screamed. "Together we can make them pay for what they've done. Why should your life be forfeit for their cowardice and deceit. It's them who deserve to suffer and die . . . not you, Stanley. Understand?"

Stan felt a great weight starting to lift from his depressed mind. Maybe he might yet have a purpose in this world. A dark, but justified purpose.

"And you can give me this revenge?"

"I can give *us* this revenge. You know I can. All you have to do is agree to let me inside, to join with me in body, mind, and most importantly . . . in spirit."

"And Jonathan? What has become of him?"

"He's still a part of me. He'll be a part of us. Together forever. Make your choice, friend. Die as a coward . . . or live as a god. What's it going to be?"

The body of the *Sabawaelnu* was changing. The image of Jonathan Blackmore was melting away, darkening into a jet-black figure of a tall, thin man made entirely of shadows. Stan knew he should turn and continue on with his plan of ending his miserable life, or at the very least run screaming away from the ancient creature standing before him, but the truth was he didn't want to. He'd never been anything more than a nobody his entire life. An uneducated, unwanted, easily forgotten person who'd been forced to scrounge through life asking for handouts or digging for scraps. The people of Beckley had kicked him when he was down, and laughed at him for as long as he could remember. Just once, Stan wished he could be the person with the answers, the man with power and authority whom everyone respected—or at least feared. Nobody would laugh at him, then.

"You already know my answer," Stan eventually said.

"Yes . . . but you must say it of your own free will."

Stan took a deep breath, knowing he was following his brother's path into horror and damnation, but today he just didn't care. "I accept your offer, *Sabawaelnu*. Join with me. My body, mind, and spirt are yours."

The dark mass of shadows seemed to smile, although it had no visible mouth. Its body transformed even further, this time into a thick cloud of black smoke. Stan's fedora with the crow feather sticking out of the hat band drifted down to sit upon the charred sand once again, and the thick, smoky essence of the beast floated out over the lake. When the dark cloud was inches away, Stan opened his mouth and inhaled in a deep breath. The creature poured its black soul into Stan's mouth, down his throat, into his lungs, and from there entered his blood stream. Its dark consciousness and spirit coursed through Stan's circulatory system and entered his brain.

Now monster and man were united.

Now they were one.

Come, Stanley . . . the demon whispered within their shared mind. *We need to hide for a while down in the dark. There are places in the flooded Shaft 3 tunnels the humans will never find us. We need time to rest. To get stronger. To change . . .*

Stan turned away from the beach and started walking into deeper water. Soon, the surface of the lake was up to his waist, then his chest, and then his neck. Without looking back, without hesitation, without fear, Stan disappeared underwater and never returned. There were ripples on the surface of the lake for a moment, outlining the spot where Stan had submerged, but as quickly as the displaced waves appeared they settled and were gone. After that, Red Spruce Lake returned to the quiet, serene oasis in the forest that the people of Beckley had enjoyed for years now, its shimmering blue water perfectly still on this beautiful summer morning.

Peaceful today, but not forever . . .

The End?

Not if you want to dive into more of the Dark Tide series.

Check out our amazing website and online store
or download our latest catalog here.
https://geni.us/CLPCatalog

Looking for award-winning Dark Fiction?
Download our latest catalog.
Includes our anthologies, novels, novellas, collections, poetry, non-fiction, and specialty projects.
WHERE STORIES COME ALIVE!
CRYSTAL LAKE ENTERTAINMENT

We always have great new projects and content on the website to dive into, as well as a newsletter, behind the scenes options, social media platforms, our own dark fiction shared-world series and our very own webstore. Our webstore even has categories specifically for KU books, non-fiction, anthologies, and of course more novels and novellas.

About the Authors

Simon Clark's novels, include *Blood Crazy* (now an entire series of books), *Vampyrrhic, Darkness Demands, Stranger, Whitby Vampyrrhic, Secrets of the Dead,* and the British Fantasy award-winning *The Night of the Triffids*, which was broadcast as a five-part drama series by BBC radio.

Weird House Press have recently issued Simon's new collection, *Sherlock Holmes: A Casebook of Nightmares and Monsters,* and the novels, *Sherlock Holmes: Lord of Damnation* and *Callisto: Blood Mission*.

He has also scripted audio dramas for Big Finish, including for their reboot of the apocalyptic drama, *Survivors* and their multi-platform *Doom's Day*.

The Cannes Film Festival 2024 saw the premiere of *Protos*, a dystopian Sci-Fi/Horror feature film, which he co-scripted with Brian Avenet-Bradley.

Simon lives in Yorkshire, England, where he can be seen roaming this legend-haunted landscape with a black and white Border Collie by the name of Mylo.

Website: nailedbytheheart.com
X/Twitter: hotelmidnight
Facebook: https://www.facebook.com/SimonClarkAuthor

Kevin J. Kennedy is a horror author, editor, and anthologist. He is also the owner of KJK Publishing and he runs the best selling 'The Horror Collection' series.

He lives in the heart of Scotland with his beautiful wife, three cats, Carlito, Ariel and Luna, and a Pomchi called Orko. He can be found on Facebook if you want to chat with him.

Gord Rollo was born in St. Andrews, Scotland, but now lives in Ontario, Canada. His short stories and novella-length work have appeared in many professional publications throughout the genre. His novels include: *The Jigsaw Man, Crimson, Strange Magic, Valley Of The Scarecrow, The Translators, The Crucifixion Experiments, Between the Devil and the Deep Blue Sea,* and *The Dark Side of Heavon.* Two other novels: *Beasts of Copan,* a time travel fantasy/horror, and *Voodoo Cowboys: The Life, Death, and Resurrection of Butch Cassidy and the Sundance Kid,* a weird western/horror/adventure novel, were co-written with the legendary Gene O'Neill. Besides novels, Gord has edited the acclaimed evolutionary horror anthology, *Unnatural Selection: A Collection of Darwinian Nightmares* and co-edited *Dreaming of Angels*, a horror/fantasy anthology.

Readers . . .

Thank you for reading *Creatures of the Night*. We hope you enjoyed this 17th book in our Dark Tide series.

If you have a moment, please review *Creatures of the Night* at the store where you bought it.

Help other readers by telling them why you enjoyed this book. No need to write an in-depth discussion. Even a single sentence will be greatly appreciated. Reviews go a long way to helping a book sell, and is great for an author's career. It'll also help us to continue publishing quality books.

Thank you again for taking the time to journey with Crystal Lake Publishing.

Visit our Linktree page for a list of our social media platforms. https://linktr.ee/CrystalLakePublishing

Follow us on Amazon:

MISSION STATEMENT:

Since its founding in August 2012, Crystal Lake Publishing has quickly become one of the world's leading publishers of Dark Fiction and Horror books. In 2023, Crystal Lake Publishing formed a part of Crystal Lake Entertainment, joining several other divisions, including Torrid Waters, Crystal Lake Comics, Crystal Lake Kids, and many more.

While we strive to present only the highest quality fiction and entertainment, we also endeavour to support authors along their writing journey. We offer our time and experience in non-fiction projects, as well as author mentoring and services, at competitive prices.

With several Bram Stoker Award wins and many other wins and nominations (including the HWA's Specialty Press Award), Crystal Lake Publishing puts integrity, honor, and respect at the forefront of our publishing operations.

We strive for each book and outreach program we spearhead to not only entertain and touch or comment on issues that affect our readers, but also to strengthen and support the Dark Fiction field and its authors.

Not only do we find and publish authors we believe are destined for greatness, but we strive to work with men and women who endeavour to be decent human beings who care more for others than themselves, while still being hard working, driven, and passionate artists and storytellers.

Crystal Lake Publishing is and will always be a beacon of what passion and dedication, combined with overwhelming teamwork and respect, can accomplish. We endeavour to know each and every one of our readers, while building personal relationships with our authors, reviewers, bloggers, podcasters, bookstores, and libraries.

We will be as trustworthy, forthright, and transparent as any business can be, while also keeping most of the headaches away from our authors, since it's our job to solve the problems so they can stay in a creative mind. Which of course also means paying our authors.

We do not just publish books, we present to you worlds within your world, doors within your mind, from talented authors who sacrifice so much for a moment of your time.

There are some amazing small presses out there, and through collaboration and open forums we will continue to support other presses in the goal of helping authors and showing the world what quality small presses are capable of accomplishing. No one wins when a small press goes down, so we will always be there to support hardworking, legitimate presses and their authors. We don't see Crystal Lake as the best press out there, but we will always strive to be the best, strive to be the most interactive and grateful, and even blessed press around. No matter what happens over time, we will also take our mission very seriously while appreciating where we are and enjoying the journey.

What do we offer our authors that they can't do for themselves through self-publishing?

We are big supporters of self-publishing (especially hybrid publishing), if done with care, patience, and planning. However, not every author has the time or inclination to do market research, advertise, and set up book launch strategies. Although a lot of authors are successful in doing it all, strong small presses will always be there for the authors who just want to do what they do best: write.

What we offer is experience, industry knowledge, contacts and trust built up over years. And due to our strong brand and trusting fanbase, every Crystal Lake Publishing book comes with weight of respect. In time our fans begin to trust our judgment and will try a new author purely based on our support of said author.

With each launch we strive to fine-tune our approach, learn from our mistakes, and increase our reach. We continue to assure our authors that we're here for them and that we'll carry the weight of the launch and dealing with third parties while they focus on their strengths—be it writing, interviews, blogs, signings, etc.

We also offer several mentoring packages to authors that include knowledge and skills they can use in both traditional and self-publishing endeavours.

We look forward to launching many new careers.

This is what we believe in. What we stand for. This will be our legacy.

**Welcome to Crystal Lake Publishing—
Tales from the Darkest Depths.**

Made in the USA
Middletown, DE
09 September 2024

60192216R00117